Graham Dix writes science fiction novels. He lives in Birmingham, near the famous chocolate factory, with his wife and teenaged daughter. Among his interests are rock and classical music, football, and tennis. Graham has run many half marathons and one London Marathon. When living abroad, he learned to speak Russian and German. He has an M.A. in Library and Information Studies and worked as a librarian for many years before concentrating on writing. He loves puns. He has a twin brother in Wales and a sister in Australia. Graham also writes children's stories.

To Mum and Dad, this is for you, with love. Thank you for all the wonderful memories. You will always be with us.

Graham Dix

Our Future Selves

AUSTIN MACAULEY PUBLISHERS™
LONDON * CAMBRIDGE * NEW YORK * SHARJAH

A CIP catalogue record for this title is available from the British Library.

ISBN 9781398480193 (Paperback)
ISBN 9781398480209 (Hardback)
ISBN 9781398480216 (ePub e-book)

www.austinmacauley.com

First Published 2023
Austin Macauley Publishers Ltd®
1 Canada Square
Canary Wharf
London
E14 5AA

I would like to acknowledge the help I have received from many people. It would have been a longer and tougher task, maybe an insurmountable one, to bring this novel to publication without their help. With apologies to anyone I may have inadvertently left out, these people are – Lynn Benn, Jill Austin, Tracy Wilkinson, Mary Hayes, Gill Walker, Jennifer Pastrana-Dix, Marlyn Pastrana-Dix, Daphne Dix, John Dix, Nigel Dix, Chris Evans, Sonia Thompson, Christina Brown, Vivian Brown, Professor Brian Greene, and the team at Austin Macauley Publishers.

"Don't grieve. Anything you lose comes around in another form." – *Rumi*

Imagine waking up inside someone else's body…in a different century. What would you do? How would the new worlsd around you react to you? This is what happens all the time to Zak Emblsin and Sarah Templeman, who are 'reincarnaters', connected across time by a shared soul.

Imagine you are a bright young scientist, Carmen Fry, who stumbles across the truth behind reincarnation. All you need is a subject to prove your theory to the world, but you can't find one. Until one day, when you are chatting online…

Birmingham, England, May 2026

Carmen and Zak were chatting online.

"So what is a good-looking guy like you doing chatting online on a Friday night when you could be out with friends?"

"I could, I suppose. Actually, I don't have that many friends."

Carmen didn't know what to say to that, so Zak's screen stayed blank for a while. Zak knew he had to do something or risk losing Carmen's attention. Something told him it would be a mistake to do that.

"Anyway," he wrote, "I could ask you the same thing. Why aren't you out tonight – I mean, I'm glad you're not, but why not?"

"Well, unlike you, I do have friends. But they're scientists. They live at the lab. Research is everything to them, even on a Friday night."

"But not for you?"

"I like to have other types of fun occasionally… Hey, Zak, can we do this on Messenger? I want to know what your voice sounds like – see if you're really the tall blond athlete in the photo you sent me."

"You mean, you want to see if I'm even the same guy! Fair enough, but I warn you, I have no clothes on."

"Shame on you. Just give me the headshot then."

"Hang on, you should be able to see me now."

"There you are. That's better. Is that a Pentatonix poster on your wall? I love their music. And you *are* the same guy, how about that! You'd be surprised how many people send a photo of someone else."

"No, I wouldn't. You look a bit different, yourself. I think it's your hair, Carmen; you have dark hair."

"Is that a problem?"

"No, of course not. It's just I thought you had red hair." The phrase *watch out for Carmens with red hair* came unbidden and unrecognised into Zak's mind. He blinked it away.

"I did, last year. The photo I sent you was taken then. Hey, you're also a liar! You do have clothes on."

"Sorry to disappoint you."

"I'm not disappointed. You look great, and your voice is sexy."

There was an awkward pause.

"Carmen, where are we going with this?"

"It's just fun, Zak. What's the problem?"

"I'm enjoying it too much."

"What do you mean? I don't understand what you mean by that."

One of Carmen's pet hates was people who did something and then beat themselves up over it. If he wasn't comfortable flirting, he shouldn't flirt. End of. She decided to give him another five minutes before giving up on him, but only because he was hot. And because of that other teasing possibility, which had led her here in the first place.

Zak let out a deep sigh. A movement caught his eye. He glanced out of the window and noticed two squirrels chasing each other up and down the Scots Pine with breath-taking 360-degree turns. Zak lived in the attic flat of an Edwardian terraced house. One advantage to this was the mature trees in the garden. He hesitated. Should he tell her? He was risking a lot. He looked in the room behind Carmen's head for some clue to her personality. There was a map of the Universe on the wall. Was that a good sign? He decided to go for it.

"Before we go any further, there's some stuff you should know about me."

"What, apart from the sexy voice and that you're illegally good-looking?"

"I'm serious. You might not want to do this once you know everything."

"Sorry, I always joke when I get nervous. You have a girlfriend? Is that it?"

"No."

"Boyfriend?"

"No!"

"Two girlfriends?"

"Please try to be serious."

"Believe me, two girlfriends 'would' be serious, for you. Sorry, I'm doing it again, aren't I? What is it then, do you have a criminal record?"

"I'm…I'm not well."

"What are we talking here, are we talking wheelchairs? I could handle that."

Carmen looked behind Zak to see if she could see a wheelchair or crutches. She saw neither but she did see a couple of hardback astronomy books which caught her attention.

"I'm…schizophrenic," Zak continued.

"Shit!"

"What?"

"Sorry, Zak. I shouldn't have reacted like that. Please tell me about it. That's if you want to."

Zak told Carmen everything. From the time he first knew he was Sarah, at about four years old. It was easy talking to Carmen, maybe because he didn't know her yet. Plus, she was cute, if a little skinny. And she wasn't in the room with him, so he could always just switch her off if things got difficult.

Carmen listened attentively without making any comments beyond sympathising with him. "That must have been such an ordeal for you," she said at one point.

At the end of it, he felt enormously relieved. It was so good just to have told someone that it almost didn't matter how she reacted. The reaction he was expecting was a question. When people found out about his schizophrenia, they usually asked how he could tell when he was Sarah and what triggered the change. Some asked if there was a cure. There wasn't.

Carmen did ask a question but an unexpected one. She said, "Are you sure it's schizophrenia? Split personality? I mean that's such an incredibly rare occurrence in schizophrenia. And there is an alternative explanation."

"What alternative explanation?"

Carmen hesitated. "You might really have a connection with this Sarah from the future."

Zak was not at all sure he liked this idea. The time when he had wanted people to believe him about Sarah was when he had been very young. It had been so hurtful to him to be treated like a naughty child simply for telling the truth. He would always carry that pain with him. Over the years, he had gradually come to accept that all Sarah's emotions and experiences, no matter how real they seemed, had to be a trick of the mind. Even when he left clothes out for her, even when she damaged his body, he knew it was really him that was doing these things. The doctors all agreed on this. And accepting it had allowed him to get on with his life. To move on.

As he thought about it, Zak realised that this was 'why' he had accepted the schizophrenia diagnosis – so that he could lead a near-normal life, so he could stop worrying that no one believed him. It was a convenient escape from isolation, but deep down, he had never really believed the diagnosis. And now Carmen was offering him a different escape route. He decided to take it.

"That's what I've always thought, but no one ever believed me."

“I believe you.”

“Why?”

“I’m actually creeped out by the whole situation. My area of research is quantum entanglement. Did you know that? Is that why you found me online?”

“You found me online.”

“Right, sorry.”

“Quantum entanglement? What is that exactly?”

“We don’t know ‘exactly’, but we do know that what we do to a particle over here affects a different, ‘entangled’ particle over there, without anyone touching it. And the distances can be huge – across whole galaxies even. Now, there is growing evidence that space (and therefore also time) can bend around on itself – or even tear – and let the fabric of another part of space through the hole, like a hernia.”

“Is that what people call wormholes?”

“Sort of. Anyway, we…I mean, I now believe that whole systems or even beings can be entangled across time as well as space. What freaks me out is that as part of my research – attempts to find evidence of different parts of spacetime connecting with each other in a non-linear way – I’ve been looking at reincarnation stories. I thought maybe the consciousness of one individual from the future might become entangled with another living individual’s consciousness. This might show itself as a ‘reincarnated’ soul. Is any of this starting to sound familiar?”

“Very. So Sarah might be real?”

“It’s possible, yes.”

“But she hasn’t even been born yet! Won’t be for over a hundred years. How can she be real?”

“I know. Weird, isn’t it? But completely explicable with what we’re now discovering about quantum tunnelling and how the Universe works. Proof would be nice, though.”

“Now you’re creeping ‘me’ out. Is that why ‘you’ found ‘me’ online?”

“Oh, sorry, Zak, no. I didn’t mean that. I meant proof in a general sense. I wasn’t suggesting you become my lab rat. I didn’t know anything about you when I contacted you.”

“That’s a relief. Just supposing I were your ‘lab rat’, do you think I could help you?”

"Well, we could learn a lot anecdotally. And your brain patterns might prove interesting, but to be honest, you're not the best subject."

Zak was almost offended. "Why not?"

"Your connection is with someone from the future not the past. Most reincarnation cases involve someone claiming to have lived before. We can visit places and check historical documents to verify these claims. What you experience as Sarah can't be proven because it hasn't happened yet."

"You don't think mine is a typical reincarnation case?"

"No. Although in one sense, it is because you say you have lived Sarah's life."

"Definitely. I can remember it – parts of it, anyway."

"When you say 'parts of it', how much are you talking about, one or two memories maybe?"

"More. For my childhood as Sarah, I can recall almost as much as I can about my childhood as Zak. What's strange is that there is nothing after Sarah's 29th birthday."

"Perhaps she will die young."

Zak's face turned white.

"God, no. I hadn't thought of that."

Silence. It was a full minute before Zak spoke again, and when he did, his tone had changed completely. Carmen could see at once that she had upset him. What a stupid mistake to have made! He had just got through telling her that he 'is' Sarah, and she killed Sarah off! Of course, he was going to feel that, even if he did turn out to be delusional.

"Carmen, I can't talk about this anymore. Text me sometime."

"I don't have your mobile…" but Zak was gone.

****

Birmingham, England, Earlier in May 2026

Carmen Fry was trawling through names of known schizophrenics on the internet, but only those with the delusion of identity form of the condition. She had started to wonder if some of these people might, like those who say they've lived a past life, be experiencing some form of quantum entanglement with another real person. She was working in the Quiet Area of the University Library as she had forgotten the swipe card she needed to get into the building where her own office was. That was OK; Carmen often used the library. There was always an assignment due in somewhere in the University, so the library was usually full of people her own age, studying away. She felt she belonged.

It was amazing how few of the schizophrenia sufferers out there were of any interest to her research profile. She felt as though she must have found them all already. And then, after hours of searching, and two coffee breaks, she found Professor James Armitage's case studies on MEDLINE about a boy who presented at age five with delusions of becoming a five-year-old American girl 'from the future'.

This was more like it. As she read on, Carmen got increasingly excited as more boxes were ticked. He lived in Birmingham, how about that? At least, he did when he was five. She checked the birth date… 1st May 2007. Let's see, that would make him, what, 19 now, just one year younger than she was herself. Even better, he had an unusual name, Zak Emblin, which should make him easier to track down. Carmen immediately searched Facebook for Zak Emblins in the West Midlands area, expecting no hits. Instead, a slender, blond, blue-eyed six-footer with a charming, crooked smile, looked back at her, along with the bonus of 'single' status. "Bingo!" said Carmen, a little too loudly, and five people turned around at once to glare their disapproval.

All she had to do now was to track him down.

Birmingham, England, 22 June 2022

Zak left school at 5 pm because he went to Drama club on a Monday. It was supposed to help with his self-confidence. So there was no one to see the trouble that was waiting for him as he stepped through the school gates on to Vicarage Road, which had long since lost its vicarage and now had a petrol station on the corner instead. The Tesco Express there was very popular with the school pupils for buying sweets on the way to and from school, and sometimes during lesson time as well, if they could sneak out. A sign in the window read 'No more than three school children allowed in the shop at any one time.' The manager of the petrol station, Darren Kingsley, hated children and had convinced himself that he had a shoplifting problem. If he had bothered to look at the figures, he would have seen that the school kids and their custom were the reason his shop showed a healthy profit every month.

Zak saw four of them coming towards him. This could be more serious than usual. Zak weighed his options. He had been attacked many times for being a 'freak' – for his multiple personality disorder, his schizophrenia – but this looked different. There was a kid he didn't recognise from Tommy's (St Thomas's), the roughest school around, and he appeared to be the ringleader.

"There he is," said Anton to Sean, this newcomer. "Or should I say, 'There "she" is'? How's it hanging, Sarah?"

"Surely, you mean 'How are "they" hanging?' if you are trying to imply that I am a woman," said Zak, pointing to his breast area. "And anyway, I am not Sarah today." Zak realised as soon as the words were out that they would not help his situation.

"You're right," said the small, wiry stranger to Anton, "he is a freak. And this is what we do to freaks where I come from." He lunged forwards in one movement bringing the knife, which was hidden up his sleeve, into his right hand and plunging it into Zak's chest.

Zak just managed a step backwards before the knife, which no one had seen or expected, entered his body. This step saved his life. The knife punctured the lower part of his right lung, where it might have entered his heart, had he not moved. He fell to the floor, bleeding profusely and spluttering, struggling to catch his breath.

Seeing how serious the injury was, Zak's red-haired attacker ran off in panic along with one of Anton's other friends. Anton himself, who had invited this unknown boy from another school to join in their Zak-taunting games, was really upset and kept apologising to Zak.

"I had no idea he had a knife, please believe me, Zak," he said, calling the emergency services on his mobile. This done, he pressed his school jacket against the wound to stop some of the bleeding and told the other boy, who was frozen still in shock, to make a pillow for Zak's head with his jacket.

Presently an ambulance arrived, and the paramedics took over. Zak would need twelve stitches and would probably have a nasty scar between the ninth and tenth ribs on his right side. More urgently, he had a punctured lung, which would take him three weeks to recover from.

****

New Palm Springs, USA, 8 March 2116

Zelda sipped her coffee and looked at the screen showing the caesarean operation taking place on her lower abdomen. She was calm and relaxed, feeling no pain. Noticing how much blood there was and how wide the cut, she regretted for a moment not using a surrogate to grow her baby. The moment passed, and she felt proud of her decision, against the advice of family and friends, to carry the baby to term in her own body – something few women did these days. She hoped it would make the bond between them stronger. She glanced across at Bron and found him looking at her already. She hated the way he caught her like this when she was deep in thought. It was an intrusion.

The doctors' excited voices brought their attention back to the child who had now emerged, soft, plump and purple, their very own brown-eyed baby with lots of dark hair. Midwife Christine washed the placenta from the infant's face and body and, umbilical cord still intact, gently placed the crying new life into Zelda's arms.

It was Bron who first noticed the scar, about four inches long between the baby's ribs low down on the right side of her chest. It was darker in colour than the skin around it, slightly raised and about a fingernail's width across.

"What is that?" he asked, pointing. "Did you cut her, getting her out?"

Everyone saw it now.

"No, definitely not," said the gynaecologist, offended. "It would be bleeding if we had. Must be a birthmark of some sort."

"Trust you to give birth to some kind of freak!" Bron yelled at his wife.

Mouths dropped open and looks were exchanged, but Zelda knew how to handle her husband.

"Don't worry, Bron," she said gently, "I've seen far worse. Don't you think she's beautiful?"

After a moment's struggle, a reluctant smile appeared on Bron's face. "I suppose she is," he said and kissed Zelda on the forehead. They were both gazing lovingly at the child now. "What do you think then, Zel, about the name? Do you think she's a Sarah?"

"I think she is very much a Sarah. 'The' Sarah. Sarah Templeman."

From nowhere, Bron produced a flask of whiskey and drank some.

"What?" he said, seeing Zelda's and everyone else's disapproving expressions. "Birth of your first child? You gotta celebrate that, even if she is a freak."

****

Birmingham, England, 20 July 2022

Zak had only been back at school for a week when Anton came up to him in the playground. Zak was taken by surprise as he'd assumed that, feeling guilty, Anton would stay out of his way. It was a very different Anton who spoke to Zak from the taunting bully he had become used to hearing.

"Thanks for speaking up for me, Zak, you know, to Mr Ford. I'm sure he would have suspended me if you hadn't told him, you know, about me calling the ambulance and that."

Zak didn't know what to say.

"You're OK, Zak. I don't think you're a freak anymore. I'm sorry about all that stuff." And with that, he rushed off.

On its own, this might not have been enough to impress Zak after all that he had gone through at Anton's hands, but he was impressed because Anton backed it up by looking out for him while he was recovering. He offered to carry his stuff between classes, asked how the wound was recovering and if it would leave a scar, and even took abuse from his former friends for helping a 'faggot who doesn't even know if he's a boy or a girl'.

Birmingham, England, March 2025

Zak was enjoying the attention of two attractive girls from the school he used to go to – they were both in the year below him – and trying to decide whether he should offer to walk them home. It was a tricky decision because, one, they had each other to walk home with, so why would they need him; two, he lived in the opposite direction, so it would take him a long time to get home, unless he took the bus; three, he didn't even go to school anymore, so it might seem a bit creepy that he was hanging around the school gates at 4 pm, if he did any more than just talk to them – after all, they didn't know the real reason he was here.

Just at that moment Zak's mind was made up for him when he saw Anton approach one of the Year 11 boys on a mountain bike, and was reminded of the real reason he was here: to check what Anton was up to. He had seen Anton a couple of times recently and had noticed a change in him. He'd become alternately withdrawn and irritable. He was particularly sensitive if you asked him what he'd been doing lately.

One of the girls, the tall one, was still chatting away, making her friend giggle, but Zak no longer heard. His attention was focussed on the transaction taking place about 50 metres away. Anton handed over something small and got notes back, which he immediately counted. This was serious. The kid was only 15 or 16.

Zak said a quick goodbye to his flirting companions, who feigned disappointment, walked over to Anton, pretended to see him for the first time and greeted him warmly. Anton did not look pleased to see Zak, so he got straight to the point.

"I'm your friend, Ant, so I can say this because I'm on your side. You're looking at a prison sentence and a criminal record if you're selling blow to school kids."

"I don't know what you're talking about."

Zak stopped walking and pulled back Anton's hoodie to make him stop cycling alongside him. "This is me you're talking to, Ant. Don't lie to me. I saw you do it."

Anton's shoulders dropped as the tension went out of him. "I'm sorry, Zak, I'm letting you down. But it's only blow, and I'm really short at the moment."

"How can you be short? I got you that job on the bins."

"Lost it."

Zak said nothing for a few seconds in case his friend wanted to elaborate but didn't embarrass him by pressing for further details. He guessed Anton had found the early morning starts too difficult.

"Who's your supplier? It's not Sean Miller, is it?"

Anton said nothing, but then he didn't have to. Zak looked really concerned.

"Listen, Ant. You must stay away from him. He manipulates people. You might only be selling blow now, but he'll soon have you pushing harder drugs."

"Don't say that, Zak. You sound like me Mam. I don't even see Sean; he's like the boss now. It's someone else, someone who works for Sean, who always gives me the stuff."

"OK, Ant, please promise me this much. If Sean ever asks to see you personally, let me go instead. He's a bully, and I know how to handle bullies. I don't want you ending up in prison, you little shit, even if you do cause me aggro."

"OK, OK, I promise. Now leave me alone." And Anton cycled off, annoyed again.

Zak watched him go, decided it was very unlikely that Anton would heed his advice, and then went home himself.

****

Birmingham, England, 20 June 2026

Carmen and Zak were eating in her favourite Italian restaurant, Marco's, which was also renowned for its wide selection of desserts from around the world, some of which were on display behind where Zak was sitting.

"Do you know how difficult you were to track down?"

"Sorry. I was just upset for a while, you know, about Sarah dying young. Didn't want to talk to anyone."

Least of all me, thought Carmen.

"You got that right…"

For a split second, it seemed to Carmen as if Zak had read her mind. Then he added, "…about Sarah dying young, I mean. It explains a few things."

"Like what?"

"There's this recurrent dream I have, both as Sarah and as me but more often as Sarah. There's a sudden impact, a flash of light, breaking glass, then a feeling of being trapped, isolated, forgotten, then total, unforgiving blackness."

"And what do you think that means?"

"I think it's a car accident…or something similar. I'm not even sure if they have cars in Sarah's world. I know they're technologically advanced."

"Could it be, well, just a dream?"

Zak played with his cannelloni. "No. I've thought about that. It's too real. Sometimes I've seen it while I'm awake. It's more like a memory. And once – I think I suppressed this knowledge before and you resurrected it when you suggested Sarah might die young – once, I 'was' Sarah, celebrating my 29th birthday. I left the party, and the last images I recall were exactly as in the dream."

"I'm sorry, Zak."

"And there's something else."

"What?"

"That time I experienced it after Sarah's party was different. It was a long time ago. I was only about seven, but it was different."

"In what way?"

"I felt pain, horrendous pain, in my head and chest. The pain disappeared as everything went black. Then I was suddenly Zak again."

"God, Zak. That doesn't sound good."

"Carmen. Do you think this means that I will also die when I reach 29? We are like one being, Sarah and I. We are connected."

"I honestly don't know, Zak. I'm not an expert on reincarnation yet." He had been hoping for a different answer from Carmen and looked disappointed. She saw this. "What I do know is that many of the documented cases where reincarnation has supposedly occurred involved two people with very different lifespans. You might have nothing to worry about."

"I hope you're right. 29, that's like ten years away. There's so much I want to do."

"I know."

"But even if I don't die, Sarah does…unless I can stop it."

"What do you mean 'stop it'?" Carmen put the fork full of radicchio leaf stuffed with goat's cheese back down on her plate, suddenly concerned.

"It's in the future, right? Hasn't happened yet. There might be a way to prevent it."

"I don't know, Zak. Sounds dangerous to me…you know, the butterfly effect and all that. You might end up changing the whole world. It could make things worse."

Zak pondered this, but not for long.

"Worse? How could it be worse? I don't want to lose Sarah. She's part of me. I wonder if I could somehow force a transfer – through my thoughts? That can't do any harm to anyone, surely? And she must be aware of me, right, as I am of her?"

"Well, I'm still not sure you should try and prevent her death. It's 'meant' to happen, in this universe at any rate; but consciously forcing a transfer – that might be interesting. How would you go about doing that?"

"Good question. I've never tried to do it before. It's always just happened. I've focussed all my attention before on trying to 'stop' it happening." Zak stood up suddenly, a mistake for someone six-feet tall, pushed his chair back into the man behind and spilled his coffee. "Got to go!"

"Wait! What do you mean? You haven't finished your cannelloni! You're not rushing off and leaving me again, are you?"

“Really sorry, Carmen, but I’ve just got to try contacting Sarah right away. I can’t wait to see if it works. I’m going to concentrate my mental energy on all the positive memories I have of her to see if I can make a connection.”

“Can’t you have dessert first? Sarah will still be…wherever she is in half an hour’s time. Marco is famous for his desserts. You’ve got to try his Olly Golly. It’s a traditional Oxfordshire recipe – it’s amazing.”

“Here, take this, it should cover my half.” Zak handed over £40. “We must do this again sometime.”

“We haven’t done it this time!”

But Zak didn’t hear Carmen’s protest, he was gone.

Carmen was left wondering how she could be feeling jealous of the only woman Zak could never form a relationship with since they always shared the same body. “Bloody Sarah,” she muttered and made for the exit, leaving no tip as if the restaurant were somehow to blame for Zak’s early departure.

"…space cannot be thought of as it once was: intervening space, regardless of how much there is, does not ensure that two objects are separate, since quantum mechanics allows an entanglement, a kind of connection, to exist between them."

Brian Greene, *The Fabric of the Cosmos,* p80.

University of Birmingham, Birmingham, England, November 2025

Carmen Fry, at 19, one of the youngest postgraduates in the history of the Department of Physics, was addressing the annual conference of researchers in the field of applied quantum mechanics, this year hosted by her own University. Her supervisor Professor Williamson was in the lecture theatre wearing a concerned frown as she reached her conclusion.

"First Einstein proved that space and time were part of one entity, spacetime. Then quantum mechanics showed that, without touching it, you can change a particle on the other side of the Universe if you change its entangled particle, here, on this side of the Universe. In more recent years, quantum tunnelling has suggested that whole entities, even universes, might be transported instantly across the Cosmos. What my research will show is that 'this really happens' across time for 'entangled' humans – people who share the same soul – and that this is what reincarnation really is, a form of quantum tunnelling."

Carmen received only polite applause and some jeers. She knew she had a long way to go to convince this audience of the validity of her chosen line of research. Her supervisor made the same point when they met for a drink after the session.

****

"You are a talented physicist and researcher, Carmen. Don't throw it all away on an idea which at best, may take decades – who knows, perhaps even centuries – to prove. At worst, and this is much more likely, you could make yourself a laughing-stock within the whole physics community."

****

"If you think that, Professor Williamson, why did you agree to supervise me?"

"It was a close thing. Your proposal was right; there is much unexplained data out there which needs looking at, but what swung it for me was that I couldn't think of a better explanation for reincarnation, unless everyone who claims to have experienced it is lying. Just be careful. Research into areas of popular interest can attract unwelcome publicity. Make sure you cover your tracks."

New Palm Springs, USA, 8 March 2145

The party had finished later than Sarah thought it would, and she was just a little drunk. What did they put in those cocktails? She couldn't remember where she had parked her gyro. This was a good thing, she decided, because it forced her to wander around the pod port of the Skytel where they'd held the party, keys in hand, breathing in the night air and sobering up. The problem was the night air was a little too fresh, so when her keys finally got a response to their beeping and she knew she'd found the right pod, she was sober, yes, but also so cold that her hands wouldn't operate the throttle.

It was a bit old and rusty, but Sarah loved her gyro. It had always been reliable, passing the Dept of Transport DOT test every year without costing too much. She managed to get it going and cruised at just above roof height to see her way home more easily as the SatNav was broken. *Must get that fixed,* she thought, humming The Laserheads' latest hit – (it was lame, but the tune got stuck in your head) – *then it could just fly me home on auto and I wouldn't ever have to worry about how much I'd had to drink.*

Sarah wondered if she had enough cat food left in the flat to feed poor old Boudicca – it had been a bit of a rush getting ready for the party, so she hadn't had time for shopping. Never mind, she could always be given a pouch of tuna. Twenty-nine, eh? 'Entering her 30th year' as some unhelpful person at the party had put it. "Sarah," she told herself, "you're getting old." Then she laughed bitterly, and finally, she cried.

****

Birmingham, England, 20 June 2026

As soon as he got home from the restaurant, Zak tried to contact Sarah. He imagined that if he could totally relax and concentrate on good memories he'd had as Sarah, this might help him to connect to her. The difficult bit would be finding a way to warn her of her early death on her 29th birthday, so that she could change what she was doing that day.

But he couldn't relax. He was too excited at the thought of doing something proactive, for the first time, in relation to Sarah. Normally, he just became Sarah without any warning and without wanting it to happen. It took him two glasses of wine, a shower and the slow movement of Brahms's *Second Piano Concerto*, the classic 1977 Pollini recording, to get into the right frame of mind. For a time, nothing happened. Curiously, it was only when he got frustrated with the whole thing, wondering what else he could possibly do to make contact, and banged the table, that it finally worked.

Suddenly he was Sarah, five years old, playing with a remote-controlled toy gyro her mom had given her for her birthday. There had been no time to warn her or connect with her in any other way, the transition was immediate and total.

****

8 March 2145

She was feeling better now. Flying the gyro with one vent open had sobered her up a bit. When she spotted her apartment block on the horizon, she felt an acute pang of belonging. She pictured herself there, steaming Fresco in hand, and the beautiful, long-haired, chestnut form of Boudicca stretched out purring in her lap.

It was then that she felt the sharp, stabbing pain in her lower ribs on the right side, just where the scar was, and heard herself call out, “Anton! Help!” as she looked up into the shocked faces of four teenaged boys, one holding a bloody knife.

“Not now, Zak, not now!” shouted Sarah. “I wanted to say goodbye to Boudicca first,” were her very last words as the old but reliable gyro, which would later be blamed for the accident, plummeted from the sky. Its cockpit shattered on impact with the streetlight which, surprisingly, stayed on for a few seconds, illuminating Sarah’s broken head and body as it bent over the gyro before going out with one last flash.

Just before dying, Sarah re-entered her own body. “Thanks a bunch, Zak,” she muttered and briefly wondered what she would have done with the decades ahead of her. Not much, in truth. Sarah didn’t know it – the kind folk at Population Control had stopped informing people – but she was scheduled to die the following month anyway…in a gyro crash.

****

Einstein: “For we convinced physicists, the distinction between past, present and future is only an illusion, however persistent.”

Albert Einstein, *Albert Einstein and Michele Besso Correspondence 1903–1955,* P. Speziale, ed. Paris. Hermann, 1972

****

Birmingham, England, September 2011

Sue Emblin looked down at her near-perfect son building a futuristic tower out of Duplo. She'd had no idea that he was this good at building things. Her eyes filled with tears. Tears of regret, mainly, because Zak's father, Robin, was not here to share the moment, having needlessly got himself killed in that car accident just after Zak was born four years ago. *Why, Robin?* Tears of joy, also, because he was so gorgeous, with his blond, wavy hair and blue eyes. And tears of gratitude for having been blessed by God with such a bright, normal, healthy child.

"You're my beautiful baby, aren't you?" She couldn't resist hugging him. "My beautiful baby, Zachary." Robin would never have agreed to 'Zachary'; Zachary, like Saccharine because he was just so sweet, and she couldn't call him 'Sugar', could she?

"Come here, Sugar!" said Sue and put her arms out to pick up the child.

Sue's beautiful, 'normal', 'healthy' baby looked at her, puzzled, pushed her away and said, "My name's not Sugar. I am Sarah. These are not my toys. This" – he pointed at the tower of Duplo – "is where I live. Can I go home now?"

Sue stared, open-mouthed. She staggered backwards and fell into the uncomfortable brown armchair which she never used. What she remembered from the Early Years Child Care course she had started but never completed, told her that four-year-olds did not play practical jokes on grown-ups. Dishonesty came a little later in their behavioural development. But that had to be the explanation, didn't it? What other explanation could there be?

"Zak darling, please don't play games. You're upsetting Mummy. You *are* home. You know that."

"No! No! No! Sarah not home. You are not my mom. You're fat. My mom's tall. I want to go home. Want *my* mom!"

The child was obviously sick. Sue was strangely relieved by this thought. It was clearly a severe illness, but this was better than what her gut instinct was telling her, which was that Zak had really become a different child. (*Wasn't that an American accent?*)

"We will take you home now, shall we? Let's pack up your toys and get your coat."

This had the desired effect. Zak calmed down immediately, knocked over the tower, laughed as it fell and started to collect the pieces. But how would he react when she got him to the Doctor's?

On the No. 47 bus, Sue went along with Zak's insistence that he was Sarah. She pretended it was a game so as not to attract attention from the other passengers. Mercifully there was no one on the bus who knew her.

"Why are we going so slow?" asked Zak. "Why are we still on the ground?"

"It's OK, Zak darling, don't worry." Sue put a finger to her lips to try and get Zak to be quiet.

"This is not a gyro. What is it? Is it a train?"

"It's a bus, Zak dear. You've been on buses before."

"No. I've never been on a bus."

Zak suddenly became distracted by the people and buildings going by the bus window, so Sue decided to leave him. While he stayed silent, he couldn't embarrass her.

At the Doctor's, Zak made straight for the Duplo box in Sue's bag and started to build the same tower, saying "Mom" every now and then and pointing at it. When they were called to see Dr West, Sue had to drag him away.

"What can I do for you?" asked Dr West, a short, plump, middle-aged man in a waistcoat who peered over his glasses.

"It's Zak," said Sue. "I don't know where to start. Zak is…having some sort of delusion. He thinks he's another child called Sarah."

The GP looked straight at Zak and smiled. "Hello there. How are you feeling?"

There was no response, only a long, suspicious stare.

"I don't think I've seen you before," Dr West continued. "Would you mind telling me your name?"

The child thought for a few seconds and the mouth came open as if to speak, but no words came out. Dr West decided to make himself less intimidating by crouching down to Zak's level and taking off his reading glasses.

"I am Dr West, Dr Adam West. What is your name? I'd love to know who it is I'm speaking to."

"Zak Emblin," said Zak, very quietly.

A squeal of delight came out of Sue and she had to apologise.

"Zak, is that really you?"

"Yes, Mum. Let go, you're hurting me!"

Sue apologised profusely to Dr West for wasting his time, although he would have none of this, and left as fast as she could, dragging Zak behind her.

Most of the way home, Sue said nothing to Zak apart from, "Oh, my Sweet!" and, "It's good to have you back," or, "I thought I'd lost you, I really did, Sugar." There was also a lot of hugging and kissing of the top of his head.

Sue was so happy and relieved that she couldn't stop smiling. But she could not help noticing that little Zak was not reacting the same way, now that his ordeal was over. He looked confused, maybe even a little scared.

"Come on, soldier, cheer up. We'll be home soon. You just had a bit of a nightmare, that's all, only in the daytime. Let's get you home and we can forget all about it."

Zak thought about this for a few seconds, frowning, then said, "I wasn't dreaming, Mummy. I was Sarah. Please don't let it happen again. I don't like being Sarah; she's upset. I want to be Zak."

For the second time that day, Sue's jaw dropped open. Only this time, she could find no words.

****

Birmingham, England, Early November 2011

Zak did not get his wish. Over the next few weeks and months, he became Sarah more and more often. It rarely lasted more than a few minutes, but apart from this, there was no pattern to it. The second time was the worst. It lasted a whole week, making his mother think she had lost him forever. The change could come at any time – when he was asleep, eating, at school, even on the toilet. Once he made a mess because he was urinating when he became Sarah. He turned and sat down, because girls pee sitting down, and sent a stream across the floor.

At first, Sue tried to pretend it wasn't happening. "He's got an imaginary friend," she'd tell people who overheard him being Sarah. When he started doing it at school and when she had friends around, she had to face the truth, whatever that was.

A few weeks after she had seen Dr West, she was invited to talk to Zak's teacher after school. There was 'a problem', Miss Chaplain had informed her over the phone, and instantly she guessed what had happened.

"We have a duty of care, not just for Zak but for the other children," she was told.

They were sitting in the Headmistress's office, three of them, Sue, Miss Chaplain and the Headmistress, Mrs Douglas. It was Rachel Chaplain who was doing the talking. It was a remarkably small office – as if the architects had just done the whole school child-sized, forgetting that the Head Teacher would be an adult. Miss Chaplain's slender knees were almost touching Sue's own.

"Some of the other children find his behaviour upsetting. You should seek medical help."

There was an awkward pause. Mrs Douglas was looking at the floor. "In the meantime, we don't think this is the best environment for Zak." Mrs Douglas looked up and spoke for the first time. "We feel he might be better looked after at home."

In other words, her son had been expelled from Reception in his very first year at school. Sue decided immediately that she would fight this. Speak to the

School Governors if necessary. And she 'would' seek medical advice. But she also felt ashamed. Ashamed of the boy who had got himself expelled at only four years old! Then she felt ashamed of herself for feeling ashamed.

****

Birmingham, England, August 2026

Zak was doing his regular warm-up slot at the Glee Club on a Friday night.

"...Unnecessary signs, they really bug me. In my local Department Store, there are signs saying 'Menswear' and 'Womenswear'. I know. We all swear, so what?"

"Instructions on medicines, they're even more infuriating. 'Shake well before opening'." Zak shook visibly. "How long before is 'well before'? What? No, it's important, I need to know when I have to do that."

"'Take one pill, three times a day'. Now that's impossible, and believe me, I've tried. It doesn't come out the other end; you can only take a pill once."

"'Library images' which are not of a library, that really bugs me, too, because I've worked in a library, so I know what they look like. Here's an example."

A news item appeared on the screen of a large ocean-going liner coming into port. Below it was the caption 'Library pictures'.

"Now, that's not a library, it's a ship. *This* is a library."

Zak clicked and the image of a typical public library came up on the screen with rows and rows of books on shelves and a PC.

"How do they make mistakes like that? My niece wouldn't make mistakes like that because she's clever. Have you noticed that some people are so intelligent, they're stupid? Yeah? It's right, isn't it? She's one of these people. They can't find things, can't dress themselves or comb their hair; they wear odd socks. Yet if you ask them what a 'charmed quark' is, they'll know the answer. Straight away, they'll come back with, 'The charmed quark has electric charge two-thirds times the elementary charge and charm C equal to +1. It is more massive than the up, down and strange quarks, a quark being any of a number of subatomic particles carrying a fractional electric charge, postulated as building blocks of the hadrons. Quarks have not been directly observed but theoretical predictions based on their existence have been confirmed experimentally."

This, which was spoken very rapidly, was greeted with applause.

"Yeah, impressive, eh?" And Zak pointed to his uncombed hair, got a laugh, then pulled his trousers up a little to reveal bright, odd socks.

"What was I saying? Oh yeah, my niece is one of these clever people. My niece Hayley is learning the cello. Beautiful instrument, but she struggled at first because she's left-handed, and you have to bow a cello right-handed so all the bows go in the same direction in the orchestra. Mind you, it also made a difference when we stopped her putting it under her chin."

"She's always been trouble for her mum, my sister. I remember once, when she was little, I had to take them both to A&E. My sister was distraught. 'Doctor, can you help my daughter, please?' she said, 'She's swallowed one of my tablets. Is it serious? Can you save her?'"

"Save her?" repeated the doctor, puzzled, "I should think so. What did she swallow? Warfarin? Thyroxine?"

"'Apple iPad', says my sister."

The audience laughed.

After his set, as he was on his way out of the club, a couple holding hands walked past Zak into the street. Without her boyfriend noticing, the girl, in her twenties, turned slightly, smiled at Zak, and put a piece of paper into his hand. It was her mobile number. He was still rooted to the spot, smiling at the good fortune his stand-up routine was bringing him, when a voice disturbed him.

"Hey, Zak."

Zak looked up to see Carmen and coloured up slightly, hastily putting the piece of paper into his pocket.

"That was really good. I had no idea you could do that."

"Thanks. You here on your own?"

"No. A friend from the Lab came along. He's in the Gents. I'm intrigued, Zak. You're so shy; how can you do that, get up in front of an audience and perform like that?"

"Dunno. I've always been comfortable with it. I find one-to-one situations more difficult. Anyway, you do the same when you deliver papers at conferences."

"I know, but I get so nervous beforehand, I practically throw up. I'd love to have a go at this, though."

"You would? I might hold you to that."

"That'd be great. Gotta go, Zak, see you," said Carmen suddenly, looking at a text she'd just received on her phone. Zak watched her cross the street and saw her link arms with a tall, muscly guy before leaving.

Birmingham, England, Late November 2011

By the time Sue's appointment with the Chair of the Governors, Mrs Douglas and Rachel Chaplain came around, she'd been back to Dr West and told him that the school didn't want Zak. The Doctor had listened patiently. Surely it was too much to expect that Zak would become Sarah while they were at the Doctor's, but just as they were leaving, he had said to Dr West, "Who are you? Where is my mom?"

Dr West had motioned to Sue to sit back down again and had talked to 'Sarah' for five whole minutes. They had left 'Sarah' playing with her favourite Duplo in the Waiting Room while the Doctor explained to Sue that he believed Zak had a multiple personality disorder and would require specialist treatment. "Does that include a Special School?" she had asked. Dr West had told her that it did, and that she would be receiving a letter of invitation from that school before long. First, however, Zak would have to see a specialist.

Because of this conversation, the appointment with the Chair of the Governors had now become an opportunity to withdraw Zak from the school without having him expelled. The teachers didn't know that yet. Before telling them, Sue had every intention of making them suffer for the way Miss Chaplain had spoken to her last time.

She listened as patiently as she could (she was an impatient person) as Miss Chaplain explained to the Chair of the Governors how Zak had refused to respond to his name when the register was taken, had denied that Zak Emblin 'was' his name and upon being asked what his name was, had replied, "Sarah Templeman." This had made the rest of the class laugh and become disruptive. At break, he had had to be forcibly removed from the girls' toilets and had burst into tears when told he had to use the boys' toilet. In Literacy, he had written nothing for the whole class 'because it wasn't his exercise book'. One afternoon several children had spoken to Miss Chaplain, crying, because all through the lunch break Zak had carried on pretending to be 'Sarah', despite being told off for doing this by the lunchtime supervisor. And it had scared them. Two more girls had started calling Zak 'Sarah' and wanted 'her' to join their 'club'.

Parents were complaining that Zak was a disruptive influence. They didn't want him in their child's class. He was play-acting all the time and preventing their children from learning. Miss Chaplain sat down a little too firmly and, it seemed to Sue, with an air of triumph. Being small and skinny, she bounced a little, which added to this effect.

"So you see," said Mrs Douglas to the Chair of the Governors, "we have little choice—"

"Too right you have little choice," interrupted Sue. "You have little choice but to follow the law. And the law says you must" – she reached into her handbag and drew out a scrap of paper, from which she read – "accommodate a child with a disability in a state school until he or she can be placed in a suitable special needs school. I know," she added, leaning forwards and jabbing her finger at the Head Teacher, "I've Googled it! I will be bringing Zak in tomorrow" – she looked directly at Rachel Chaplain – "and you *will* teach him."

It was Mrs Douglas who spoke next. "Now, just a minute, Mrs Emblin, did you say 'disability'? We haven't been informed of any disability—"

"I'm informing you now. He's—"

"And we certainly weren't aware of it when excluding him."

"No, you sure weren't aware – but you weren't looking either, were you? You just assumed he was a badly behaved boy."

"OK, let's take this down a notch." Mrs Douglas paused and glanced at the Chair of the Governors for approval. She got the faintest of nods. Gerald Jones was renowned for saying very little, which made his colleagues feel uncomfortable. "Zak can stay," she continued. "For now, he can stay. Can you please tell us the nature of his disability?"

Sue looked from one teacher to the other, decided to give them a chance and explained. "He has a multiple personality disorder, the doctors think possibly schizophrenia, although he's too young for them to be sure and they need more tests."

"And how does this disorder manifest itself?" asked Mrs Douglas. "I mean, what do we need to look out for?"

Sue was incredulous. "It's what she's been talking about!" Sue pointed at Rachel Chaplain. "You can't miss it. He believes he is an American child – I think from the future – called Sarah, Sarah Templeman. She is slightly older than Zak and lives in some sort of tower block. He will suddenly become this person and simply be unable to respond as Zak. He can be Sarah for hours at a time or just for a few minutes. Once, it was a whole week. I thought I'd lost him. We have no idea yet what triggers it."

All the tension had gone from the room now. Sue could sense only sympathy and it made the tears come.

"What do we do?" asked Rachel Chaplain, kindly.

"Tell the other children – as much as you can. And welcome Sarah as a new member of your class. You know, give her own exercise book, drinks bottle, book bag, stuff like that."

Miss Chaplain and Mrs Douglas whispered together for a minute.

"We can do that," said Mrs Douglas.

Rachel Chaplain asked, "What makes you think this 'Sarah' personality is from the future?"

"When Zak becomes Sarah, he talks about strange things – 'light pens' and 'gyros' for instance, which seem to be small, personal helicopters that are very good at hovering. But I expect he gets it all from TV. They do, don't they?"

"Oh, absolutely. At this age, they just soak everything up," said Mrs Douglas, reassuringly.

But neither of the teachers, who both had children, could remember hearing about gyros or light pens on any children's programme or on the internet.

****

Birmingham, England, Late November 2011

Sue was waiting in the Consultant's Room with Zak. They were seeing the main man today, the senior consultant who, they had been told, had taken a personal interest in Zak's case. He, a Mr James Armitage, had already introduced himself, had sat reading Zak's file in front of them for at least five minutes and had then gone into the room next door to talk in hushed tones with the doctor they'd seen last time, Dr Shepherd. Zak was playing with puzzle pieces on the carpet which smelled very new.

Sue was not in a good mood. The bus journey had been difficult. Zak had changed into Sarah for several minutes (which probably meant he wouldn't switch now, in front of the consultant, when she needed him to) and had embarrassed her by making excited little comments in a higher-than-normal voice about driving along the ground in a bus, so close to other vehicles. "Wasn't it dangerous?" "Surely flying was safer?"

"Sorry about that," said Mr Armitage, in a Jamaican accent, bringing Sue out of her daydream. "What's unusual about your son's condition is the degree of his delusion of identity, the form his particular schizophrenia takes. I've just been talking to Dr Shepherd about it. It's a myth, you know, that schizophrenics have multiple personalities – they generally experience voices or intrusive thoughts which they don't see as their own. And yet here is your son, going through life as two completely different people. Very, very rare in schizophrenia."

"So, it definitely is schizophrenia, then?"

Mr Armitage paused. "We think so. He is certainly delusional. But there are some traits we might expect to see which are absent, maybe because he is a child and they haven't developed yet. Tell me, has his behaviour when he is not Sarah, when he is himself, changed at all?"

"No, I don't think so. Changed in what way?"

"Schizophrenics often suffer social adversity – for instance, bullying – which can lead to a loss of confidence. Has Zak experienced anything like this?"

"No. He doesn't get bullied. The other kids think it's cool when he changes into Sarah."

"I see. Maybe that will be different when he gets older, Mrs Emblin. We must warn you that the public perception of schizophrenia is very negative, thanks to the media. These sick people are portrayed as if they all pose a physical threat. In fact, schizophrenics are much more likely to harm themselves than anyone else, and that is mostly sufferers of delusions of persecution rather than delusion of identity – Zak's form of Schizophrenia." Mr Armitage took a deep breath and Sue wondered where he was going with all this.

"Now Zak's classmates admire him for being able to switch personalities. It's a skill they envy him. This will change. As Zak gets older, particularly into his teens, he is likely to be perceived as much more of a threat by his peer group. People fear the unknown. Zak's schizophrenic episodes will be understood by very few people he knows. Not understanding it, they will fear it, and Zak may have some abuse to put up with. We feel we should warn you about this."

Now Sue understood, although she didn't want to.

"But you'll be able to cure him long before then, won't you, now that you know what it is? Can't you just give him a drug to stop it happening?"

"I'm afraid not, Mrs Emblin. At present, there is no cure for schizophrenia. All we can do is help people to live with it."

He gave Sue a leaflet with contact numbers on it for self-help groups and a charity. Then James Armitage took Sue back to talking about what was special about Zak's illness which, for him, was the main part of the interview. Zak became this other person so totally, rather than experiencing partial loss of identity, which was much more common. He went on to explain, in some detail, the tests they would like to carry out on Zak.

Sue heard none of it. All she could think of was that there was no cure. She was going to have to live with this craziness! It wasn't until they had got home that Sue wondered what treatment for her son she had just agreed to at the hospital.

****

Birmingham, England, 8 April 2016

"How is Uncle Clark?" asked Zak, waking from a daytime nap on the sofa. "Will they be able to fix his robot arm?"

Here we go again, thought Sue, a chill rising through her.

"You don't have an Uncle Clark!"

"Sarah does. He fell down the stairs yesterday and broke his robot arm, and they're going to try and fix it for him. He's in a rock band and he needs it to play the keyboard."

This was too much for Zak's mother.

"ENOUGH! Enough of this nonsense. You're creeping me out. And you can't get fixable robot arms anyway, it's just rubbish!"

"You can too! Where Sarah lives, you can."

"Oh, yeah? Sarah, Sarah, Sarah. Always f***ing Sarah. I've had it to here with Sarah, do you understand? You're not ill; you're making it all up! So, just where does this f***ing Sarah live? I bet you don't even know that."

"New Palm Springs, USA."

"What?"

"She lives in New Palm Springs, USA."

"Now I know you're lying. I've been to America and I know there's no such place. It's just 'Palm Springs'."

"They had to build a new one after the earthquake destroyed California."

Sue looked as if she might explode. After a few moments, she calmed down enough to say, "You'll be the death of me with all this Sarah nonsense. Why couldn't you be more like David and Lily? They never give me any trouble. Now go and tidy your room!"

****

Birmingham UK, Friday 4 March 2016. Zak Is Eight and in Year 3.

Zak was in the playground when he heard, “Hey, Freak,” and looked up to see who was shouting and who they were shouting at. He looked straight into the eyes of Owen Flynn, from Year 6, who was only in the playground to help the Lunchtime Supervisor, a role which came with his status as School Councillor.

“Yes, Freak, I’m talking to you. Mrs Gould has gone inside, so there’s no one to help you, is there?” He grabbed Zak’s chin and forced his head this way and that, so that he could see there was no one to call on.

“No, no one,” said Zak, not knowing what to say or even if he was expected to say anything.

“Shut up. I’m talking.” Owen shoved his face right up close to Zak’s, so Zak could only see one eye.

“We don’t want freaks like you here. You scare people with all that future stuff. Stop it, do you hear? I know you’re just doing it to get attention. Well, not anymore. ’Cos if you do, I’m gonna smash your skull in, understood? And if you tell anyone, you’ll get the same treatment. Do you hear?”

Zak said nothing, knowing that he couldn’t control it, that Sarah just took over sometimes. Owen still had Zak by the arm and was right in his face when Mrs Gould came back out and saw them. Hope rose briefly in Zak’s chest, but Owen acted quickly.

“Mrs Gould,” he called. “I just caught this one calling them names, you know, the new black girls in Reception. Bad names.”

“OK, Owen, I’ll handle it,” said Mrs Gould, and led Zak away. She bent down and peered into his face, holding him firmly by the wrist.

“Now, Zak, what’s got into you? You’re normally such a good boy. How would you like it if someone called you names?”

“I don’t like it, Mrs Gould. Owen just called me a freak. Then he said he would smash my skull in. And I didn’t say anything to those girls.”

For a moment, Mrs Gould looked shocked, then her usual smile returned to her face. “I think you must have misheard him, Darling. Owen is a good boy and the best School Councillor we've ever had. His mother is a Governor, you know. Lovely family. Now go inside and we'll say no more about it."

Zak learned that day that the world was not a fair place. Grown-ups don't always protect you, although they say they will. He realised that he would have to deal with Owen himself and this made him sad, but it also made him more determined to put things right.

****

Birmingham, England, Wednesday, 9 March 2016

It was a Wednesday which meant swimming. Zak loved swimming, Sarah too. So it didn't matter if he transferred in the middle of the lesson, but it did mean that he had to wear a rather strange swimsuit which covered his whole body, Edwardian-style, just in case he transferred.

Year 6 were getting out of the pool as Year 3 arrived. Zak caught sight of Owen Flynn, and his heart sank. He knew what was coming because bullies are predictable. Owen spotted him and broke into a smile.

"Hello, Zak. What's with the bodysuit, have you grown tits? Is Sarah taking over your body now, as well as your mind? Come on, then, get 'em out and show 'em to us! Hey, look guys – Zak's got tits!" and he pulled Zak's suit down over his shoulders so that it pinned his arms to his waist.

All the Year 6 boys and some of the girls laughed, stopping only when their teacher came over. She had no idea that they were laughing at Zak. She noticed Zak's swimsuit hanging down and bent down to speak to him. She spoke at a low volume, but it wasn't low enough for the Year 6 pupils not to hear.

"Zak, I know you don't like the full bodysuit, but you'd better keep your top half covered. You're already eight; if you changed into Sarah now, she might feel embarrassed. Now put your swimsuit back on."

Miss Fleming turned to see the Year 6 boys staring and laughing again.

"What's the matter with you lot? Hurry up and get changed or you'll miss your lunch." She marched them off to the changing rooms.

Finally, Zak was free to swim. He felt like crying but managed to stop himself. He didn't enjoy swimming at all because his mind was somewhere else. He spent most of the rest of the lesson devising a plan to get back at Owen. By the time they were in the minibus on their way back to school, he'd worked it out. If teachers were stupid and didn't see what was happening right in front of them, then maybe he could turn that to his advantage. But the conditions would have to be exactly right for it to work.

Tuesday, 15 March 2016

On the evening of football practice, Zak's neighbour was supposed to collect him. Her son Joseph also went to football practice. This arrangement allowed Zak's mum to work the whole afternoon in the hairdresser's shop. But Joseph was not at football practice, and Joseph's mum forgot about Zak. She didn't even phone or text him or his mum, so no one came to collect him. Zak decided to walk to the shop where his mum worked – it was only ten minutes away. Unfortunately, Owen Flynn's house was along the route, and as soon as Owen saw him pass by the window, he had other plans for Zak.

"Get away from my house, Future Freak!" yelled Owen as he shot out of his front door.

"'Future Freak'? Is that the best you can do?" Zak replied. He carried on walking and spoke these words over his shoulder.

Owen floored Zak with a left hook from behind which he hadn't seen coming. "No, 'that's' the best I can do."

By the time he got to the shop, Zak's left eye had closed completely. It was purple. His mum went ballistic when she saw it, demanding to know how and when it had happened. Zak usually felt grateful to his bullies for having the common sense to bruise him only in the body area. This was easy to hide. He could keep it covered up, and if he winced as he moved, he could invent an excuse such as stubbing his toe. A black eye was different. You just couldn't hide it.

Zak's head was throbbing, and he felt a bit sick. He took a long time to answer his mum's questions, making her even more annoyed. Eventually, he said he had been punched by a boy he didn't know, from a different school. The last thing he wanted was his mother marching around to Owen's house. That would only make things worse. He could see she didn't believe him, but at least she stopped questioning him. No more was said about it at all that evening, even when his mum was treating his eye with an icepack, and Zak drew a line under it. His eye would heal; it was no big deal, really.

The next morning was House Point Assembly so the whole school was there. Sue Emblin had dropped Zak off as usual that morning, and he thought she'd left, so he was very surprised to see her walk out at the front of the Hall with Mrs Douglas who was looking uncomfortable. The Head Teacher gave everyone a forced smile and said:

"Where is Zak Emblin? Zak, can you come up to the front, please?"

Zak was mortified. His mum was embarrassing him in front of the whole school. Why couldn't she just let it go? The walk to the front seemed to take forever; he felt everyone's eyes burning into him. It got worse. His mother put both hands on his shoulders as he reached the front, turned him to face the school and said, in a loud, stern voice:

"Who did this? I know it was one of you. Mrs Douglas has given me permission to find out who injured my son."

At this, Mrs Douglas, who had given no such permission, looked surprised. No one answered for a very long time.

"Who the f*** did this to my son?" shouted Zak's mum at the children.

Mrs Douglas spoke in a whisper to Mrs Emblin and persuaded her to leave the room, but not before she had turned to face the children once more and shouted:

"I'll find you, whoever you are!"

Mrs Douglas ushered Sue Emblin out, leaving her son on his own, facing the whole school. Zak tried to get back to his place quickly, but Ryan Bailey started laughing, and soon everyone was joining in. Zak just sat there, head in hands to hide his tears, praying for Mrs Douglas to come back into the room soon. He'd take getting beaten up by Owen anytime over this.

****

Monday, 21 March 2016

One of the good things about being eight was Zak could say goodbye to his mum at the top of the drive and walk the rest of the way into the school. Some mums and dads hung around watching until their child was safely inside the playground. Zak's mum was no longer one of these.

"What's going to happen? Are aliens going to swoop down and kidnap me?" he had asked. This had finally convinced his mother that Zak was old enough to walk into school on his own. It was cool, walking into school on his own, just like Year 6 kids did. That's how he felt until Owen found out that his mum disappeared quickly every morning. The very next day Owen was waiting for him on the driveway into the school with two of his cronies from Zak's own class, Ryan Bailey and Kyle Evans.

"Monday is homework hand in day, Sarah; let's see yours."

"I'm not Sarah today," said Zak.

"Sorreee, I should have said 'Mummy's Boy'. Now hand over your homework, 'Mummy's Boy'."

Ryan and Kyle both laughed. Knowing no good would come of it, Zak handed over the homework book.

Owen didn't have to leaf through many pages to see that Zak's assignments were nearly always correct and that he frequently earned house points and glowing comments from the teachers, something he never saw in his own homework book. He frowned.

"I'm holding on to this. As School Councillor I have a right to inspect it."

"But I've got to hand it in today!"

"You'll get it back at break time, Freak." With that, Owen Flynn walked away. His two pals followed, looking back to enjoy the effect their leader's behaviour had had on Zak.

Zak did get it back at break time, all wrinkly and smelling of pee. He guessed Owen had dropped it down the toilet and then dried it on the radiator. He handed it in to Miss Chaplain anyway; what else could he do? The next day Miss Chaplain summoned him and Owen's friends, Ryan and Kyle, to stay behind in the classroom at lunchtime. She spoke to Zak first, holding his homework book by the corner between her forefinger and thumb.

"What do you mean by handing in your homework in this state? It looks like you dropped it down the toilet—"

Kyle and Ryan laughed at this.

"—and smells like it too!"

More laughter.

"I don't know what you two are laughing at! You're all in trouble, all of you. Do I look stupid?" No one answered. "You must think I am. Zak, I nearly didn't mark your homework in this state, but I'm glad I did, because by some strange coincidence your sentences for spelling are the same, and I mean word for word, as Ryan's and Kyle's. Please don't copy each other's work, boys. I don't know whose sentences are the original ones, so I'm taking two house points off each of you. Now go!"

Zak tried to stay behind to explain that it wasn't his fault, but she was in no mood to talk, and Owen was watching him anyway from the doorway with a look on his face warning Zak not to tell Miss Chaplain the truth.

Out in the playground, Owen, Kyle and Ryan were laughing. Ryan was boasting that the two lost points meant he now had a total of minus three points for this week. They didn't care about losing house points. It was a badge of honour. Zak did care. He wondered if he would be able to keep it a secret from his mother. But worse than this problem was the knowledge that Owen's gang would probably repeat this trick. Getting out of doing homework was far more important to them than winning house points. Once again, he was going to have to find his own solution. It didn't take him long to think of one.

****

Monday, 28 March 2016

Zak was right about the trick being repeated. The following Monday, Ryan was waiting for him on the driveway into school. Zak made sure his face looked disappointed.

"Don't tell me you haven't done your spellings again, Ryan."

"I don't need to. I have you," Ryan replied. "I also have you to do my project. Did you choose Roman Army or Roman Baths?"

"Baths."

"Good. Now hand it over."

For a while, Zak made a pretence of being really upset and reluctant to hand over the project, before giving Ryan the same wrinkled homework book he and Owen had taken from Zak the previous week. "Only don't copy it word for word this time. Miss Chaplain will spot that, and we'll both be in detention again."

Ryan thought about this. "Thanks for the advice, Sarah, but I really don't mind detention, especially not if I have you for company." Ryan turned and walked away looking pleased with himself.

As he walked into his own classroom, Zak was also smiling. *Sometimes being bullied could be quite enjoyable,* he thought. Making sure Ryan was still outside, he went up to Miss Chaplain's desk and handed in the new homework book she had given him the previous week. He was really pleased with his project work this week, on the Roman Army.

Two days later the class were discussing their projects.

"Ryan, stand up, please," said Miss Chaplain.

Ryan leapt to his feet, wondering how many house points she was going to give him. Zak's homework was the same, of course, but he was always getting house points, so she'd probably miss him out this time.

"Your work was…interesting, Ryan. I thought you might like to share some of it with the class. How did the Romans heat their baths?"

When Ryan didn't answer, she added, "Shall I remind you what you wrote?"

He nodded.

"They just turned the hot tap on."

Everyone laughed except Ryan. It dawned on him that he wasn't going to get any house points. Being so tall for his age made him feel really exposed as he towered over all the other seated children in his class.

"How about soap, Ryan? Shall I share your thoughts on what soap the Romans used?"

Ryan said nothing.

Miss Chaplain read from his homework book. "Herbal Essences shower gel, because it gives you orgasms, plus it was buy-one-get-one-free back then."

This time the laughter was so loud that Miss Clarke came in from the next classroom to see what was happening. Ryan realised too late that he should have read what Zak had written instead of just copying it out in a rush while laughing about what he was doing with Kyle and Owen. He did not like being laughed at himself one bit.

"Do you know what an 'orgasm' is, Ryan?"

"Yes, miss…I mean, no, miss."

"So why did you write it then?"

"I didn't write it, miss. Zak did."

"Zak did? In your exercise book? In your handwriting?"

"I mean I copied it from him."

"You copied it?"

"Yes."

"After I warned you last week about copying from other children?"

"Yes, miss."

"Don't lie to me, Ryan. I've marked Zak's homework. His project isn't even about the Roman Baths."

Ryan shot an accusatory glance at Zak, who was smiling back and nodding, his arms folded.

"It is an excellent project on the Roman Army."

"But, miss—"

"Don't 'But, miss' me. You need to learn to admit when you are wrong, Ryan. Now, stay behind during lunch break and do some proper work on the Romans. I'll be here to make sure you do."

Ryan tried to protest, but Miss Chaplain wouldn't listen. *One down, one to go,* thought Zak, for he still had to pay Owen back for the swimming baths humiliation.

Birmingham, England, Wednesday, 7 April 2016

Zak had to wait another week for an opportunity to do that. It was changeover time at the swimming pool again. Zak looked behind Owen to see if Miss Fleming was watching. She was, so he smiled at Owen, as a good friend would. He knew Ryan had told Owen about being humiliated for copying Zak's homework because he'd overheard Ryan asking Owen to come up with a plan to get his own back.

"Enjoy your Roman Bath?" he asked Owen. "Did you use Herbal Essences, like Ryan?" This had the desired effect.

"What are you smirking at, Freak? That's not funny. Wipe that expression off your face or I'll wipe it off for you! Show me some respect; I'm a School Councillor!"

As Owen shouted this, Zak felt his lower jaw being grabbed and his cheeks being painfully squeezed to remove the smile. He felt like punching Owen but willed himself to appear calm, although he was far from calm on the inside. This made it crystal clear to Miss Fleming who the aggressor was. She came rushing over.

"Owen Flynn, I'm surprised at you! Leave that poor boy alone."

"He was teasing me, miss!"

"Teasing you? This boy is about half your size, Owen. You're big enough to look after yourself without resorting to violence on a boy who is two years younger than you!"

"But he called me names!"

"Enough excuses! I was watching. All I saw was him smiling at you – he was trying to be friendly. Owen, your behaviour is a disgrace to the School Council. I will speak to Mrs Douglas straight away about getting you removed!"

"You can't do that; my mum's a Governor!"

"I can and I will. Governor or not, your mother will get a letter from me explaining why you've been removed from the School Council."

Never underestimate the power of a smile, thought Zak, and gave Owen another one as Miss Fleming ordered him back to the changing room.

The look of pain and shock on Owen's face made up for all the bullying Zak had suffered at his and Ryan's hands in recent weeks. Or rather, it would have done, had he seen it.

Miss Fleming turned solicitously to Zak and asked, "Are you OK, Dear?"

"Yes, I'm fine," replied Sarah, rubbing her face, which was sore where Owen had squeezed it, and adjusting the swimsuit to make sure she was completely covered. "Oh, good, swimming. I love swimming."

****

Snowdonia, June 2013

"You'll see, this is what's so good about living in the country," said her father excitedly as Carmen Fry pulled on her wellies. "I know you'll miss your friends, but with a house this size you can have them over at weekends, you know, for sleepovers. And you just don't get clear skies like this in the city."

They stepped outside.

"Wow," said Carmen immediately. There was absolutely no wind, no clouds in the sky and no pollution haze. Thousands...no, millions...no, billions of stars were visible in the sky. She had never seen anything like it before – before last night, that is...

It had all seemed so different yesterday...not an adventure at all, not the 'New Beginning' her mother had tried to sell her – more of a sad end. She had stood in the communal gardens and taken in the mature trees, the four Scots pines and the two pear trees for the last time – especially the pear trees. Every year around April, she had examined the beautiful white blossoms and tried to guess whether it would be a good or bad year for fruit. In good years, in September, she had enjoyed hours in the garden picking the fine Conference pears no one else on the estate seemed to want (one mother had banned her children from eating them after Carmen had offered them some). She had even made her own tool for getting to the out-of-reach ones, consisting of a pond-fishing net tied to a tent pole.

That first tree had been special. It alone had borne the edible fruit. Only it had been climbable. People had sat under it for private moments with a cup of coffee or a cigarette. The same stone which people had sat on for this purpose had also served as a goalpost, with the trunk as the other, for games of football. Foxes and cats had hidden behind it at night. Over the years she had avidly watched long-tailed tits, gold crests, jays, tree creepers, nuthatches and woodpeckers on that tree and, of course, hundreds of squirrels. She had been helped in this by the same father who was now trying to introduce her to the wonders of a clear, countryside night sky. One evening she had even watched a peregrine falcon rip apart a wood pigeon under that tree. She could never think of birds of prey in the same way again after that, seeing them from then on for what they were – living, carnivorous dinosaurs.

This place held so many memories. She had learned to ride a bike here – the pink one, one of her many pink possessions. She'd had years of anti-pink battles with her mum, finally getting through to her that blue was her favourite colour, not pink, and being allowed to choose at least some of her own clothes.

She and Callum, from number 38, had gone on bug hunts at dusk, scaring Callum's younger sister with slugs, spiders, woodlice and moths. Then there was the snow caterpillar, which had delighted so many people on the estate and brought them closer together. One particularly snowy winter, Carmen, her friend Tamara and Callum had decided snowmen were boring. They had set about making an igloo instead, only it had proved too difficult. Three huge balls of snow, as tall as the children themselves, were all they had had to show for their efforts. So they had put a face on one of them, made feelers out of branches, pushed the balls together into segments, made one or two more segments and called it a Snow Caterpillar. The result had been so good, you could pretend to ride on it, which the photos proved was exactly what they had done!

Once Tamara had moved into the flat opposite, Carmen had played less with Callum and his sister Georgia. She and Tamara had spent as much time in each other's flats as they did in their own. They had collected Moshi Monsters. They had danced together, sung together, written songs together, including a Moshi Monsters one (which they had uploaded to the Moshi Monsters web site), and practised for shows their school had put them into.

OK, she would be chatting online and sharing all sorts of stuff with Tamara, but it wouldn't be the same as seeing her every day. She looked up at Flat 42. Tamara was the one she was going to miss the most.

A hand rested gently on her shoulder – her mum's hand. The other hand held a tissue out to her, and it was only then that she realised that she was crying. "Come to the van now," said Betty Fry. "It's best to just turn and keep walking. Don't look back."

****

And so the seven-year-old Carmen had left the only place she had ever lived, feeling very sad and expecting the sadness to continue indefinitely. What a surprise to her it was, then, that her spirits rose almost as soon as they came off the motorway and entered the Shropshire countryside. Wales beckoned. Snowdonia beckoned. The glorious sunset seemed to last forever because they were heading west, straight towards it. Now it did seem like an adventure.

And then the stars came out, one by glorious one, each brighter and more distant than the last, and Carmen was spellbound. This was the beginning of her lifelong love affair with the stars.

Her father's voice recalled her to the present. "See these seven stars in a lopsided W shape, that's—"

"Cassiopeia," said Carmen, confidently.

"And these three there, close together in a straight line, that's—"

"Orion's Belt," chimed in Carmen again.

"Wow," said her father, "I had no idea you knew so much astronomy."

"You bought me the encyclopaedias!" She took his hand. "Dad, listen. You don't have to worry about me. I'm going to love it here."

****

Gwynedd, Wales, July 2013

Shortly after her eighth birthday, Carmen and her dad were stargazing. They were using the telescope he had bought her against his wife's wishes. She had wanted to buy a party dress. Betty, it seemed to Martin, was not allowing Carmen to grow up. Martin, it seemed to Betty, was forcing Carmen to grow up too quickly. "Why do you want to fill her head with all that stuff? She's only eight," she had said.

With the new telescope, Carmen could make out stars, even whole galaxies, she had never seen before. It would be great fun trying to identify them.

"What do you see?" asked her father.

Carmen focussed on a spiral galaxy with bluish edges and a bright white centre and gestured to her father to have a look.

"Awesome," said Martin. "I'm not sure, but it looks like Bodes Galaxy, which is bigger than the Milky Way, where we live."

"I know where we live, Dad." Carmen sounded slightly annoyed. "How far away is it, do you know?"

"I'd guess about eleven and a half million light years."

"Amazing. What's that in miles?"

"Can't be done that way, Carmen, the number would just be too big. That's why we use light years."

"What's a light year again?"

"A light year is the distance it takes light to travel in one year."

"But that's enormous! Light travels at 186,000 miles a second! So that would be 186,000 × 60 to get minutes, × 60 again to get hours, × 24 for just one day, × 365 for a whole year! And you say we would need eleven and a half million of them?"

Her dad nodded, smiling. Carmen tried to calculate the figure in miles on her calculator, but it just wouldn't work. Her dad was right, the numbers were just too big. (Later she tried again on her laptop and ended up with 67,455,504,000,000,000,000 miles! She had no idea how to even say this number).

"It's amazing we can see it at all, that far away. I wonder what life is like there. If they have people-like beings, I wonder what they are doing now."

"Who knows? Bodes Galaxy might not even be there anymore."

"What do you mean? Of course, it is, we can see it." Carmen pointed to the telescope.

"No, no, we can't, not exactly. What we see is the light which started its journey towards us 11,500,000 years ago. If that galaxy has been swallowed up by one of its suns going supernova at any time in the past 11.5 million years, we wouldn't know. You're looking into the past."

"Amazing. So that means if *they* are watching *us*, they'll see mammoths and ape men wearing fur clothes?"

Martin laughed. "Not mammoths, no. They weren't around until about 5 million years ago. Ancestors of humans? Possibly. They'll see us exactly as we were 11.5 million years ago."

When his daughter was in this mood, Martin Fry felt he could tell her anything. He had no need to 'dumb down' or 'jazz up' the science; she just soaked it up. Carmen was looking at him quizzically, humming almost inaudibly. He knew that when she did this, she was either about to ask a very difficult question or to try and prove him wrong on something.

"So that means," said Carmen, "it *is* possible to look back in time. You said it wasn't."

"No. I said we couldn't *travel* back to the past; I didn't say we couldn't look back in time at someone else's past."

Carmen thought about this. "I remember now. Didn't you also say we *could* travel to the future?"

"Now, that one you've got right, Darling. The only thing preventing it is we haven't built a rocket fast enough yet. But then again, we probably never will. You'd have to go at nearly light speed to make a significant difference."

"Difference to what exactly?"

"How fast time goes by. If you're travelling that fast through space, Einstein's equations show that you must necessarily be travelling proportionately slower through time. Time slows down for you when you're travelling very fast, although you don't notice it."

"Why does that happen?"

"Why does it happen? I'm glad you asked me that. This was one of Einstein's great breakthroughs. He discovered that space and time are inextricably linked. They are part of the same thing, properly called 'spacetime'."

"I still don't understand." Carmen stood up so quickly from behind the telescope that she bumped her head on the sloping ceiling of the attic bedroom. Warming to his theme, her father didn't notice this.

"Nothing can travel faster than light, OK? Have you heard that?"

"OK."

"But we are all, in fact, travelling at light speed through spacetime. Now, if almost all your light speed travel is through space, that gives you only a tiny portion left to travel through time, so you travel through less time. For you, time goes slower."

Carmen nodded, but she was still frowning.

"If you were sitting at home, instead of hurtling through space at near light speed in a rocket, most of your travelling at light speed would be done through time, as you're not travelling through space, you're stationary (except for the speed the whole planet is travelling at). So time would go much faster for you."

"I think I get it." Carmen flicked hair from her face with her hand, a habit she had recently developed which would stay with her throughout her life. "But this doesn't affect us, right, on everyday scales?"

"That's exactly why people don't know about it!" Martin was getting excited now. Carmen loved to see that she could have this effect on her father. "It's been tested, though, back in the seventies. They took two state-of-the-art caesium atomic clocks and set them to precisely the same time. They kept one in the lab and flew the other one around the world a few times on a fast, commercial aircraft. Then they compared them. The one that had been travelling showed a slower time."

"How much slower?"

"Er, two millionths of a second."

"Is that all?"

"I know it doesn't sound much, but if you increase the speed of travel to near light speed, believe me, it makes a significant difference. They got it right in the 1950s' version of *Planet of the Apes* but not in the 1970s' or 1990s' remakes."

Oh, no, thought Carmen, *he's going to go on about classic old films again.*

"After a long mission, Charlton Heston lands on a strange planet ruled by apes, when he thought he was returning home. Of course, at the end of the film, when – in a classic moment of cinema history – he stumbles across the decaying Statue of Liberty, he realises he has been 'home' all the time. Only things have changed because 2,000 years have passed since he left Earth in his spaceship at near light speed at the start of his mission. For him, only two years have gone by."

Carmen opened her mouth to speak but heard her mother's loud voice calling them for dinner instead. She sounded very concerned that they were having to eat so late because she and her dad had been in the attic room for such a long time. Carmen was disappointed. She might tease him, but she loved spending time like this with her father. He knew so much, and she didn't think she would ever be able to learn enough to know as much as he did. They packed up the telescope and went down for dinner.

****

Birmingham, England, Early June 2016

To coincide with the Brazil Olympics, Zak's new school was having a Family Fun Day. As a special school, they relied on such events for extra funding. Zak was excited because the theme was going to be 'the mini-Olympics' and he was a good runner. He was not the quickest sprinter in his school, but over one or two laps of the field, no one could touch him. He was expecting to win. They had been told that there would be a trophy for every event, so he was anticipating being presented with a trophy in front of the whole school, a first for him.

Most of all, he wanted his mum to see him win. She was always saying that, unlike his brother, David, and sister, Lily, he was no good at anything. This was his chance to prove her wrong. Zak was a little nervous when he brought the letter home about the Family Fun Day, but he had no need to be; she agreed to go. What she actually said was, "I suppose so," and then added, "I need to check with Lily and David first, that they haven't got anything on that day." This made Zak nervous again, but when he checked with her later that evening, his mother said, "What? Oh, yeah. They said they had nothing on. It's OK."

"So, you're coming then?"

"Yes, I'm coming! Now let me watch this!"

Zak breathed a sigh of relief. His mother's eyes returned to *The Only Way Is Essex* on the 52-inch television with cinema sound bar which dominated their small and sparsely furnished living room.

In 2013, Zak asked for a guitar. "You're too young," his mum told him.

In 2014, Zak brought home a letter from the Birmingham Schools Music Service. Excitedly, he told his mum how he had been allowed to try a violin at school and how he had really loved it. He loved the feel of it beneath his chin, the way it shone and even the smell of it. Above all, he was spellbound by the beautiful music the violin teacher had produced from it and longed to be able to do the same thing himself. He asked his mother if he could learn the violin. It was only £9 a lesson, he told her.

"£9 a lesson?" His mother exploded. "I can't afford that. I'm a single mum with three kids! I've already got Lily's gymnastics exams and David's football coaching to pay for."

"You can use Child Care vouchers! Shauna's mum does," Zak protested.

"Forget it, Son. Ain't gonna happen. I can't be doing with all that form filling."

Later in 2014, Sue Emblin got a letter from Mrs Brooks at Zak's school. It read:

At Radcliffe's, we strive to let every child reach their creative potential, regardless of disability. As you will know, your son Zak Emblin has been attending choir practice at lunchtimes. We have now decided to make this increasingly popular activity an official After School Club, from 3:30 to 5 pm, on Tuesdays. The children are working towards a concert before Christmas. Each session will cost £13. Please complete and sign the form below if your child can attend.

Attached to this letter was a handwritten note which Sue Emblin couldn't be bothered to read because the handwriting was a bit florid. It read:

Zak has a really beautiful tone to his voice, combined with a natural sense of rhythm. I do hope you can bring him to the Tuesday sessions. I see him as a possible future soloist in the City of Birmingham Choir.

This time Zak didn't even need to ask the question. His mum looked up irritably from the letter and said, "No way! £13 a time! For singing! I wish someone would give me £13 every time I sing in the bath. It's too much!"

Zak protested, "Don't Lily's gymnastics classes cost £16? I saw the receipt."

"Don't be so cheeky! You've no right to go looking at that. Anyway, it's different. Lily has real potential. Her trainer says so. He said if she didn't have such big hips, she'd be one of the best gymnasts in the club."

Sue Emblin picked up from a dusty shelf a framed photo of Lily holding a medal and gazed at it with pride. She had cropped and enlarged it from a group photo of Lily's entire class, who had all been given a medal for taking part in a regional competition in which they had come next to bottom.

Zak sighed. "Don't you see, Mum? He's just trying to tell you both, gently, that Lily's too fat."

"Don't be so rude! Of course, he isn't. He said she had real talent, which is more than can be said for you, you cheeky little bastard!"

Zak just sat there with his arms folded, frowning. What was the point? It was just another disappointment to put alongside all the others.

Seeing him frowning, his mother added, "And don't get doing things at lunchtime without asking me. Honestly, what's the point of you singing in a choir? You'd be a laughing-stock if your voice suddenly changed to Sarah's halfway through a verse. Haven't thought it through, have you? There's no sense in you at all. What am I going to do with you?"

She reached for her cigarettes. "You'll be the death of me, you will, with all your Sarah nonsense."

****

Birmingham, England, 12 June 2016

The day of the mini-Olympics had arrived. Zak was doing the one lap of the field race. He was really looking forward to impressing his mum and wanted her to be there on time. "Don't forget, Mum," he said, "the races start at 12. Please don't be late."

Sue Emblin registered that her son was talking to her but didn't understand what he was saying. She was about to ask him when David, her eldest son, stomped into the room, carrying a shirt. He threw it on the table in front of her.

"Look at the collar!" he shouted at his mother. "Burn marks! I can't wear that. One of my favourite shirts, and you've ruined it with your lack of ironing skills! What am I going to wear to the party now? It's tonight!"

"David, you have dozens of shirts!"

"Not this colour! It needs to match my new shoes and trousers, which I bought to go with this shirt!"

Before she knew it, Sue had agreed to going with David into the city centre to buy a replacement shirt.

"You can't," protested Zak. "What about my race?"

David and his mum stared blankly at Zak.

"You're coming to watch my race, remember? Family Fun Day? 12 o'clock? I've been going on about it for weeks."

"Of course, I remember," said Zak's mum, although she had, in fact, forgotten. "Only, David has this shirt crisis now. It must be sorted for this evening. I can't let him down now, can I?"

"Why not? You're letting me down. Just like you always do." Tears were in Zak's eyes. "Only this time it's worse, because you promised."

This annoyed his mother, who protested that she'd only said *he* could go, and he still could – he could go on his own.

"Why can't David go shopping on *his* own? He's older than me; I'm only nine," replied Zak.

"David loves getting my advice when choosing clothes, always has done. Such a smart boy, he is. Makes his mum proud."

"But I wanted you there" – Zak was crying now – "to see me win."

David laughed. "Win? Someone's very confident. Do you know what I say? So what if you do win? It's only a bunch of freaks running around a field; it's not like it's a real race!"

Zak's lips tightened, and he ran to his box room, slamming the door behind him.

"You've upset him now," said Sue Emblin, matter-of-factly, and started discussing the style of shirt he wanted with David.

****

Sarah opened her eyes to find herself in Zak's box room in his family's two-and-a-half bedroomed terrace in Birmingham in the year 2016. She had been there before quite recently and recognised some of the posters. Two were of popular rock bands not-smiling for the camera. Another showed a teenaged violinist sitting backwards way around on a chair, proudly holding a very expensive-looking violin. Her name was Miranda Harper.

Aged nine now, Sarah no longer found these swaps scary. Now they were, depending on her mood, either an adventure or an inconvenience. She spotted an A5 flyer on Zak's table, advertising a 'Family Fun Day' on June 12. It had a map on it to Zak's school, so she put it in Zak's pocket. She wondered if the date today was June 12. It would be on one of the computers, she remembered. They didn't have holography and light pens yet in the twenty-first century, so she'd have to find a computer to check the date. This could be tricky. One thing Sarah had learned was to stay away from Zak's mom, who hated her for some reason…presumably for taking over Zak's body, but then she seemed to hate Zak too. Sarah had noticed that he had the smallest room. And his was the only room without a TV (were they called TVs?) or a computer. Or even a rug on the rough, wooden floor.

The best thing would be to just head out, looking down, and hope no one stopped her. Anxious though she was about being on the streets on her own, it was preferable to being shut in the box room by Zak's mom, while being shouted at from the outside that she would stay there until she 'snapped out of it' and became Zak again. This was what had happened the last time she had been there. She'd even had to pee out of the window, which had been a new experience and one she didn't want to be repeated.

Sarah's escape plan started off well. She hunched Zak's shoulders and walked through the small lounge and even smaller kitchen as fast as she could, towards the back door, which was closer than the front. She paused, briefly, to check the date on a computer screen – today was the 12th June – and that's when Mrs Emblin noticed her.

Zak's mom shouted at her back, "Be grateful I'm even letting you go to the Fun Day, after that show of cheek!"

She was at the back door now but couldn't remember how to open it and seemed, to herself at least, to be making a huge amount of noise trying.

"Oh, and Zak," added Zak's mom suddenly. Sarah was convinced she had been discovered and stepped gingerly back into the kitchen, fearing the worst, "you'll need some money. Here, have this fiver."

Sarah took it and left, relieved, through the front door, which she could remember how to open. As soon as she was on the street, Sarah took out the flyer and examined the map carefully. It was too far to walk, but the bus route from the city centre to Radcliffe's was clearly marked. She needed the number 116 service, which was half-hourly. All she had to do was to get herself to the city centre.

She was looking forward to seeing where Radcliffe's, the Special School Zak now went to, was and what it looked like from the outside. She already knew it from the inside, from previous swaps. It was OK, pretty much like other Birmingham schools from Zak's time, really, old brick buildings with draughty rooms and high ceilings, not as 'special' as she'd expected. Her own parents had chosen a very different solution to her frequent reincarnating behaviour – home schooling. If she swapped, as she just had, they simply sent the tutor home early. There was no point in Zak doing her lessons. For instance, how could he learn twenty-first-century history for events which, for him, hadn't even happened yet?

Sarah made for the nearest shops which she could see in the distance. Shops meant people. Logic told her that this was where she might find a bus. She was right. There were people standing under a shelter although it wasn't raining. This was promising. There was moving text at one end of the shelter which read: "Next No 45 service to City Centre due in five minutes. On time." This text, in green, kept repeating itself. She had no idea how to pay for the journey or if the £5 Zak's mom had given her would be enough. She didn't want to ask an adult as she didn't want to draw attention to the fact that she was a nine-year-old child, travelling alone.

When the blue double-decker bus came, people got on, said where they were going and put coins into a box. Sarah told the driver that she was going to Radcliffe's Special School, gave him the five-pound note and said, "Is this enough?"

The driver snapped back at her, "Exact fare only. Stand aside," and looked past her to serve the person standing behind her.

She must have looked surprised, for an old lady standing in the queue spoke to her.

"I overheard that," she said, "dreadful man, this driver. I've had him before." She said this loud enough for the driver to hear. "Are you coming back by bus, Dear?"

"Yes," said Sarah, who hadn't yet thought about the return journey. "I suppose so."

"Then you'll need an All-Day ticket. It's cheaper. It's £4. Don't lose it. Just show it to the driver when you come back. Wait, I think I might have change for that fiver."

She took Sarah's £5 note and gave her five heavy gold-coloured coins instead which, to Sarah, seemed much more valuable than the note. She thanked the lady profusely and paid the driver, who showed her, rudely, where the tickets came out. She went upstairs on to the top deck for a better view of the journey and because, used to gyros, she felt more comfortable higher up.

Sarah got a bit lost in the City centre. It wasn't obvious which stop to get off at. Once off, she had to find the number 116 bus stop. She wandered around for what seemed like ages, passing old-fashioned looking cafés and restaurants with strange names like Starbucks and KFC, shops, lots and lots of people, and even a bronze statue of a startled bull. Things got better once she'd got on the bus. The friendly driver promised to tell her when she had reached her stop. And once there, she could easily follow the map all the way to Zak's school. It was an imposing, large, old house, but before Sarah got a chance to wonder if she had the courage to go in, a boy came running out, shouting:

"Zak, Zak, where have you been? Your race is about to start. Come on, no time to change. Those trainers will be fine."

He ran off, and Sarah broke into a trot to follow him through the old Victorian building and out to the field the other side where the Fun Day stalls were all visible, with parents and children crowding around them.

At first, she was nervous. Sarah knew that Zak would be able to get his body to go faster than she could manage. He was much more attuned to it than she was. Plus, she lacked confidence because she hardly ever ran anywhere at home in 2125. No one did. Most of her life was spent high above the ground, so there was just no call for it. Sarah looked around the busy event and noticed for the first time that people were generally much thinner, and probably fitter too, than in her own time.

For Zak's sake, she decided to give the race a go anyway. Just don't fall over, she told herself, and everything went well. She won easily. It was a truly exhilarating experience. What a wicked machine Zak's body was; she was hardly even out of breath at the end of it! Marcus and Luke, both very out of breath, slowly came across to congratulate her.

"Well done, Zak. I reckon that was a pretty fast time. We thought you weren't going to make it," said Luke.

"I didn't. I mean Zak didn't. It's Sarah you're talking to."

Luke's and Marcus's faces broke into broad grins.

"F***, Sarah, that's great!" said Luke.

Marcus added, "And you didn't even fall over once! Zak will be really proud of you when we tell him."

"Thanks, guys," said Sarah, and they hauled her off to throw wet sponges at their teacher who was in the stocks, until it was time for their award ceremony.

Back in Zak's box room later that day, Sarah wrote on a post-it note:

"To Zak, look what I won for you! Love, Sarah," and stuck it on the small pewter trophy of a running man which, an hour earlier, she had enjoyed receiving in front of the other children and their parents. She looked forward to hearing his reaction.

Who knows, perhaps note-leaving might have become a habit between them at this stage, as it did much later, if Sarah had received a reply. She didn't. Sue Emblin came into Zak's room looking to find fault. She saw the trophy and the note, which incensed her. "More bloody Sarah nonsense!" she yelled, waking Sarah up, but not before she had screwed up the note and put it in her pocket.

Seeing Zak's mom shouting and grabbing at her annoyed Sarah so much that she re-joined her own body immediately, leaving Zak staring at the trophy and ignoring his mother. He was very disappointed.

"*I* wanted to win that trophy," he said under his breath, and he shed a tear.

****

New Palm Springs, USA, 15 June 2120

Zelda Templeman was bathing her four-year-old daughter, Sarah. She was always the one who did it, as it required patience, and Bron, her husband, had none. He had mustered enough enthusiasm for the role of fatherhood to share the job of bathing the baby for the first nine months of her life. Once her eczema had become a problem, you couldn't see him for dust or, rather, for empty Extra Strong lager bottles. Sarah's eczema meant that special ointment had to be added to the sparkly transparent bath in just the right quantity. If there was too little, she wouldn't get the benefit from it and would be itching so much come bedtime that she wouldn't fall asleep. If there was too much, Sarah would be as slippery as a bar of soap. Although this could be amusing – Sarah squirmed with delight whenever she popped out of her mom's grasp – Zelda knew it was also dangerous; she could easily slip on the bathtub floor and injure herself.

"How ya doin', Babe? This water too hot for you?"

Sarah shook her head. "It's fine, Mommy."

Zelda sponged the bumpy scar on Sarah's chest.

"This is a strange birthmark. I wonder if it will fade as you get older?" she commented.

"What's a birthmark, Mommy?"

The mother explained to her daughter that it was an unusual mark you were born with, and Sarah thought about this, before saying:

"I got it when the bad man cut me with the knife. It's better now."

Zelda dropped the sponge and stared. "No, Honey, you've always had it. It was there when you were born; your daddy spotted it right away (well, he would, wouldn't he?). What's all this about a bad man with a knife? Wherever did you get that from?"

"It hurt bad for weeks. They put special glue on it in the hospital. My other mommy was angry. She said it was all my fault."

Zelda was horrified, and it showed on her face.

"Are you angry too, Mommy?"

"No, Honey, no! Don't think that."

Zelda rushed to hug her daughter, soaking her T-shirt in the process. What did that matter? Her daughter, Sarah, had a mental problem and her mom's heart was breaking for her. At the same time, she felt relieved that Bron hadn't overheard their conversation. He would not have taken it well at all, no sir. He wanted his child to be perfect in every way and made sure she knew that.

Sarah's comments upset Zelda. She said no more about it to her daughter and forced herself to focus on the bedtime hologram story and on singing the little one to sleep. Zelda could hold a tune better than most and loved the fact that Sarah appreciated her singing (Bron certainly didn't. You'd have to sing every song in a Thrash Metal style to impress him). Singing was one of the few things which distracted Sarah enough from her itching legs and back to allow her to drift off.

Once Sarah was safely asleep, their bath time conversation came back to her. What had she meant by 'her other Mommy'? All that stuff about being stabbed and treated in hospital, it sounded like a memory. Perhaps it was a premonition? But she already had the scar. Weird. And a bit creepy. Zelda made her mind up to ask Sarah for more details. If she hated the scar so much, that it was giving her nightmares, surely talking about it with her mom could only help.

When they were playing in the communal rooftop garden of their apartment block two days later, Zelda braved the subject. Sarah was planting begonias in pots, or rather, thought she was. Her mother was discreetly adding or removing compost as necessary after Sarah had finished her bit. A constant buzzing, like an angry swarm of bees, came from the gyros darting in all directions above their heads.

"Sarah Darling, what did you mean the other day when you said a bad man gave you the scar, you know, the one on your side?"

"It's OK, Mommy, it doesn't hurt now."

"I know, Darling. Did it hurt before, then?"

Sarah frowned. "Yes, when I moved and all the blood came out. Anton thought I might die. He was crying because it was his fault."

Zelda wanted to ask who Anton was but said instead, "How do you mean, his fault?"

"He brought the bad man to me, the one with the knife."

"And why did he do that?"

"He thinks I'm a freak. They all called me a freak. What's a freak, Mommy?"

"Someone who is a bit different, Darling."

"Is a freak a bad thing to be?"

Zelda found herself hugging her daughter again, this time covering herself in potting compost.

"No, Honey, it's not. Listen, do you have this dream often? Because talking about it can help it to go away, you know, so you must always tell Mommy—"

"It's not a dream, it's real."

"Real? So when did it happen?"

Sarah thought about this for a long time but could only say, "Before."

Zelda steeled herself. She hadn't yet broached the most painful part of what Sarah had said the other day.

"And what about your 'other Mommy', was she there before?"

"Yes, she picked me up from the hospital."

"But who, who is she?"

"My mommy when I was a boy."

When…I…was…a…boy! The words hung in the air and Zelda found herself unable to process them. *I mean, were we talking past lives here? Fuck.* She felt a sudden urge to down one of Bron's lagers, if there were any left, and made for the refrigerator. Sarah was holding Mommy's hand and got pulled inside, still clutching her tiny yellow trowel and wondering why they hadn't planted the last begonia.

Birmingham, England, 13 July 2026

For the tenth time that day, Zak tried Carmen's mobile. He'd left messages for her, but she was probably still too mad at him to phone back. Unfortunately, what he really wanted to talk to her about would be, he sensed, a touchy subject. But there was no one else who 'got' Sarah the way Carmen did. She picked up. She said nothing, but at least she had picked up. Zak said he was sorry. Still no answer.

"Can I come over? We can sort this out face-to-face."

Still no answer, but at least she hadn't hung up. Zak decided to chance his arm.

"OK, Carmen, unless you tell me I can't, I'm coming over to see you right now. I can't bear to have you mad at me. If—"

She hung up. Was that good or bad? She hadn't told him not to come. She must know his reaction would be to drive straight over there. It was a three-hour drive, so she had plenty of time to contact him if she changed her mind. He went straight to the car and punched Carmen's address into the SatNav. She had sent it to him, without hesitation, a few days before their first date when he had told her that he wanted to send her one of those personalised cards for her birthday, for which he needed her address and a more up-to-date photo. He had been surprised at how readily she had agreed to this.

Two hours, forty-five minutes later the Queen's voice said, "One turns left here," and, "One has reached One's destination," and Zak changed the voice setting on his SatNav to Ozzy Osbourne for the return journey. This was only to put off going to the door, which he was a bit nervous about. The drive had been straightforward in his reliable old BMW, and he'd found her house quickly and easily for a country residence.

Big house. Impressive house. A house which spoke of quiet achievement and confidence. What a view! The Mawddach Estuary was visible below, a Victorian-looking iron and wooden railway bridge spanning it. To the west was the sea, probably Cardigan Bay; and to the North, mountains, lots of snow-capped mountains. Zak wasn't sure, but he thought one might be Cader Idris, the second-highest mountain in Wales.

Carmen was staying with her parents because it was a vacation. If she'd been at Uni, it would have been a five-hour rather than a three-hour drive. All Zak knew of Carmen's parents, Martin and Betty, was that he was some sort of manager in the social care service, and she made and sold greetings cards as a business. When he had found this out, he had wondered whether he should have bought Carmen's birthday card from her mother, but Carmen had said no, she sold the 3D 'crafty' ones, mostly, and not online yet.

So this was the house she had grown up in. As a child of the city, he was envious of the spectacular views she had been able to enjoy throughout childhood. He realised he was prolonging his enjoyment of these views because he was feeling nervous. He knocked the door. Maybe one of her parents would answer. Zak wondered what he would say if that happened. He needn't have worried. It wasn't one of Carmen's parents who answered. It was a well-toned man, over six feet tall, in his thirties, bronzed and with dark wavy hair, who was naked from the waist up.

"I was looking for Carmen," was the first thing that came out of Zak's mouth.

"The question is, is Carmen looking for you?" replied the semi-naked man in a surprisingly high yet confident voice.

"Who is it, Karl?" Zak heard Carmen's voice coming from another room.

"I've obviously come at a bad time. I should go now," said Zak, turning to leave.

"No, wait, please!" Carmen said, pushing in front of Karl, who had one hand on the door frame. "I didn't think you'd get here that quickly."

"Yes, well, it seemed important. Never mind." Zak turned to leave again.

"Seemed important? Zak, you didn't call me for three weeks – and now suddenly you want me to drop everything?"

"Zak?" said Karl. "Is this the dude who's been messing you around? Can I punch him?"

"That won't be necessary, Karl. And please put a shirt on."

"Messing you around? Have I 'messed you around', Carmen?"

"I didn't want to do this in front of Karl, but since you ask, Zak, let's take a look, shall we? You walked out on our first date because you simply had to contact Sarah that instant. And I haven't heard from you, not a single call or text, for three weeks, until today when you can't stop calling me! You aroused my curiosity about what would happen if you tried to contact Sarah, then left me in limbo. I'd say that's messing me around, wouldn't you?"

After a few seconds, it was Karl who broke the silence.

"Hey, who's this Sarah babe? Are you guys into threesomes?"

"Oh, shut up, Karl. Zak *is* Sarah. He becomes her in the future when he reincarnates. She's been connecting with him since he was four."

Karl looked delighted. "You're shitting me. This is the guy you want to put in your thesis, the reincarnater you told me about, who no one believes except you? Hey, I'm really pleased to meet you, pal. I'm pleased to meet both of you." And Karl enclosed Zak's hand with both of his in a very warm handshake.

Zak was not impressed. It was Carmen he spoke to, not Karl. "You want to put me in your thesis? And you've discussed this with your…boyfriend…before telling me?"

"Yeah, sorry. Maybe I might have mentioned it if you'd bothered calling me! And Karl is not my boyfriend. He—"

"He is semi-naked!"

"Karl has an aversion to clothes."

"What's the point of doing the time in the gym if you don't show it off?" said Karl, pointing to his rippling pecs.

"As I was saying, Karl works in the lab with me. Meet Dr Karl Frideriks, astrophysicist. He's come over uninvited, as usual, to go over some equations with me. He often does. Our relationship is entirely mathematical."

"You mean 'physical'," said Karl. "We're physicists."

"I most certainly do not mean physical! I have no interest in Karl's body, semi-naked or not."

"Aw, you're just saying that. I know you do, really." Karl flexed his abdomen in a way which made Zak feel sick. Suddenly he put on a T-shirt, a tight-fitting one, of course, beamed at Zak, and said:

"Do you know how important you are?"

Zak's expression gave away that he didn't.

"You are evidence; proof, in a nutshell. My dearest Carmen here has this wonderful theory about quantum entanglement and future echoes, but without any evidence to back it up, she was on the point of losing her funding. She can build a whole case study around you, Zak."

"Don't Karl, I haven't asked him yet."

"No, you haven't! In fact, you said someone who connected with a past life would be a better option than me." Zak sounded annoyed.

"OK, I can see you two have plenty to talk about, so I'll leave now. A word of advice first, my lovebirds: if you really want this relationship to work, you've got to stop arguing with each other and start connecting."

Karl's words had the effect of making Zak and Carmen look into each other's eyes. Embarrassed, they quickly looked away again. They didn't notice Karl leaving or hear his red sports car driving away, spitting gravel. For Karl, this made it the perfect exit. He was not always the selfish attention seeker many took him for.

"He's right, Zak, we do need to talk."

"I know."

"About the thesis. I was going to tell you, I mean, ask you. I just got annoyed when you didn't call. I—"

"It's OK, Carmen, really. Tell me now."

Carmen told him that she had so little evidence to back up her theory that even an unprovable case-study – a reincarnater who connected with a future self rather than a past one – would be better than none.

"The person I'd really like to interview is Sarah – she connects with a past self – but that's not going to happen. I'd have to be living in her time, or she in mine."

"She sort of does. When she connects with me, I become her, as you told Karl. You could interview her then, I suppose, if she agrees."

"Could I really, Zak?" Carmen hugged Zak spontaneously and kissed his cheek. He was starting to enjoy the closeness of her and her scent, when he suddenly turned away, remembering the reason he had come to see her today.

"Except you may not be able to."

"What do you mean?"

"There's a problem."

"What problem?"

"I think she's dead. The connection is dead. I haven't become Sarah for three weeks now, since that day I left you in the restaurant. It's never been that long before between episodes."

"So, you did connect with her that day?"

"Oh, definitely."

"Tell me, Zak." Carmen sat down on a dark green sofa with wooden arms which seemed old-fashioned even for her parents' tastes. She took Zak's hands and pulled him down with her.

"At first, I connected with her as a child. I was suddenly about five, playing with a toy version of one of those gyros. As she was playing with a gyro, it could have been the ideal time to warn her about them, in case the older Sarah dies in a gyro crash."

"And did you?"

"How could I? I was stupid to think I could help Sarah by forcing a connection, I didn't think it through. When we connect, we become each other. I was Sarah, with the mentality and knowledge of a five-year-old and some of Zak Emblin's memories, but no memory about what might happen to her when she's older."

"Yes, of course. So you couldn't get a warning to her."

Zak slumped into the sofa. He stared out of the French window, beyond which were pastures rolling down to a river estuary, book-ended by mountains. Zak saw none of this.

"It's worse than that, Carmen."

"How do you mean?"

"Just before I became myself again, I had two nightmares. Except they weren't dreams; they were real. I was living these experiences, not imagining them. And…something different happened, that's never happened before…"

Carmen could see tears welling in Zak's eyes. "Go on, Zak. I know it's difficult, but you must tell someone about this. You have to tell me."

"OK, OK." He took a deep breath. "Suddenly, I was the older Sarah, in a real gyro, returning home from my 29th birthday party, tired and a little drunk, but happy. And then it changed. I saw myself again, being attacked by Anton's gang. And I kept changing, like a flickering light, between one experience and the other." Zak stopped, looking horror-stricken.

Carmen was holding his hand now. "What is it, Zak?"

"The last thing I recall as Sarah was that old recurrent nightmare of the shattering glass, the pain and the sudden darkness, only real this time. The pain in my head and body was much worse than before, so bad, I passed out. When I woke up, I was me again and the pain had gone."

"And you haven't heard from Sarah since?"

"Nothing for three weeks. I think I've killed her, Carmen. She was flying a gyro; what if she became me at the same moment as I became her? If she was dealing with that knife attack, she would have crashed the gyro."

"We don't know that that's what happened, Zak."

Without realising he was doing it, Zak hugged a cushion with ducks on.

"I've had three weeks to think about it, and I'm pretty sure. By trying to connect with her and warn her about the danger she would face on her 29th birthday, I've become that danger and killed her."

Carmen stroked his hand as he continued.

"All my life, I've dreaded becoming Sarah, fearing it might happen at an embarrassing moment. I should have been worried about danger not embarrassment. She probably felt the same about me. And now I just wish she'd connect again. I miss her, and I need to know she's OK."

"I know, Zak, I know." She put a protective arm around him.

And suddenly they were hugging. And kissing. And tearing at each other's clothes. Carmen had promised herself not to do this again so early in a relationship, but she liked Zak a lot and sensed that he needed distracting from those awful visions of Sarah's death crash.

Zak had been tainted with death, possibly his own. He needed to feel alive. Carmen gave him this. Becoming one with her body, making her cry out in pleasure, this confirmed his real, physical presence in the world. He was a man. He was Zak and he was alive even if part of him had died with Sarah.

****

Birmingham, England, 2019. Zak's 12th Birthday. David Is 16 and Lily Is 17

The Emblin family were sitting around their huge television but only half-watching it. *The Bank of Mum and Dad* was on, a reality TV show revealing the shocking amounts of money some parents lavish on their ungrateful children. Zak complained to his mother that he didn't even get pocket money.

"You told me I'd get pocket money when I reached 12. You said Lily got pocket money at 12, and I could have some when I reached the same age."

Lily overheard this protest with interest. Teasing her freaky little brother was more enjoyable than what was on TV at that moment.

"Hey, Nerd. *I* got pocket money at nine!"

Zak looked accusingly at his mother. "I asked you when I was nine. Why did you lie to me?"

His mother explained that she couldn't trust him with his own money because of his schizophrenia.

"What would you spend it on?" she asked, lighting a cigarette and, seeing no ashtray nearby, flicking ash on to the carpet.

Zak answered honestly that he would spend it on music or save up for a keyboard.

"You see? You'd waste it on things that can only do you harm," said his mum.

"What do you mean, 'harm'? Music is great. I have Bach's *Double Violin Concerto* in my head all the time recently. Miranda Harper is playing one part; she's brilliant."

"Exactly. 'In your head'. And your head isn't right, is it? The doctors say you should avoid music; it could trigger more multiple personality episodes. And you haven't become…another person for weeks now."

"Her name is Sarah, Mum. Why won't you say her name? And that's bullshit anyway. I think you're making that up about the music. No doctor has ever said that to me."

"It's not bullshit. It stands to reason. It's the same with white knuckle rides at theme parks; you just can't do them. Too risky, could bring on an attack."

****

Birmingham, England, 21 July 2026

Despite her jealous feelings, Carmen was almost as desperate as Zak was for Sarah to make contact again. If the connection really were dead, she would have lost an unprecedented opportunity, potentially a career-saving opportunity, to interview someone from the future.

She was in the lab now, black blinds down against a bright sun, sitting at her desk trying to prepare the questions for such an interview, just in case. What did you ask someone who had so much knowledge? Merely by being born over a century later, Sarah knew (or had access to knowledge about) what happened next in some of our longest-running mysteries. Did we solve the global warming problem? Or was it still a big issue? Was there any falsifiable evidence yet for the existence of multiverses? Had we found out what dark matter and dark energy really were? Was the Universe more likely to end in a 'Big Chill' or a 'Big Rip', both effects of the Universe expanding at an accelerating rate? Had we discovered the extra spacetime dimensions predicted by Superstring theory? There were so many questions from her own field alone.

Yet Carmen knew she would have to waste some questions on getting proof that Sarah was real and not some twenty-first-century student acting out the part of a reincarnated soul. Even this part was trickier than you'd think. It was no good simply saying, "Tell us what happens in the future." Anyone alive today could have a plausible stab at that. Sarah would have to demonstrate knowledge of events or facts which were about to happen, so that when they did occur, Carmen could use this as evidence. And it would have to be more than one, a lot more, or the critics would say she'd just got lucky. So Sarah might have to do some research to prepare for a second interview, unless Carmen found a topic which she was interested in. Music maybe? Zak had told her that when he was Sarah, he often had songs floating around in his head.

None of that mattered, of course, if Zak and Sarah never swapped places again. Carmen thought about Zak and his distress. The priority now was to reassure him that the connection was not lost. She had no idea at all if it were lost or not, but she had to pretend to be an expert for Zak's sake and, she freely admitted, for the sake of her research. It was possible that if Zak thought he'd lost Sarah, then he might really do that. She had to prevent this. She had to convince Zak that although Sarah was dead, she was also alive, as it all happened in the future anyway. Zak might still be able to connect with a younger Sarah.

Even if he did, she realised that – assuming they always (or nearly always) connected when the same age as each other – she only had access to just under ten years' material from Sarah before she died because Zak was already 19. She'd better make the most of it. Better get Sarah to swap with Zak as much as possible – once they knew how the connection worked. And better record everything she said while in Zak's body. It was a pity, really, that she liked Zak so much. There was a lot to be said for not getting involved with your research subjects.

Carmen reached for her mobile to call Zak and arrange a date but hesitated before doing so. She thought hard first about what she was going to say to him. She looked for inspiration to the framed photo of her father, with her behind the telescope he had just bought her for her eighth birthday. His advice had always helped her. Giving Zak advice could do no harm and might help him. She decided to offer some theory that his body swaps with Sarah were normally with a Sarah who was the same age as he was, but that occasionally, maybe when either one was in a particularly stressful situation, he might swap with a different aged Sarah. As evidence, she would cite some of the primary school episodes Zak had told her about when they had been a few years apart in age. She decided to speculate also that he and Sarah would learn how to control and plan transfers. Satisfied, she called Zak.

Carmen's theories were pretty much guesswork, but she was a good scientist and good scientists excel at positing theories. In this case, her theories turned out to be true. It was a double whammy; they also succeeded in reassuring Zak. Before long, he was transferring with Sarah again.

****

Birmingham, England, August 2026

As soon as Carmen and Zak walked into the terraced house where Zak had grown up, looking only at Carmen, Sue Emblin said, "Very nice, Zak! I didn't know you had it in you." Still looking at Carmen, she added, "I didn't think anyone would have him with his disability. You have told her about it, haven't you, Zak? He has told you?"

Carmen assured Zak's mum that he had told her about his schizophrenia.

Sue's dark brown hair, tinged with red, had been dyed peroxide blonde. An inch of dark hair was showing at the roots. She asked Carmen why she didn't go blonde.

"I'm a natural brunette with a hint of red; it just wouldn't work," replied Carmen.

"Sure, it would. Look at me, it's the same as my natural colour. And why does a pretty, slim girl like you want to hide her legs away in jeans. You should show them off, wear a short skirt!"

Carmen was not in the least offended, but Zak got embarrassed on her behalf. He looked at his mum's fat thighs, thick with varicose veins, bulging out of shorts which were two sizes too small.

"Perhaps you should wear jeans more often, Mum."

"I am, aren't I? These shorts are denim. Don't be so cheeky!"

Birmingham, England, 6 April 2016

As she marked books in her classroom one day after school, Rachel Chaplain was pondering the enigma that was Zak Emblin. His proposed place at the special school Radcliffe's had been in question for a while now. St Francis' School had been coping well again, and his mother, Sue Emblin, had begun to wonder whether he might not be better off staying there after all. The other children, with a few exceptions, were amazingly good with him, not at all scared when he changed personality, and just as friendly to Sarah as they were to Zak.

Today all that had changed during the geography lesson. She had wanted to introduce the children to the concept of government. She had asked them if anyone knew the name of the Prime Minister. Quite a few did. Encouraged by this, she had asked if anyone knew the name of the American President. She recalled what had happened next. Only Zak had put his hand up.

"Yes, Zak, who do you think it is?"

Zak looked around to see if the teacher was talking to someone behind him.

"I'm not Zak, I'm Sarah."

There were a few sniggers, but the children in Year 4 were used to Zak becoming Sarah by now.

"Sorry, Sarah, go on."

"It's President Bullock, miss."

"Good try, Sarah. It's actually President Obama."

"Wait, miss, is this a trick question? At my other school, we did about him in tenth grade. Wasn't he the first black president?"

"Yes, absolutely."

"But that was, like, over a hundred years ago!"

Quite a few children laughed. Others listened intently.

Sarah continued, "That was back when there were 52 states, right?"

"Correct. Impressive that you should know that. How many are there now?" asked Rachel Chaplain, unable to contain her curiosity, an impulse she regretted as soon as Sarah replied.

"Forty-eight, of course. Hawaii was given independence. Louisiana, Mississippi and Alabama got completely flooded in the '80s due to climate change. A quarter of a million people died. Everyone knows that."

Alarmed at the upsetting information coming from Sarah, Miss Chaplain felt she should change the subject quickly.

"Well done, Sarah. So who becomes President after Obama?"

"I can't remember that from my other school. But I know that exactly ten years to the day after Obama finished his second term, President Herzog was assassinated."

"What?"

"Climateers claimed responsibility. They said he was opposed to moving away from a fossil-fuel economy, which we needed to do to save all human life on Earth. 'One life for everyone's life' was their tweet after they shot him."

Several children were now looking scared; others just confused. Rachel Chaplain decided to remove Sarah/Zak from the classroom.

"This is so interesting, Sarah, that I'd like you to tell Mrs Douglas all about it, right now, in her office. Come with me. Children, while I'm gone, please continue with the decimal places work which we were doing just before this, and if you have any problems, ask Miss Thompson here" – she pointed to the classroom assistant.

The quickest route to the Head Teacher's office was through the playground. Despite the drizzle, they took it. As they passed through it, Rachel spotted workmen putting in a big new metal security gate with a combination lock. This was supposed to deter deranged people who might want to force their way in to kidnap or kill schoolchildren. *Such is the world we live in,* thought Rachel. Today, however, the threat to her children's security had come from within, from the information, supposedly from the future, which Zak, in a schizophrenic episode, had shared with the class. No amount of extra security could protect them from that.

"You need to hear this," said Rachel Chaplain to her friend, Lesley Douglas, without any greeting, once inside the Head Mistress's tiny office. She prompted Sarah to repeat what she'd said in the classroom. A look of shock and surprise spread over Mrs Douglas's face as the 'child' obediently did as she was asked, even adding that California was now split into two halves, as most of it had fallen into the sea during the 2039 earthquake.

It was one thing to get the children to accept that Zak Emblin experienced regular delusions in which he became an eight-year-old American girl from the future. This was different. How could the delusional Zak imagine in such detail? He was only eight. 'Climateers'? Only 48 States? Where was this information coming from? The voice now speaking through him was clearly much older, probably that of a teenager. No, this was something different, something frightening. Both Miss Chaplain and Mrs Douglas found it creepy. They could not allow the other children in Zak's class to be exposed to such talk of natural disasters causing death on a massive scale and of assassinations. It could be upsetting for them. Fortunately, most of it had gone right over their little heads, but they couldn't take the risk in future. Zak's doctor was right after all: Radcliffe's was the best environment for him now. He could not stay at St Francis's any longer.

When all the children had left for the day, Zak now himself again, Rachel felt a sense of relief that the decision had been made to place Zak in a special school. She would inform Sue Emblin herself. His delusions were clearly very deep-seated indeed. Yet something bothered her, something she hadn't dared discuss with her friend and colleague, Lesley Douglas. What bothered her was the possibility that somehow Zak had really become this girl, Sarah, from the future. She removed her iPad from the desk drawer at the front of the classroom, created a new folder which she called 'Sarah' and wrote:

2027 – President Herzog assassinated?
2039 – California falls into the sea after earthquake?
2080s – Four US States flooded, quarter of a million killed?

Then she went back to her marking.

****

Birmingham, England, August 2016

Sometimes when she was bored, Rachel Barrett (nee Chaplain) surfed the news channels. Today was such a day. CNN had a story about the US election. Hilary Clinton was still leading. Donald Trump, the Republican candidate, was facing allegations of sexual abuse against women. The face on the screen playing down these allegations was that of the unfortunate member of Trump's campaign team who had been given the job of answering media questions. His name rang a bell with Rachel Barrett, but she was not quite sure why. It was William Herzog Jr.

****

Birmingham, England, August 2026

Zak's stand-up act was going well enough for him to pay a stooge for part of his routine. This person pretended to be a volunteer from the audience, so it had to be a different person each time so regulars didn't get suspicious. When Carmen heard about this, she volunteered.

"Are you serious?" asked Zak.

"Absolutely. I do get nervous, but I love performing, and it will be such a change from the Conference Circuit."

You got that right, thought Zak, because he was thinking of using slapstick in the act and he hadn't seen any at the two conference presentations he'd had to sit through while waiting for Carmen one day. Both performances could have used some in his opinion.

The very next Friday they were on stage upstairs at the Glee Club. Zak was speaking. Carmen was standing next to him, holding a plastic bucket full of water and a cheeky grin.

"And now, here is Saturday's weather. It will be fine." As he said this and held up a large orange above his head, Carmen threw water over him from the bucket. He added quickly, "but with scattered showers, obviously."

He yanked her aside roughly by the elbow and said in an irritated stage whisper, "I said, when I say 'Sunday, it will rain', you throw the water over me. Got it?"

Carmen nodded, looking a bit sad because she'd been told off.

"Saturday is fine. On Saturday, I hold this big orange above my head and we both smile. Got it? It's when I say, 'Sunday it will rain', that—"

Zak stopped speaking because Carmen had just thrown a lot of water over him again. He was drenched.

"What did you do that for?" he protested.

"You said, 'Sunday it will rain'," replied Carmen, simply.

"I did say that, yes, but only because you have to know when in the act, I am going to say, 'Sunday it will rain'. I didn't—"

Zak stopped again because a lot more water had just been chucked over him. He glowered at Carmen.

"Tell you what," he said. "Let's just do the act. Are you ready?"

Carmen nodded.

"And now, here is Saturday's weather." Zak held the large orange above his head and Carmen pointed to it, smiling. "It will be fine." After a pause, he added, looking across at Carmen, "On Sunday it will rain." Nothing happened. Carmen was still smiling but didn't move the bucket. Zak repeated, a little louder, "On Sunday it will rain." Still nothing. He repeated it again and this time pointed to his head.

When he repeated it again, Carmen interrupted calmly but assertively, "No, on Sunday, it will be fine."

"How do you know that?" asked Zak. "*I* am the weatherman."

"Because there's no water left," said Carmen.

To prove this, she threw the remaining drops of water from the empty bucket over the audience, which squealed at first, then laughed, and finally applauded as Zak and Carmen took a bow and left the stage.

Fifteen minutes later, outside the Glee Club, Carmen was still buzzing. She and Zak had both changed out of their wet clothes.

"I'm so glad I did that; that was such a rush!" said Carmen, and Zak agreed. They went back to Carmen's and had the best sex they had so far had in their still very young relationship.

New Palm Springs, USA, 3 July 2121

Five-year-old Sarah Templeman was flying her remote-controlled gyro around the spacious, metallic living room of her parents' apartment. She was good at it. The Fly, as the manufacturers had called it, was very robust to cope with the many crashes they thought it would have to endure at the hands of five-year-olds. But Sarah had taken to it from day one – her fifth birthday – and had proved her daddy wrong. He had complained that it was a waste of money buying a boy's toy for his little girl as she would probably never play with it.

"It's what she wanted," Zelda, his wife, had countered.

Now they were both watching her with pride as she flew the little craft in and out of the Duplo tower blocks which she had created, based on their own apartment block in New Palm Springs, California Peninsula.

"That's a boy's toy, Darling," said Bron, smiling. "You might turn into a boy, playing with boy's toys all the time!"

Zelda started to protest but she was smiling too, until Sarah suddenly spoke over her in a voice they had never heard before.

"I *am* a boy. My name is Zak."

The gyro crashed into one of the tower blocks, and a little chrome pilot came tumbling out.

"This is too hard. I want *my* helicopter, the police one. Where is it? Where's Mummy?"

"What do you mean, Sarah? I'm right here," said Zelda. "That is your gyro, your favourite toy."

Sarah looked at Zelda and started crying. "You're not my mummy! I want to go home."

Instinctively, Zelda's long gibbon arms scooped up Sarah to comfort her, and she knew immediately that she wasn't holding her own child. Yes, Sarah's body was the one she was familiar with, but the way the child moved and held herself was completely alien to her. She gripped her daughter's shoulders tightly and stared into her eyes. "Sarah, Sarah, where are you?"

"Ow, that hurt. I'm not Sarah, I'm Zak. Let me go. I want to go home – NOW!"

In the space of a few seconds, Zelda's world had been turned upside down. One moment she had been in an idyllic family scene where parents were watching proudly what their young child could do. The next moment that same daughter had gone, replaced by an imposter in her own body, and Zelda was already thinking fast about how to deal with this unwelcome new situation, this new world. She knew instinctively that this was not her child and she needed to know who had taken over her child's body – it might be the only way to get Sarah back.

"Where is your home?" she asked of the child who was now pulling at Sarah's fluffy blue top in disbelief.

"Don't listen to her, Sarah. You're just feeling a little sick, is all," said Bron. "We'll get you to a physician, and you'll be back to normal in no time." To his wife, when out of Sarah's earshot, he added, "What are you saying? We gotta pretend nothing's wrong – for Sarah's sake."

Zelda recalled with a chill how, about a year ago, Sarah had talked about being a boy 'before' and had described how, as a boy, she had got the scar on her chest. Somehow the moment had never seemed right to tell Bron about this little episode. As nothing like it had happened since – until now – she had decided he was probably better off not knowing. Now she regretted that decision.

"But that's not Sarah," she replied. "Can't you tell? She's been possessed. That's not even her voice."

Holding the child's hand, she repeated, "Where is your home, Darling?"

The child looked very dubiously at Zelda and said, quietly, "Birmingham."

Zelda and Bron stared at each other in disbelief. Birmingham, Alabama had been under water since the 2080s' floods, 35 years ago. Was the child now possessing their daughter's body a ghost from that tragedy? A flash of inspiration came to Zelda because Sarah had been talking in a funny accent since she'd been acting strange.

"Do you mean Birmingham, England?"

"I think so. Mummy taught me my whole address in case I get lost." The child looked suspiciously out of the window. They were very high up and lots of small helicopters like big flies were buzzing this way and that, narrowly missing each other. "Am I lost now?"

"I think you might be, Sweetie." There was a tear in Zelda's eye as she said this. It was so difficult being nice to a child who had just taken over her own daughter's body. She wanted to scream, yet this child seemed so helpless too.

"Tell me that address now, Honey." She motioned to Bron to get her a light pen, so that she could record the details. He didn't understand at first but then handed her one.

Zak/Sarah spoke, "I live at 14 Churchill Avenue King's Norton, Birmingham B17 8ZQ England. My phone number is 0121 458 9310. You can phone my mummy there and tell her to pick me up."

This all came out in a fast monotone suggesting that the child had learned it all in one go. As s/he was saying it, Zelda copied the details in mid-air with the light pen, leaving a trail behind like that left by sparklers but which stayed there.

Seeing it, Zak/Sarah's jaw dropped open. "How did you do that? That's where I live, and, and the letters are flying!" S/he tried to touch one, but it had no substance.

"It's just an ordinary light pen," said Zelda to the child. She then spoke to her useless husband, who was looking confused and repeating, "What's a 'phone'?"

"Don't you know any history at all? It's a cell. Cells used to be called cell phones about a hundred years ago when they were invented. We have an address and a cell number now. This might help us get Sarah back."

"How?" asked Bron sarcastically, "Are we going to England?"

"Maybe, yes. Don't you see? If this child has entered Sarah's body – what did you say your name was, Honey?"

"Zak."

"That's right, Zak. Then Sarah might now be in Zak's body. They might have changed places!"

Bron was looking unconvinced, but said, "We could call the number and find out."

Zelda thought for a moment. "No, no, it wouldn't work."

"Why not? It's worth a try surely?"

"Bron, don't you see? This child, Zak, is from the past – I know, I know it sounds ridiculous. And I don't know how it's happened. But you saw how fascinated he was just now with the light pen. No one's used the words 'phone' or 'helicopter' for over a hundred years. That number won't exist anymore."

Bron tried the number on his cell anyway but he got the number unobtainable signal every time. While he was doing this, Zelda probed a bit more. Holding Zak/Sarah's hand gently and looking into the child's eyes, she said:

"Zak, did your mummy teach you the days of the week, too?"

Zak, who was starting to like this tall but gentle lady, recited all seven days of the week.

"How about the year, Zak, did she tell you how to write that?"

Zak shook his head. Zelda would have to try another tack. Then it came to her.

"What year were you born, Zak, do you know that?"

"Yes, I was born on 5 May 2007. I am five years, two months and two days old," said Zak proudly.

This proved two things to Zelda. It was not Sarah in there – her fifth birthday had been six months earlier. And this child really was from the past. Born in 2007, he should be 114 years old! Was he some sort of ghost, possessing Sarah's body?

All the time they were talking, the address Zak/Sarah had recited hung in mid-air.

Zelda now picked up the light pen, which looked like a very slim stapler, and collected this information by waving over it, like using a whiteboard rubber to erase words.

"I'll just save this," she said, "and see what comes back. It might help us to find your mommy."

"She's called Mummy, not Mommy."

"Mummy, yes. I'll try and remember."

A hologram of Birmingham, England in 2012 suddenly bubbled out of the light pen, expanded, the buildings distorting, and shuddered to a halt in front of them.

"Wow," said Zak. "I live there!" And he didn't just mean Birmingham. The very flat which Zak called home had rotated around to the foreground of the hologram.

"Is this Google Earth?" asked Zak. He got blank looks from Zelda and Bron.

"Write that down!" exclaimed Bron suddenly, in an unnaturally loud voice. "The things Sarah says which make no sense to us are likely to be from the past. They might help us to find our Sarah."

'Write it down yourself!' Zelda was tempted to say. Until she noticed that he couldn't because he had a large bottle of Extra Strong in one hand and a bottle opener in the other. *Shit. This crisis was going to be the perfect excuse for him to start drinking again.* She would have to deal with that later. For now, finding Sarah was her priority. She turned to the child, light pen in hand.

"Did you say 'Doodle Earth'?"

"No. Google Earth. I saw Mummy go on it once. It's really cool."

"And this map is like it, is it?"

"Yes. You can see your own house and walk around the streets."

"OK. Shall we do that?" Zelda clicked something on the light pen and a life-sized avatar appeared just outside Zak's flat.

"Who's he?" asked Zak/Sarah.

"Oh, he's always the same to start with. Today we will make him you or me."

"I want him to be me."

"OK, he's you. Just step into the body shape and after a few seconds it will look like you. Shall we go into your flat, see if Mommy – I mean Mummy's there?"

The avatar wobbled into a human form. Zelda couldn't help gasping for it looked like a little boy, a blond, blue-eyed boy, and not like Sarah. She supposed this must be what the boy Zak had looked like. It was chilling having confirmation come from a computer that her daughter's body no longer contained her daughter.

The Zak avatar walked up one flight of stairs and rang the bell for No. 13. Zelda's heart was beating fast. She hoped Zak's mommy would be there with Sarah inside Zak's body, not knowing where she was or what was happening to her. But there was no answer. She wanded the light pen at a corner of the hologram and a calendar appeared. It read Tuesday 3 July 2012. Today was also 3 July. That made sense; she hadn't requested any specific date, just 2012, so the computer had taken her back exactly 109 years.

"Can we go in there? Adrian might be in. He plays the piano." Zak/Sarah was pointing at the door to No. 14, opposite, which was ajar.

"Why not?" said Zelda. As the block was laid out symmetrically, it would at least show her the layout of Zak's parents' flat. The avatar took them on a tour of a squeaky clean flat, very white and sparsely furnished, which did indeed have a piano – a baby grand – but no people. Zelda instinctively bent her head to avoid bumping it on the ceiling, although this was not necessary in a hologram. How annoying that everyone was out. Zelda checked the time in the bottom right-hand corner of the hologram. It was 7 in the evening; surely someone had to be around. As the weather was fine, Zelda moved the avatar Zak into the communal gardens, hoping to find someone outside they could try and talk to – empty, except for one figure taking down washing who seemed very static.

Zelda realised what the problem was at the same moment as her annoying husband shouted:

"You won't find anyone in there. We didn't have trackers then. They only came in in the 2080s after so many were 'unaccounted for' in the floods. Don't you know any history?" Bron laughed until he made himself cough. "The only people there are those who were there the day the film was made, and they're not active."

Zelda felt frustrated. She had hoped to get a family name from Zak's flat that she could look up in *Who's Who?* – the universal database of biography which had entries on everyone whose birth had been registered in the past 300 years (although some of the nineteenth-century ones were a bit sparse). She looked at the child.

"What's your full name, Zak?" she asked.

"Zak. Zak is my name."

"Do you have another name which comes after 'Zak', your family name?"

Sarah's face wore a puzzled frown. "Zak Em," he said eventually. "Mummy sometimes calls me 'Zak Em'."

"Zak M," Zelda repeated. His family name probably began with an 'M'. Matthews, Moore, Morris, there were so many of them, it wasn't much of a lead. She pulled *Who's Who?* Out of the light pen.

"What are you doing now?" asked Zak.

"Wasting time while Sarah gets further away," said Bron, swigging his beer.

Zelda ignored him.

"I'm going to look you up in this big book, Zak. See if we can't get you home."

Zak stepped closer to see what she was doing. Zelda put in 'Zak' and '2007' as keywords and got back 20,000 hits. She narrowed it down by entering 'UK'. This reduced it to 4,000 hits – still a huge task. She was about to add part of Zak's address into the mix when she got lucky. She spotted the corner of an envelope sticking out from under Zak's front door in the hologram of his flat which was still open. OK, so interaction with living beings was impossible. What about inanimate objects? She reached into the hologram and tried to grab the envelope, but it was too small. She came back out and enlarged the section including the front door. She tried again. This time the letter came away between her forefinger and thumb.

In her excitement, she tried to pull it out of the hologram, which was impossible. Her hand came away empty. *Shit,* thought Zelda, before realising that she might not have to pull it all the way out of the hologram to be able to read what was on it. She put her hand back in, grabbed the envelope again and, taking care not to pull it past the edge of the hologram, read what was on it. "Sue Emblin, 13 Churchill Avenue, Kings Norton, B17 8ZQ." Bingo. She had Zak's family name now. "It didn't start with 'M' at all. 'Zak Em', not 'Zak M', was short for Zak Emblin. Better confirm it, though."

"Zak, do you know what your mummy's name is?"

Zak thought for a moment before saying, "Sue. Sue Emblin."

"So you do know your full name! Thank you, Honey. Now let's look you up in this great big book."

The entry for Zak Emblin, born in Birmingham, England, on 5 May 2007, was three paragraphs long. There could be some leads there. And it gave her another name to try – in 2027, Zak had married one Carmen Beatrix Fry. Without hesitating, Zelda clicked on that name as well.

"Very interesting," she said.

"What is, for Christ's sake?" snapped Bron, between swigs.

"The woman Zak married in 2027 is still alive – there's no end date in *Who's Who?* Perhaps we could talk to her."

"She must have slipped under the radar. I thought the Eternity treatment was only given to those 35 and under back in the '70s. She must have been in her 60s by then."

While Bron was talking, Zelda was reading through Carmen Fry's entry in *Who's Who?*. "My God," she said, "she went to prison for fraud, and they still let her enter the Eternity Programme. I told you it was interesting. Here's the reason. It says here she qualified for Eternity as she was 'engaged in important government research into wormholes and quantum entanglement'."

Bron said something about Carmen now being one of the oldest people alive, but Zelda wasn't listening – her mind was racing. Wormholes...in popular fiction they were associated with time travel. They had a one-hundred-year-old child in their daughter's body, who later (earlier?) married this same researcher into wormholes. Zelda decided she really needed to meet Carmen Fry and the sooner the better.

But where to find her? The latest entry in her biography was ‘Semi-retired since reaching her hundredth birthday in 2105, Carmen Fry now lives in Wales, UK, in the house where she grew up.’

****

Birmingham, England, 21 January 2027

Rachel Barrett (nee Chaplain) felt stupid switching on CNN. She sank back into the new flat pack sofa bed she had bought the previous week, sipped her mug of Horlicks and sighed. Something had been bugging her for the past 14 years which tonight would be resolved one way or the other. In 2013, a boy in her class had predicted some horrific future events with exact dates while possessed by another personality. Her brain had told her that these were just wild imaginings from the mind of a schizophrenic (she was pretty sure he had been diagnosed with schizophrenia). But there was so much detail, he'd made it sound so real, that she'd opened a file called Sarah – the name of the child supposedly possessing him.

If the events turned out to be true, it would be remarkable, of course. It would probably turn accepted scientific thinking on its head, if only the scientists knew about it. But that wasn't what concerned Rachel. She was a teacher. Teaching was her vocation. You did the best you could for every child, just as she, as a mother, had done the best for her own two children, Maisie and Grace (now both at university), with absolutely no help from her husband. If the predictions came true, it would mean that Zak had been telling the truth and that they hadn't believed him. They would have let down a child who had trusted them to look after him. She made the decision to stay up late and watch CNN to be sure. As the hours wore on and her husband, Charlie, finally stopped demanding to know when she was coming to bed and fell asleep, she relaxed a little. The Horlicks helped. Nothing was going to happen. The President was safe. She fell asleep on the sofa bed.

When she woke up, it was already 3:30 am the following day. OK, so the US was five hours behind the UK, but even so if anything was going to happen, it would have to happen in the next hour and a half, and that seemed unlikely. She stood up, stretching. There was no way she could put off having to join her husband in bed any longer. And there it was, suddenly, a simple line of text going from right to left across the bottom of the screen:

Breaking News: President Herzog injured in assassination attempt while on board Air Force One. Assailant detained.

Just like with President Kennedy in 1963, they were announcing it as an injury first. Rachel suspected he was already dead.

"William Herzog," she said to the screen, "Rest in Peace."

Zak had been right. Rachel wanted to contact him immediately to apologise. She had no means of doing so and felt too guilty anyway. Children that young always tell the truth; why hadn't they listened to him? Ugh, it was just too weird, she had met a person who had been possessed by someone from the future. She didn't want to think about it anymore. No one would believe her if she told them anyway, so she resolved to put it out of her mind and joined the snoring Charlie in bed.

Even when he was asleep, she wasn't safe from Charlie's temper. Rachel gently used her fingers to open his fists without waking him. She interlaced her fingers with his to keep his palms open. This way, if he tried to lash out in the night, he wouldn't be able to form a fist and she might be able to stop him. Uncomfortable though it was, this was the only way Rachel Barrett could get to sleep each night.

England, Wales, 5 July 2121

It had been a gamble just dropping everything and flying to the UK. Before she had left the US, Zelda had tried everything to contact Carmen, but she had been simply uncontactable. Her publisher had described her as a recluse. His advice was helpful, though; he told Zelda that Carmen stayed in most days and would 'probably' answer the door.

"She says she's waiting for a visit. As if anyone's going to visit the Old Bird up there where she lives!"

There was nothing for it but to go to Wales on the off chance. When they crossed the border from England, there were no checkpoints or anything like that, less than on some State boundaries, just a notice saying 'Croeso y Cymru' which Zelda assumed was 'Welcome to Wales' in Welsh.

And the landscape was the same as it had been in Shropshire, England – hilly. But after about another hour of painstaking progress along winding narrow roads, small mountains appeared. Tense and desperate as she was, with Sarah missing, Zelda could still acknowledge that in happier times, this would be a spectacular landscape. And it must have been even more so back in Zak's day because he kept asking where all the wind turbines had sprung from. Small by American standards, they were nonetheless 200-metres tall white needles which punctured the land in patches for miles around. Zelda thought of it as Wales receiving Divine acupuncture. This led to the fanciful hope that if the country were 'cured', this might mean that she would get Sarah back as part of that cure!

To someone used to travelling everywhere by gyro (there were precious few of these yet on this side of the Atlantic) the journey seemed interminable. At last, their hire car climbed the final mountain, groaning its displeasure as it went, turned a corner onto a roadway wide enough for only one small vehicle, and Zelda recognised the old Welsh farmhouse ahead, from pictures she'd found online. The road, which now had grass growing in the middle, led them into a tarmac car park. It was the only choice, apart from reversing. There were no other roads turning off it. Zelda got out and opened the gate and drove in, wondering if she had been watched from the house.

As soon as Carmen Fry answered the door, Zelda knew the gamble had paid off. Zelda was greeted extremely warmly. Carmen said, "I've been so looking forward to this meeting!" as if Zelda really had managed to arrange it. She looked remarkably upright and spritely for 116, but then Zelda remembered that, as she had qualified for the Eternity Programme, she had set at 60 once the cure for the disease which is ageing had been discovered.

At first, Carmen got very emotional, hearing Zak's voice again, even though he was only five. She couldn't resist telling him that he would marry her one day.

"But you're old," said Zak.

Carmen smiled. "How old do you think, Zak?"

A frown of concentration appeared on Sarah's face as Zak thought about this.

"Very old, at least 30," he said at last.

Carmen laughed. "What if I was to tell you that I am 60, or even 116?"

"That's very old. I don't want to marry you."

"Don't worry, I'm only 20 when we meet. And you're 19. Watch out for Carmens with red hair!"

A tear came into Carmen's eye. Zelda didn't know what to say. She just wanted Sarah back. She sensed that to achieve this she needed to keep Carmen focussed and stop her reminiscing about Zak. The old lady had no incentive to swap Sarah back to her own body while she was getting so much out of hearing Zak's voice again (possibly for the first time in decades). A question came to Zelda from nowhere.

"Is there any truth in the rumour about death squads? I mean, back in the States, you never meet any older people, like yourself. Everyone looks about 25 now, of course, but no one even admits to being 35 or more."

Carmen thought carefully before answering.

"That's because there are very few people over 35 left. I wasn't happy about the Eternity Programme when it came in, but now they've gone too far the other way. I wasn't happy about Eternity because of the effect it had on my work. If people don't die, they can't reincarnate. They are not being allowed to reach the fullest potential of their multi-personality souls."

"Excuse me for asking, but in that case, why did you choose not to die?"

To buy some time, Carmen offered coffee and started to make it. She smiled. She could see where her friend, Sarah, had got her famous directness from, although physically she hardly resembled her tall, leggy mother at all.

"I wanted to see how long 'immortality for all'– well, for all young people – would last, and of course, it hasn't lasted. Death programming came in in the 2100s. And," she added mysteriously, "I also knew I had to be around to meet Zak."

Zelda missed the significance of this last remark because the truth about death programming was such a shocking revelation to her. She wanted to know immediately when Sarah would die (but not herself or Bron) and if it was now. Carmen explained that she still had Government Research Level clearance to the Mortality Programme classified data. She made a few keystrokes on her tablet, mainly for show. She didn't really need to look anything up. She had been anticipating this conversation for so long that she was ready for any direction it might take. She told Zelda that Sarah did not die yet.

Zelda sank into a chair. *Sarah was not dead. Did not die yet. Even if I never see her again, she lives.* Tears were in her eyes now.

Oblivious to the change in Zelda, Carmen advised her on how to return Zak to his own time and body.

"Transfers require a heightened emotional state," she said. "Anger is best – no one knows why. You've got to upset him – big time." She handed Zelda a brand-new-looking light pen. "But first, give him this."

"It's a light pen," said Zelda, drying her tears. "You want Zak to take this back with him? That's transferring physical matter through time. Does that work?"

"In theory," Carmen began, "there is nothing to prevent Zak taking something physical back through time, provided it is small enough to fit into the hand he thinks is his at the time his emotional state is heightened. In practice, I have no idea how it works."

"No idea? Then how do you know it *will* work?"

"Ah, I've had this light pen for 94 years."

Carmen let that information hang for Zelda to realise the significance of it.

"Not possible," said Zelda. "That's a Smart Slimline light pen. Even I can't afford one. They only came out last year!"

"Exactly!" was all the old lady said.

"You mean, you mean you got it from Zak? Back when he first met you? That's unbelievable!"

"A year afterwards to be precise – he'd forgotten all about it. Typical Zak," – her eyes met the child's – "always remembering the insignificant things and forgetting the important ones."

She held the child's hand and put the light pen into it. "You see, I always knew this meeting would take place this year. I just didn't know when. I've tried to be in for at least part of every day, just in case you came by. I also knew that transportation through time is possible, simply because I have the light pen. It was this light pen which secured me the funding I needed. Well, not exactly this one. I must confess I've replaced it with a shiny new one, for better effect. I couldn't give the Research Committee this rusty old thing,"– Carmen held up another light pen. It was the same model but was discoloured, chipped and dented – especially as it doesn't produce holograms reliably anymore. "I know this new one works. With my retinal scan and some hairs – showing my DNA aged at least 60 years – on it, the Research Committee gave me the benefit of the doubt, although some on the committee accused me of making myself up to look older. It also helped that they couldn't trace either of you two; there were no exact DNA matches – at least, not to begin with."

"What about Sarah? What does this mean for her?"

Carmen thought about the Sarah she had known, as she placed a mug of coffee in front of Zelda on one of the oldest oak coffee tables Zelda had ever seen.

"Yes, you've been very patient. I forgot; you must be worried sick with her missing. I'm afraid I don't know exactly what happens to Sarah, and I'm not going to insult your intelligence by guessing."

Zelda looked very disappointed with this academic's answer and sunk deeper into her chair, pulling the complaining Zak down with her.

"There are some things I *can* tell you. I have witnessed Zak and Sarah swapping places much later in their lives. This means that at some point, Sarah *will* return to her own body; I just can't be sure when."

"Can you give me an estimate? Is it days? Weeks? Years?"

"Definitely not years. Zak didn't like to talk about it because, when it happened, it was the longest time he had ever spent outside his own body and time, plus he was so young, of course; we mustn't forget that. Still, I'm pretty sure he said he was back in 2012 within a couple of weeks, which implies that Sarah returned to her own body at the same time – but we can't be sure of that."

"Why not?" Zelda was still looking very worried.

"I believe the soul that is both Zak and Sarah, has a strong connection between its multiple personalities. We are witnessing that now with the interchange between the two children we know. But there may be others—"

"Others?"

"Yes. I have found no evidence that souls live only two lives. Given the strong connection, Sarah could just as easily 'swap' with another of her soul's multiple personalities as come home to her own body. She could enter into the body of a past personality who lived before Zak, or into that of someone in the future."

It was worse than Zelda had feared. She became aware of something tugging at her jeans. Zak, who was still holding the light pen, said:

"When can I go home? You said if we found this lady, I could go home. Why can't I go home? I want Mummy."

Carmen recognised at once that Zak was in just the sort of emotional state that might allow a transfer. But she knew that she had to include a photo of the three of them on the light pen before Zak took it back to 2012. She had switched on the record function as soon as she had seen Carmen pull into the car park, so having his voice come out of Sarah's mouth was already covered. She snatched the light pen from Zak, making him cry, took a quick selfie of the three of them and, forcing the light pen back into the child's fist, shouted to Zelda:

"Tell him he can't go home. Ever. Quickly, tell him now!"

Zelda was quick enough to realise what Carmen was trying to do. Tears in her eyes, she said:

"Zak, you must stay in this new world now. Forever. You can't go home. You can never go home."

Her last words were drowned in her own sobs. Zelda knew with as much certainty as she had ever known anything that she would never look into those deep brown eyes again and see her own daughter looking back at her. How would she ever be able to bear so much pain? A small voice made her look up.

"Why can't we go home, Mommy? I've been to England. Are we staying in England now?"

****

Birmingham, England, 15 March 2039

Zak looked at his mother in the hospital bed. She was asleep, which was a rare release for her from the lung cancer which was killing her. Her breathing was now so shallow that she found it difficult to get to sleep. She cut a tragic figure: her cheeks sunken, morphine drip wired up to her arm, grey eye sockets, no hair. She was 57.

Why couldn't he feel sorry for her? Was it because she had contributed to her own death by smoking – and death was now inevitable? Or that she had blamed him for this? ("You started me smoking when you were a kid, with all that bloody Sarah nonsense. I was fine before then, never needed the cigarettes. All through David and Lily's time at junior school, never needed them. Mind you, they were good kids, David and Lily. You had to be different.")

Maybe it was because she had never accepted Carmen who, with her doctorate, university career and high salary, would have been the perfect catch for most mothers.

Even that was not the real reason, although it was getting closer to it. The real reason, he knew deep down, was *why* she had never accepted Carmen. To accept Carmen would have been to embrace her theory of reincarnation and the connection across time between personalities sharing the same soul. That is, of course, a tall order for anyone to believe. But his mother wasn't 'anyone' – she had seen evidence – the light pen. Once Carmen had worked out how to use it, she had seen the hologram pictures of Carmen, much older, with Sarah and her mother. She had heard his own voice, crying, pleading for her, his mummy, coming from Sarah's lips. It might be understandable for an average member of the public to dismiss all this as some sort of magic trick. But Susan Emblin knew what Zak had been through all his life. She knew that he had always experienced Sarah as a living, breathing person, entering his own body, despite – for public consumption – sticking to the schizophrenia explanation.

The inescapable conclusion was that his mother rejected the truth because she preferred a son who was mentally ill. She hated and feared mental illness, always had. She had this in common with about 25% of the population. To justify this hatred to herself, she always apportioned blame to the mentally ill for their own condition. In her eyes, mental illness was something you brought upon yourself; or, in extreme cases, it might be divine retribution for wrongdoing. If her son were mentally ill, she could blame him and absolve herself. If he were abnormal only in the sense that he had the rare ability to transform himself into a future embodiment of his soul, she would have to accept him, love him, feel guilty about all the blame she had laid on him as a child for embarrassing her and for making her life difficult. She could not do that. And he hated her for it.

They had not spoken to each other for years. That had only changed when he had provided her with grandchildren, something David and Lily had yet to manage. She had contacted him then, but Zak knew that it was really his children, not him, that she had wanted to see.

Six months ago, she had got the lung cancer diagnosis. The doctors had made it clear from day one that the prognosis was bad. Since that day, they had seen each other nearly every day. David had showed up twice, once with irises, the only flowers she was allergic to, and got praised for it by his ever-doting mother. Lily had not shown up at all, not once, since the day her mother had been diagnosed with terminal cancer.

If she were a weak woman, that would have made it easier for him to forgive his mother, but she could be brave. Dealing with terminal cancer had brought out a certain courage in her. She had also defended him, at least to begin with, when he had been convicted of fraud and gone to prison. When he was a young child, she had even stood up for him on occasion when he had been treated badly for becoming Sarah. And he knew now what that must have cost her.

So why wouldn't she believe him? Why couldn't she admit that she had lived a lie during all the years she had put his behaviour down to schizophrenia?

She stirred, and he reached for her hand. Yes, he felt sad that she was dying, but it was only the same sadness he would feel for any fellow human in that situation. He even felt resentful that she was going to get away with not having to admit that he had been right all these years. Then he felt guilty for feeling this way.

She coughed. Automatically he reached for the cardboard vomit bowl before she had fully woken, knowing that she would cough up large amounts of mucus and blood.

"Mum, it's me. It's OK, I'm here. Do you want the television on?"

She found this more soothing than listening to her own son and having to make conversation. She wanted him there, yes, but she did not want him talking to her. Oh, she would chat away to David or Lily, but not to him. So, if his sister and brother were so wonderful, where were they now? Why weren't they at her bedside like he was, when she needed them?

He helped raise her into a sitting position so that she could cough more easily and more productively. She sank back, exhausted, against the hospital pillows, and nodded almost imperceptibly. Understanding the nod, he switched the television on. It was very old and tiny, a 40-inch flat screen, not even 3D, but it was functional. Susan Emblin's tired, green eyes settled on the screen, and Zak sensed the calm flowing through his mother.

She watched about 20 minutes of an antiques programme, then said, "News," to Zak, who immediately switched channels to CNN. Susan Emblin was not one of those dying people who sought solace in old films or children's TV. She found comfort in the news. You could depend on it for death and destruction. She was not alone, not singled out. Everywhere people were dying. Every moment someone just like her was dying somewhere else. This was why Zak chose CNN; you could rely on it for in-depth coverage of disasters across the globe.

Today it proved exceptionally reliable. There was nothing but disaster coverage; all other news was pushed to one side. There had been an enormous earthquake in the USA itself. It was along the San Andreas Fault and had reached point 9.0 on the Richter scale. It had happened in the early hours of the morning, mercifully taking many as they slept. Almost all of California had broken off into the sea, creating a new island, a new coastline and leaving a peninsular where the inland town of Palm Springs had been before. The death toll was expected to rise to about 9,000. It was especially high on the new island part of California, which included San Francisco. Emergency services from outside the area were now cut off by the sea. The only way in was by chopper.

Zak was horror-struck. But it also dawned on him that this was the very event, unfolding before his eyes, which Sarah had predicted while occupying his body as a child. He remembered having to tell the head teacher about it and fearing he would be expelled. He remembered his mother getting annoyed, telling him – telling Sarah – that there was no such place as 'New Palm Springs' when she had said they had renamed it after the earthquake.

There was no need for him to say anything. He knew she remembered as well; saw on her face that she was fighting the implications of that recollection – that he, Zak, had been right about Sarah all along.

“Why resist it, Mum?” he said as she fought for breath. “It means our souls live on. It means you will live on.”

He thought she had closed her eyes to deaf him out, as she usually did during arguments, but she never opened them again.

****

Nottingham, England, 15 March 2039

Rachel Barrett was looking forward to her retirement from teaching in four years' time. She knew exactly what she would do: get a horse and ride it every day. Her eyes studied the many framed paintings of idealised horses which adorned the walls of her lounge. Kids were lovely (didn't she have two wonderful daughters and three grandsons?) but horses were noble and beautiful creatures in a way a human could never be. We only get one chance at life, so she was determined to realise this long-held ambition. She loved living in the city but missed the countryside. She would find a stable in a village near Nottingham (probably Laxton – she loved its castle and twelfth-century church) and drive out there every day, sometimes twice a day. Nothing beat the freedom she felt when riding; plus horses were so much more reliable and loyal than men.

Unfortunately, this brought her thoughts flooding back to Charlie and how she had finally left him after 25 years of abusive marriage. This was another reason for moving to Laxton. She would at last have an address Charlie did not know about. This would make her feel a lot safer than she did now, protected only by a court order. This was a subject she had been trying to avoid thinking about. A tear came into her eye.

She did not have to endure it for long, as a news item on television penetrated her consciousness. They were talking about a massive earthquake along the San Andreas Fault. Thousands were dead. California was now an island.

Rachel looked at the calendar, but she already knew what year it was. She found the old iPad which she had kept expressly for this purpose, opened the file named 'Sarah' and read:

2027 – President Herzog assassinated?
2039 – California falls into sea after earthquake?
2080s – Four US States flooded, quarter of a million killed?

Two down. One to go. Since that terrorist had killed President Herzog on the very last day of his presidency in 2027, she hadn't needed any proof. Zak Emblin, a little boy she had taught briefly, had seen the future, was probably possessed by a soul *from* the future. Then, back in 2027, she had felt so uncomfortable, so guilty. He had been an innocent child and they had not believed him. They had let him down. Now she felt mainly curiosity. She wanted to meet him. See how he was doing. Apologise. Find out more about his experiences as Sarah.

She wondered if he had married or had children. Or was his – what? Affliction? Disability? Special power? They all seemed to fit – was it preventing him from leading a normal life? It can't be easy to be the family member of someone who suddenly becomes another person entirely. Rachel guessed he was probably still single, a loner, if he was still alive. To have a successful relationship, he would have to meet someone who completely understood what he was going through, and that was unlikely. It was difficult enough for anyone to find a soul mate, let alone someone with Zak's problem. *Look at me,* she thought, *I have no disabilities at all and look who I ended up with.*

On a whim, she googled him. Most people preferred the new style *Who's Who?* now for finding out about someone, but old habits died hard with Rachel. She found him in Wales. A small glow of satisfaction pulsed through her when she saw that he *was* married to someone called Carmen Fry. *Good for you, Zak!* That name and face were familiar, perhaps she had been on a TV documentary – she *was* a scientist. Rachel noted down the name of the town. There was a picture of their house on the web with Zak and Carmen standing in front of it. It looked like an old stone farmhouse. Rachel printed this out. Her next holiday would be in Wales. The pony trekking was lovely, apparently.

****

"This life is but a tenure, one of many perspectives a spirit must experience in the quest for eternity."

– Brian Rathbone, *Call of the Herald.*

Birmingham, England, September 2026

The service dog had been a great idea. He wasn't mad keen on Labradors but that was all they'd had available, so that was that. Normally service dogs were used with epilepsy, but it was not unheard of for a dog to prove useful with schizophrenia as well. Psycho, as he had christened her, did not just bark at him when he got angry or emotional, she was much better than that. He could recognise for himself when he was in a heightened emotional state and therefore might become Sarah. Where Psycho was brilliant was that she knew when he would really become Sarah. She could smell the change. This meant that, when upset about something, Zak could stop worrying about swapping with Sarah, on top of everything else. It was not going to happen unless Psycho barked six times, and then repeated it. And if she did that, he knew 100% for certain that he would become Sarah. He could prepare himself. He had learned always to have a sports bra, T-shirt and jeans in Sarah's size within grabbing distance. At least, he could dress like a boy even if he were trapped inside a girl's body.

He knew by now that Sarah was a lot less well organised than he was. In fact, she seemed to live her life on a whim. So he left clothes out for her too. A top and a longish skirt in his size which Carmen had helped him to choose from some specialist tall girls' web site. He also left a voicemail, set to repeat, so she was bound to hear it until she worked out how to switch it off. And that might take some time, as his state-of-the-art iPlay would seem antiquated to Sarah, who was familiar with twenty-second-century technology. The message said:

"Hey Sarah, it's me, Zak. You're in my body again, sorry. If you don't believe me, look inside your pants! I've left some clothes out for you – I get a warning now; I've got this dog. See you. Or rather, I won't. Be you, I should say."

****

Birmingham, England, Two Weeks Later in 2026

Sarah opened her eyes and knew instantly that she was in the past, probably in England. She was in a dark street she did not recognise and wondered what the hell Zak could have been doing here. But then safety issues were different for boys. There was a bus stop in the distance and Sarah started to walk towards it, finding Zak's black Doc Marten's boots very heavy. She did not get there. She came alongside a pub called the Cross Keys. It had a flat roof and was entirely built of concrete, now covered in graffiti. It was one of the ugliest buildings Sarah had ever seen. Had she been a local, the Cross Keys would have told her that she was in Campsfield and, more importantly, to get out of there as soon as possible. A small yet muscly young man with red hair came out of the pub and noticed her. Two other bigger men came out at the same time and looked as though they were with the first one. Sarah did not like the look of recognition which appeared on the first man's face. She tried to walk past him. He grabbed her arm.

"What are you doing here, Emblin? This is my patch. Didn't I teach you enough of a lesson that time back at your school, with that wimp Anton? Why hasn't he come himself? Why has he sent you again?" He produced a medium-sized kitchen knife from a sheath attached to his belt.

Sarah said nothing and tried to break free. She could smell the alcohol on her assailant's breath. He pulled her back, motioned to his two friends, who looked equally unwelcoming, and shouted:

"Take him around the back to the car park, behind Eric's van."

Instinctively, Sarah dropped to the ground and screamed, but they dragged her along anyway, the ringleader's hand now over her mouth. She was getting grazed knees, so she stood up again and went with them.

"I asked you a question, Zak! Why are you here?" The assailant took his hand from Zak's mouth to let him answer.

"I'm not Zak," Sarah managed to say, which brought a vile smile to her attacker's face.

"Oh, we are Sarah now, are we?" he taunted.

So this guy knew Zak and knew about him changing into her.

"Don't think that's going to help you. I think it's a try-on, to make me let you go, you f***ing weirdo."

"No, I really am Sarah."

"Prove it."

Sarah tried frantically to recall some future facts which might at least confuse her assailant (who she recognised now as the same guy who had stabbed Zak before) and buy her some time to escape, but it was too late. They were behind the van now, a clapped-out Ford. The cars around it, by contrast, were new, expensive sports cars.

"Pin her down, boys," said Sean to his henchmen. "You can prove it by showing me how you suck off like a real lady, bitch!"

The other two forced her down to her knees again, and Sean Miller forced her to fellate him at knife point. Another van sped into the car park just as he came, forcing all three of them to run off. While Sean was stuffing himself back into his pants, Sarah did manage to spit the semen back into his face.

"I'm coming back to kill you for that, Emblin," Sean yelled back at her as he ran off.

Sarah was in shock and feeling desperate for a mouthwash and a shower, but she did manage to run fast in the opposite direction. Zak's boots did not feel so heavy now. Shocked and frightened as she was, she noticed again how much more athletic Zak's body was than her own, running faster than hers would have done for the same amount of effort. *Damn you, Zak, for getting me into this.*

****

Suddenly Zak wondered what he was running from and hated the fishy taste in his mouth which made him keep spitting. He became aware of a sharp pain in both knees and looked down to find them grazed and bleeding through torn jeans. He wanted to know what Sarah had been through but had no way of asking her. Should he go back and get the package Anton had paid him well to collect from Sean, who was supposed to be in the Cross Keys in Campsfield? Something told Zak to give it a miss and he went home to nurse his knees instead.

Wales, UK, March 2039

It was only two days ago that Zak had accepted her as a friend on Facebook, and now here she was ringing the bell at Zak and Carmen's old farmhouse in Gwynedd. It was good to be a long way from Nottingham at an address Charlie did not know. Carmen answered the door, two toddlers wrapped around her ankles. Her friendly, welcoming smile quickly turned to a look of concern and surprise.

"Are you OK? Come in, come in, please. Have you been in an accident?"

"Yes," said Rachel, remembering her counsellor's advice to tell the truth about the abuse she had suffered, as it was out of her control and she should not feel guilty about it.

"Yes, an accident called marriage. My ex-husband paid me an uninvited visit two nights ago." Rachel touched the bruises on her eyes and cheeks. "He saw Zak's face on the PC screen and just lost it. I tried to explain that Zak was a former pupil who had just accepted me as a friend on Facebook, but he doesn't hear anything when he's in a violent rage."

"Did you call the police?"

"Afterwards, yes. He's in trouble. He's not supposed to come near me. There's a court order against him. I'll have to change the locks again now."

"Well, you're safe here, and you can stay as long as you like. He doesn't have this address, does he?" asked Carmen, suddenly concerned for her children. Rachel assured her that he did not.

With this exchange out of the way, they introduced themselves properly. Carmen was particularly friendly because she was dying to hear from Rachel what Zak had been like as a child. She was also impressed that, upon first seeing her, Rachel hadn't said (as so many did), "I know you. Aren't you the one who was in that fraud scandal that was all over the front pages a few years ago?" or words to that effect.

"Can I meet Zak now?" asked Rachel.

"Yes, and no," said Carmen. "You can meet his body, but Sarah's in it today. It's an unplanned swap, so Zak couldn't warn you about it. Come and meet Sarah—"

"I'd love to. I've already met her a number of times, but she was a child back then."

"Oh, well, in that case, I'm sure you two will have plenty to talk about. Do you want some coffee?"

"Tea, please, if you have it," said Rachel, and Carmen ushered her through a narrow, old stone corridor into a surprisingly spacious living room on two levels with open Spanish arches between them.

The view from the end of the lower level, which was almost all glass, was spectacular. You could see mountains on both sides of the Mawddach Estuary, on this side, rising behind the house. Far below, a long wooden railway bridge crossed the river from Fairbourne towards Barmouth. In the middle distance were sheep-dotted hills. Straight ahead was the open sea of Cardigan Bay. On a clear day, you could see a silhouette of Pembrokeshire rising from the ocean horizon. Today was one of those days, and Rachel was impressed.

Sarah could see Rachel taking it all in.

"I know," she said. "Carmen's so lucky, living here. She grew up here, you know. It was her parents' house. Still is Martin's, really, although he's already passed it on, legally, to Carmen and Zak, as he's been ill recently. He lost his wife, Betty, last year."

"I'm sorry to hear that," said Rachel. "I have great countryside in Nottinghamshire, but I have to confess, this beats it."

Martin Fry came charging in through the French windows, chased by very noisy twin boys of about four. Rachel guessed these must be his grandchildren (and Zak's children) and that he must be Carmen's father. He did not look ill, but he was a bit thin, and out of breath.

When the children allowed it, introductions were made. Coffee, tea, and biscuits were served.

Rachel was curious to know if it was difficult to accept having someone else in his son-in-law's body. He told her that it had been at first, but that he had got used to it surprisingly quickly. Zak always brought him back a small memento from the future. And he, Martin, gave Zak tips on what to look out for in the American night skies some hundred years from now, but Zak said the visibility was not that good in the city. And anyway, how could you not like Sarah? She was so blunt and spontaneous.

"Hey, Martin," said Sarah (she pronounced it 'Marden'), "who are you calling spontaneous? Do you want a fight?"

"Yes, yes, fight! Fight! Auntie Sarah, fight!" chorused the twins and leapt on top of Zak's body as Sarah was sitting cross-legged on the floor.

"Be careful," said Carmen, returning from the kitchen. "Get off her! Your Auntie Sarah's not used to that body yet, someone might get hurt!"

"It's OK, Carmy, I'm 22. I'm well used to Zak's body. It's your delightful boys that are new to me. I must meet them in a later reincarnation…a later swap, I mean, not a whole 'nother person. That *would* be complicated."

Oh, sorry, Sarah, I didn't realise. And I meant you weren't yet used to Zak's body *in this swap*, as you've only just swapped. This reincarnation business can be confusing. Well, this is James, he's four. And this bundle of energy is Stephen, he's just five minutes younger.

"And Rachel, I've just realised, you won't have a clue what Sarah looks like. Do you want to see some pictures Zak brought back last time?" Rachel nodded, her mouth full, but Carmen hesitated. "Oh, no, I've just thought, we can't do that. These were taken when you were 25, Sarah, it hasn't happened yet for you."

"Bring 'em on," said Sarah. "I'd love to know what clothes I've got to buy and how I wear my hair in three years' time."

"Er, it's luminous yellow," said Carmen, showing everyone the selfie Zak had taken on his mobile during the last planned swap. Like everyone, Rachel was taken with the hair which was in a Richard III style as well as being bright yellow, but she was just as intrigued to see that Sarah was short and slightly squat, a world away from Zak's six-foot lanky frame. How did they manage? She looked at Zak's body. Jeans and a loose shirt. It could be worn by a girl. Rachel understood why Sarah had not bothered changing her clothes.

While Rachel was unpacking, Sarah came in to talk to her. She asked how long Rachel would be staying, and Rachel said she didn't know yet. Sarah explained that she was concerned about Carmen.

"She needs a break. I was talking to her just before you arrived. She's had a tough year, first with Betty's sudden and unexpected heart attack, then Martin's cancer diagnosis, and now she's so worried about the boys, she's neglecting her research."

"What's the worry with the boys?" asked Rachel. "Is it losing their grandmother?"

Sarah hesitated before speaking and played with the velvet curtain sash as she was standing by the window.

"Carmen and Zak think they might also be reincarnaters. Zak and I were four when it first happened to us. Believe me, it was scary. We joke about it now – only the other day I was boasting to Zak about being one step nearer to Nirvana than he is, as I am a later reincarnation. But if it is true, if they really are reincarnaters, they're going to need all the help they can get. Carmen has taken to watching them all the time. If there were someone else here besides Martin, she could get a break. Martin's fine with Stephen and James but he's frail and needs frequent rests. Zak and I are too likely to become each other which makes us unreliable."

"You mean you want me to stay a while and look after the twins?" Rachel could not keep out of her voice her surprise at the sheer presumption of it.

"Oh, I know, I know it's a lot to ask. It's not even me asking. I've only just got here from 2138, but Zak put this note in the pocket of his jeans for me, in case we swapped." She handed Rachel the note. It read:

Rachel Chaplain, my old teacher, is coming. Ask her to watch over James and Stephen to see if they swap with anyone. She's perfect. She knows about us; she's seen us swapping as children, so she knows what it looks like. And Carmen needs the break.

Rachel looked up at Sarah and, of course, saw Zak's eyes looking back at her. So this was how they communicated. In an age marked by rapid technological change, they wrote notes on scraps of paper for each other which they hid in their clothing. Rachel felt sorry for them. This, added to the guilt she felt for not having believed Zak as a child, led her to agree to watch over Stephen and James for a couple of weeks. Maybe feeling safe from Charlie also had something to do with it.

"Are there any signs I need to look for? Have we got any names for people either of the twins may have swapped with?" she asked.

"I have absolutely no idea, but I'll ask Zak." Sarah reached immediately for a pen and paper.

It still seemed very odd to Rachel to hear, "I'll ask Zak," coming out of Zak's mouth. She decided to ask Carmen herself as it might be a while before Sarah and Zak swapped back and were able to communicate with each other.

Rachel found herself alone with Carmen in the kitchen when they were loading the dishwasher after dinner. As a mother herself, she knew that Carmen would never allow someone she had only just met to look after her boys, so she told the truth, dropping Zak in it, because she was pretty sure he hadn't discussed his intention of asking her to babysit with his wife. If Carmen were surprised, she did not show it. She looked hugely relieved and thanked Rachel profusely.

"I haven't been able to go in to work for ages because I'm worried about them. Stephen seems very distant sometimes. And I'm under pressure at work to 'produce' another reincarnater, as if you can somehow magically do that. It's not that I don't try. I have interviewed hundreds of potential candidates. I've even checked out all the schizophrenics I can find."

Rachel just nodded and listened.

"My worst fear is that my boss, Commander Levy, will find out that my own children reincarnate and try to get her hands on them, I'd hate—"

Carmen put her hand to her mouth, realising that she had said too much. Rachel was indeed at that very moment wondering who Commander Levy was and why an academic was line managed by someone with a military title. Fortunately for Carmen, she was discreet enough not to ask.

Wales, UK, March 2039, Two Days Later

Stephen and James were on the floor playing Connect Four. They seemed as interested in opening the base of the stand, to let the counters noisily spill out, as they were in the game itself.

Sarah, pretending to read, was watching them. She was fidgeting a lot and looked bored. Rachel was also watching the boys, more intently than Sarah was. The boys were not aware anyone was watching them. Stephen picked up the brown cardboard box where they kept the games which had loose parts and put it over his head. He put his arms out in front of him and strode forwards, despite not being able to see where he was going.

"Who are you?" asked James, giggling.

"I am an astronaut. In space. It's dark in space."

The two adults looked at each other, concerned. Rachel put out a hand to stop Stephen walking into the wall. Rachel heard a few faint woofs coming from an ancient and arthritic Labrador, lying in a basket in the kitchen.

Zak's happy voice suddenly said, "What are you doing, James, you'll walk into something."

In a weird, croaky voice, Stephen said, "I am not James."

"No, sorry, I can see that now. James is on the rug. You're Stephen; now be careful—"

"I am not Stephen. I am Andre. I am from the future."

Zak looked at Rachel. They had not said hello yet, but that would have to wait. Their faces both wore the same concerned expression. Zak grabbed Stephen's arm but tried to keep his tone gentle. He didn't want to alarm the child.

"Stephen, this is your daddy speaking. Who are you? Where are you from?"

"I am Andre. I am an astronaut. My spaceship is green. I am from the future." The same croaky voice was coming from Stephen's mouth.

"Andre, where is Stephen?" asked Rachel, but the child was preoccupied, looking for something, and did not reply.

The Andre voice said, "Where is my spaceship?"

With more worry showing in his voice, Zak asked, "Is Stephen on the spaceship? Where is he?"

James looked up from where he was sprawling on the carpet, with a puzzled frown, and said, "It's only a game, Daddy. Stephen's here," and he pointed at the cardboard box-head.

"Yes, I'm here," said Stephen, taking the box off his head and looking up at his daddy.

Oh, Thank God! Thank God, you're back! You had me so worried then. Where did you go?

"Space," is all that Stephen would say.

Over the next few days, this episode was much discussed. Rachel was asked to watch the boys even more closely, but hardly needed to because both parents were so worried that they were doing the same thing. On the fifth day of her stay, which also happened to be Carmen and Zak's wedding anniversary, Rachel put her foot down.

"I won't be here long," she said, "so I want you two young people to go out and enjoy yourselves this evening, while you can! I'll watch the boys. They'll be fine."

At first, Carmen protested, saying that Stephen was bound to swap with the astronaut as soon as their backs were turned, but between them, Zak, Martin and Rachel persuaded her to go out. An hour after they had gone, Rachel wondered what she had let herself in for. She had never come across such noisy, boisterous children in her life (and as a teacher, she had met many boisterous children). They were exhausting. When James broke an ornament trying to hit Stephen with a cushion and missing, she gave in and switched on the television. She asked them which channels they were permitted to watch.

"ChildNet," chorused the boys excitedly.

Rachel switched it on, and very soon the boys were glued to it and she had some peace and quiet. *Martin would appreciate it too*, she thought. He was upstairs in his room, trying to rest.

Rachel managed to read for about 20 minutes before something on the TV caught her attention. A cartoon was beginning. A boy of about four put a cycle helmet on his head which changed immediately into a space helmet. "I am Andre, the astronaut," he said in a croaky voice. "My spaceship is green." He pointed to the green sofa which turned into a rocket. "I am from the future. Join me on my space adventure."

Rachel laughed. She thought about phoning Carmen and Zak but decided against it. Let them enjoy themselves. If she called, they would assume that something was wrong. She would tell them later.

****

Birmingham, England, 2026.
Zak's Untidy Bachelor Flat

She had finally worked out how to operate the antiquated voicemail system and played back Zak's message three times. "Hi, Sarah, it's me, Zak. You're in my body again, sorry. If you don't believe me, look inside your pants! I've left some clothes out for you – I get a warning now; I've got this dog. See you. Or rather, I won't. Be you, I should say."

Sarah replaced the cell on its charging cradle, but not before curiosity had got the better of her and she had checked his recent messages and calls. Two things leapt out at Sarah, who had known Zak since he was a child. Zak's mom had not contacted him for weeks. And there were quite a few recent calls and messages from Carmen. *Good job, Zak!*

Sarah was thrilled on hearing Zak's message. It was exciting that Zak was communicating with her rather than just invading her body unannounced as usual. She could see possibilities here. Now that they both had some control over when to become each other – Sarah had realised that anger worked best – they might be able to talk and even plan things together. Suddenly the future looked brighter. A way appeared before her of turning to her advantage something which had always been a burden. Plus, the Labrador was cute. It was watching her now from its basket and licked its lips as she held out her hand to stroke it. She wished she knew its name.

It was also great just to hear Zak's voice – they'd never spoken *to* each other before, only *through* each other's bodies. And he clearly had a sense of humour which was good news.

Birmingham, England, 2026

Over the following weeks, they perfected the art of controlling their anger by thinking of particularly annoying episodes or people. This meant that they could flit in and out of each other's bodies to leave notes to read. They also agreed times for longer swap overs, so that they were more prepared. Sarah grew very fond of Psycho, but Zak never really warmed to Boudicca nor she to him. Zak quite liked cats normally, but Boudicca's air of superiority got under his skin. He particularly hated the way she padded around in circles forever with her claws out, before settling on his lap, only to jump off if he made the slightest sound or movement. He even focussed on her sometimes to force a transfer, although he never told Sarah this.

The more planned transfers they had, the more comfortable they felt in each other's bodies. For a laugh, once, Sarah even went into the men's changing room at the gym. One tall blond guy looked particularly cute as he pulled his jeans down over his tight buns. She got a real surprise when Zak's penis twitched into life. So even the slightest thought of sex produced a visible erection! How difficult life must be for guys, especially if they really did think of sex every six seconds, as popular myth held.

As soon as Zak got back into his own body from one of these planned swaps, he selected his Miranda Harper playlist which included her new recording of the Sibelius *Violin Concerto* which he particularly wanted to hear. He made coffee and brought up the latest proof he had been correcting. The deadline was fast approaching. Unsurprisingly, his employer made no allowances for unscheduled three-week stays in twenty-second-century New Palm Springs. He'd got through so far without telling them about his 'schizophrenia' and wanted to keep it that way. But it did mean that he had submitted a few assignments late. When this happened, they complained bitterly, but they always kept him on because his work was good.

Zak was a natural proof reader. He was the first to notice typos and always saw mistakes others missed. When he was 16, instead of a job interview, they had sent him a sample proof to correct. It had taken him five minutes. Then he had corrected the covering letter. Just for good measure, and with the bravado of youth, he had also corrected a chapter from one of their recently published novels which had, of course, already been proofread several times. Zak had found five mistakes.

Two weeks later he had found himself employed and working on his first proof – a boring, technical article about different types of concrete. He had felt great that he was earning already while David and Lily were still a drain on the family income. His employed status at such a young age had gone unnoticed by his mother, apart from her taking a sizeable cut to help with bills. She had still told him regularly that he would never amount to much, implying that David and Lily were destined for greater things.

It did not take long for Zak to spot the alterations Sarah had made to his text. It was a town planning document containing the expression 'committed city-dweller'. Sarah had replaced this with the word 'fup' and had marked the original term 'old-fashioned'. *How dare she?* Zak glanced anxiously at Psycho. It was all right. She was lying in her basket. He did not want to end up back in Sarah's body again so soon. He kept a lid on his anger and checked what else Sarah had changed. She had made some stylistic alterations. The effect was to make the document punchier and less technical.

When Zak re-read the brief at the beginning, he noticed something he had missed before. As well as the usual proofreading request, the client had also said, "If you have any comments on the style, we'd welcome them. We want this to be a public document, readable and accessible without expert knowledge."

Sarah had helped him – apart from the word 'fup' which must come in at some point between now and Sarah's time. Zak thought hard but could not remember hearing it while in the future. He decided to ask Sarah about it and wrote a note straight away. He also thanked her for helping him and gave her permission to do it again, provided she never sent anything off to the client before he had seen it. Next, he imagined the pain of Boudicca's claw in his thigh so he could get Sarah here to read the note. When she swapped back ten minutes later, by focussing on his lack of food shopping skills (in either century!), he found this note.

"This is great, Zak! We have a job we can do without fear of being fired for sudden disappearances. I'm not sure how long I can last in the prison service. You're right about 'fup' by the way. I remember when it became popular now. It was after a big Government report on changing city services came out. It referred to 'fully urbanised professionals' and their need for more gyro lanes higher in the sky. It soon got shortened to fuppies and then fups. I think I might be one."

Birmingham, England, 2026.
Two Months Later

Sarah had planned a swap without consulting Zak, to deal with some unfinished business.

Nice of him to leave the clothes but she wouldn't be needing them this time, she decided. This time she wanted to appear to be Zak until the last minute. Sarah's plan was simple – get close to Sean and stab him. Not with a knife as he had done to this, Zak's, body, at the same time giving her own body the 'birthmark' she hated. She would have savoured such revenge, but no, she would stab him with the syringe in her hand which she had brought back with her, inadvertently, from 2140.

Sarah would never have dreamed that the connection she had across time with Zak was anything other than a link between consciousnesses, hardly a physical thing at all. And yet here, in her hand, was the phial she had been clutching just when her anger had risen to a high enough pitch to bring her back to Zak's body in 2026!

And what an opportunity it now gave her. Sarah thought of herself as a strong person, but she had found it difficult dealing with being raped by Sean (and it wasn't even her own body which had been violated). She had begun to fantasise about getting revenge by somehow humiliating him. And it was in one of these fantasies that she had picked up the syringe containing a drug she occasionally had to use on sex offenders she came across in her work as a prison service doctor. And now here she was, still clutching it.

She checked Zak's pockets. Good, he had money. Then she fiddled around with his phone for what seemed like ages before she found the app for local taxi services. If she was going to do it, she could not hang about, or she might swap back with Zak. She ordered a taxi in Zak's name, walked out to the street for some fresh air and to try and calm down. The most difficult thing would be to stay cool enough to attack Sean without getting angry. That could force a transfer at an awkward moment.

The taxi driver was reluctant to go to Campsfield but changed his mind when she gave him another of Zak's £50 notes. Now she needed some luck. She needed Sean to be in the Cross Keys, and she needed to get close to him, unnoticed.

He wasn't there. Nor could she see any of his cronies. The pub smelled of warm British beer and dust from the ancient carpet. She ordered a pint of cider and waited. Alcohol relaxed you but also dulled your reflexes, so it was a risk. She chose a seat to the left of the front door. She kept Zak's back to the window. Here she felt concealed enough and close enough to the door to be able to attack Sean from behind as he came in. All it needed was one swift jab. It would work, as long as he came in through the front door.

He came in through the back door directly opposite from where she was sitting. She was almost the only person in the pub, so he looked straight at her. Sarah was too slow to remove the 'Oh, shit' look from Zak's face before Sean saw it. He smiled.

"You have some nerve coming here again after last time. Come back for more, have you? It is Sarah, isn't it, not Zak?"

She made an instant decision to be herself – if he liked raping her, maybe he wouldn't kill her.

"Yes," she said. "And I've brought you something." Thinking quickly, she held out the hand with the syringe in it. Sean took it and was clearly curious.

"I know you like recreational narcotics, Sean. This one is special. No one else in the world has this. At least, not yet. It's from the year 2140, where I come from. I work with narcotics. The problem is distribution. I could get rich back in my own time, except security is too tight." She pointed to the syringe. "You just can't get them out of the building. We'd have to bring clients into the lab itself – it's too risky."

Much as she hated doing it, Sarah leaned in closer to Sean to develop the air of conspiracy between them. "Now I've found a way to get them out of the lab – *by becoming Zak* – and I want you to handle the distribution. You've got the contacts and the, er, management skills and, of course, you'd get a percentage."

"A f***ing big percentage. Why me?"

"I don't know anyone else here, in this time. Don't get me wrong, I still hate you for what you did to me. But this is a business proposition, pure and simple."

"What does it do, this narcotic? What thrills am I selling?"

"Try it."

"You want me to shoot up, right now?"

"You gotta know it works, right? You might not believe I really brought it from the future. You might think I'm still Zak being a f***ing schizo."

Sean thought for a moment then suddenly looked up, away from Sarah.

"Hey, Skunk, get over here! I know you're listening."

From the dark recess behind the bar, a man stood up. He was fortyish, with a ponytail. In all the time she had been sitting there, Sarah hadn't noticed him. This was not a good development. She felt out of her depth. She had to stop Sean giving the amphycetylene to Skunk. She forced herself even closer to Sean and touched his arm.

"Are you sure that's a good idea?" she whispered. "This is for leaders, Sean, not followers. It makes you feel confident. Doubles your energy. And…it has a real effect on women. I brought this for *you*, Sean, not for some foot-soldier!"

"Hey, I'm no foot-soldier!"

Skunk had got closer to them than Sarah had realised. "*I'll* try it," he said and tried to snatch the syringe from Sean's open palm. Sean was too quick for him. Something he was already on had sharpened his reflexes. In what seemed like one motion, he closed his fingers over the syringe and plunged it into his own forearm.

"You work for me, Skunk, don't forget that. I decide who tries what merchandise and when, got that?"

"Yeah, Sean, sorry."

****

Relieved that she had succeeded in getting Sean to take the drug, Sarah smiled.

"What are you smiling at?" demanded Sean and, almost immediately, started gasping for breath. He threw an accusing look at Sarah, who stared straight back.

"I think he's poisoned you, Sean," said Skunk, unable to keep out of his voice the relief he felt that he had not taken the drug himself.

"Don't worry," said Sarah. "Breathlessness is only a temporary symptom which will wear off in a few minutes." Sean looked a little relieved until she added, "Unlike the other effects."

"What…other…effects?" he gasped, suspecting from Sarah's expression, that these might not be the ones she had described.

"I didn't lie to you, Sean. Amphycetylene does have a real effect on women. It stops them getting raped by shits like you. You've raped your last victim. You will never again experience an erection. Viagra won't help you. This impotence is irreversible. Oh, I tell a lie. Doxyprosanol will correct it. Good luck getting hold of that. It's not developed until 2095. You'll be in your nineties by then. You've had this coming to you ever since you forced your smelly cock into my mouth. Goodbye and good riddance."

Sarah turned to leave but her little speech had brought back to her mind in graphic detail all the horror of the attack that night and she could not stop herself getting angry. She came to her senses with such a start that her cat, Boudicca, leapt off her lap and ran across the room. She looked around to confirm that she was safely back in 2140 and laughed.

****

Zak blinked. The room he found himself in was very dark, probably a pub. It smelled like a pub. As his eyes adjusted to the lower level of light, he recognised it as the Cross Keys in Campsfield. He turned to see the gasping form of Sean Miller, his least favourite person on the planet, being tended to by one of his gang, the one with the ponytail whose name he always forgot. The look of malevolence on Sean's face was worse than he had ever known it. He was trying to say something.

"Bitch!" shouted Sean eventually. "I'm not finished with you."

He reached down and grabbed something – was it a syringe? – and threw it at Zak, all in one graceful movement. The first time Zak had experienced Sean's quick hands, he had ended up scarred for life with a punctured lung. This time he ducked just in time and started running. What had Sarah got him into? She would have a lot of explaining to do. He really did not want Sean Miller as an enemy, but now did not seem like the right time to negotiate. The Ponytail was looking around for something, a gun maybe. He needed to get the hell out of there as fast as he could.

The first thing he did when he got home was bolt all the doors and windows. Then he wrote an angry note for Sarah.

"What the hell are you doing? You could have got me killed! For God's sake – no, for *my* sake – stay away from Sean Miller when you're in my body!"

Even as he was dotting the exclamation mark, Zak felt himself transferring again. *That's what you get for writing an angry note,* he thought, noticing Sarah's legs and the bloody cat looking daggers at him (how he hated that long-haired, flat-faced, pedigree monster). At least, she would read it straight away.

Sarah did read it. And felt compelled to write one of her own.

"Sorry, Zak, I'm glad you're OK. I didn't mean to get so angry while I was there, but I did need to teach the Shit a lesson for raping me. For raping you, really, it was your mouth he forced himself into while we were transferred. Oh, you're shocked, are you? Probably vomiting this very minute, now you recognise the bad taste you had in your mouth that day? Excuse me for not showing much sympathy but I'd say it was *you* who first put *me* in a dangerous situation. Everything bad that's happened since is because you left me in Campsfield at Sean's mercy! Anyway, you should be thanking me. Sean's never going to bother you again."

That'll show him! thought Sarah, and immediately felt herself stroking Boudicca. "This is getting ridiculous," she said to the cat. "I don't think we've ever had so many transfers in one day before. I hope he doesn't get angry again reading my note."

Zak read Sarah's reply as soon as he re-joined his own body. He managed to keep a lid on his emotions this time but not on his stomach contents – she got that bit right.

Zak was annoyed with Sarah for most of the rest of that day, but not enough to force another transfer. Then, as he was getting ready for bed, it dawned on him that they had had a conversation. OK, it had been an argument, but it was still a conversation. He and Sarah were getting better at communicating across 117 years, without technology! Amazing!

****

So some good came of Sarah's horrifying experience in Campsfield – more planned swaps between her and Zak. Although Zak did have to move to a secret address to get away from Sean Miller, Sarah was wrong about him not bothering Zak anymore. He was desperate to get a cure for his impotence, and Zak was the only person who could get it for him. Zak found this out the very next morning.

****

Birmingham, England, September 2026. The Day After Sean Injected Himself with Amphycetylene

The buzzer to Zak's flat door went. As he unbolted the door and opened it, Zak was thinking about telling Carmen that she could interview Sarah more easily now that he and Sarah had perfected the art of planned swaps. He saw Skunk but had no time to react, his mind elsewhere. The single punch broke his nose and floored him.

"I wanted to kill you," said Skunk. "Unfortunately, Sean needs you alive to get the antidote from Sarah for whatever you gave him yesterday. You got three days. Bring it to him at the Cross Keys at 2 on Thursday. If you don't show, Sean will get angry. That's not pretty."

With that, he was gone. It was only then that Psycho decided to bark.

"Is that the best you can do?" complained Zak, holding his nose, "It's too late now."

Psycho eyed him with an expression which Zak interpreted as: 'Service Dog, not Guard Dog. Intruders not on my job description.'

All Zak could think of was how stupid he had been to answer the door. He had bolted the doors and locked the windows for a reason! He looked in the mirror and saw that blood from his nose had spattered all over his T-shirt. He pulled it over his head and used it to soak up the rest of the blood still coming from his nose. Strangely, his nose was not painful until he touched it. Then it was very painful. And what was that sideways movement? That shouldn't happen. He needed to go to hospital and get an x-ray. And that would eat into his three days.

Christ, only three days, what was he going to do? Sure, he could probably get the antidote from Sarah, but wouldn't Sean then kill him anyway? He liked his chances better if Sean Miller still needed him. What he had to do was to move. And quickly. To somewhere Sean and Skunk could never find him. Carmen, maybe? He was almost certain Sean knew nothing about Carmen. Yeah, that was a good plan. Should he go to the police too? No, things would only get complicated when they found out that 'he' was in Campsfield yesterday. Funnily enough, he didn't think that saying he was in someone else's body in the year 2140 would be an acceptable alibi to the police. They might even commit him again as it would sound like a schizophrenic episode.

Zak fed Psycho, packed a few things and set off for Carmen's. He would tell her the truth. On the way, some blood dripped through the tissue paper he'd stuffed up his nose on to his lap, at just about the same time as he passed a sign to the hospital. Should he head there first? He was sure his nose would need resetting. Above all, he needed sympathy and someone to take over. The hospital experience would be easier to bear if Carmen were with him. He went to Carmen's first.

A shirtless Karl opened the door. This was becoming a habit. A bad one.

"Look at you, man," said Karl. "Your nose is all sideways. We've got to get you to a hospital. What happened?" He was already ushering Zak away from the house towards his car. It occurred to Zak that Karl was one of the few people he could tell everything to – Karl knew about him connecting with his reincarnated self. But just now he didn't want to tell Karl anything about anything.

"I'll be fine. Carmen in there?" asked Zak and realised that talking also hurt his nose.

"No, she's at the lab. I'm just texting her now to get her to meet us at the hospital."

"So, what, you have your own key now?" Carmen had not yet given Zak a key to her apartment.

"She lent me her key, so I could drop off this heavy houseplant she's just bought. Sweaty work," he added, pointing to his shirtless upper body. "You're lucky I was there."

Zak did not feel lucky. Karl was awkwardly silent for the rest of the journey to the hospital. Zak didn't mind. He just wanted to put his head back, close his eyes and sleep. But when he tried this, he felt sick, so he opened his eyes a little and watched the road. Karl was driving slowly, probably thinking vibration would give Zak more pain. At one point, Zak thought he saw Carmen's car overtake them on the dual carriageway, but he must have got that wrong, Karl had just told him that she was at the lab which was on the other side of the city from the hospital.

When they arrived, Carmen was already at the hospital. She was every bit as attentive and caring as Zak had hoped she would be. While they were waiting in

A&E, she packed Karl off to the cafe and got him to tell her exactly what had happened.

When he had finished, Zak paused. He was hoping Carmen would realise independently that he needed to move and would offer to take him in. She didn't. Surely this was proof that she and Karl were living together? What was he going to do? He needed to get out of his house; his life might even depend on this. And Karl, now wearing a shirt, was already coming back with three coffees. Carmen had been caressing the back of Zak's neck out of sympathy for his ordeal and injury. Seeing Karl approaching, she removed her hand and leaned back in her seat. More proof.

"I've decided to move into a hotel," said Zak suddenly. "I don't feel safe at home anymore."

"Of course, you don't," said Carmen, realising this for the first time. She looked searchingly at Karl. "I suppose you could stay at mine, Zak, I mean temporarily, until this 'Sean' thing blows over. Or, or better still, he could stay at yours, Karl. Then he wouldn't have the hotel bills. Sean Miller would never trace him there. And if he did, well, you're pretty big and strong."

"Karl is not the only man with muscles, you know!"

Karl and Carmen stared open-mouthed at Zak, their expressions saying, 'Where did that come from?'

"OK, sorry," said Zak. "What I mean is Sean's guy, Skunk, is even bigger and stronger than Karl here. He could hurt you, Karl. I don't want you taking that risk for me."

Karl made a point of handing Carmen her coffee and starting to drink his before placing Zak's in a position where he would have to reach for it, which would probably hurt his nose.

"And I don't want Carmen taking risks for you." It was the most serious Zak had ever heard Karl sound.

"Whoa, wait a minute, guys – the testosterone levels here are rising, less of the chivalry, please. I can look after myself. And seriously, Karl, I think Zak has a point. We know this guy Skunk is violent, I think he would see you as a challenge. I think I will be safer around Zak than you would be. Change of plan. Zak, you're coming home with me."

Karl did not get a chance to argue because Zak was called in to see a doctor at that moment and Carmen went with him.

It was messy. The bridge of his nose was fractured. They could see the splinters of bone on the x-ray. The doctors reset it as straight as they could, but Zak was warned to expect problems with his sinuses in future. Carmen managed to stay with Zak the whole time by saying she was his girlfriend. Zak was in hospital having painful treatment for a fractured nose, and he was enjoying himself.

They told him to come back in three weeks and prescribed painkillers. What now? Karl left in a hurry and, it seemed to Zak, a sulk. Zak and Carmen decided the best time to move him into her flat was straight away, before Sean started watching it. She was OK about the dog. Apparently, she had not been allowed to keep pets at the estate of flats she'd grown up in and had always wanted one.

In case Sean's gang was already watching Zak's house, they took Zak's car to Carmen's flat first, then, without going in, drove to Zak's flat in Carmen's car. "Don't bring too much stuff," said Carmen. "If they are watching, we don't want them to suspect you're moving out."

"Not yet anyway. I don't mind Sean thinking I've moved in a couple of days. It might make him give up looking."

"If someone castrated you, would you stop looking? I'll say this for Sarah, she knows how to live for the moment. She doesn't worry about the consequences; she just does what she feels like doing, what she thinks is right. I sort of admire her for that."

"Really? Personally, I wish she'd done a bit more thinking and planning before pulling off a stunt like this. I like my flat."

"You'll like my place, too, I promise."

They spent the next hour collecting Psycho and some essentials and driving to Carmen's flat. Everything was the same as Zak remembered it. Except that there were two half-empty coffee mugs in the kitchen, the bed was a mess, and Zak could not see any new, heavy houseplants anywhere.

****

Birmingham, England, Late September 2026

Should he talk to Carmen about Karl? If he didn't, how would she know how important their relationship was to him? He would talk to her, he decided, just not right now. He was too annoyed with her. It would come out wrong. What really got to him was that he'd been spending so much time with Carmen recently, both at her workplace, as a research case study, and at home, as her lover, that she should not have needed another man in her life. Was her relationship with Karl as important to her as what she had with him? Why did she need Karl, even as a casual boyfriend? Was he, Zak, somehow inadequate?

Psycho barked six times then stopped.

"This is not a good time, Sarah," said Zak under his breath, before realising that it was he who had forced the transfer, annoyed as he was with Carmen. Surely enough, Psycho barked six times more and stopped. Zak just had time to shout, "See you later, Carmen!" before finding himself naked in a surprisingly comfortable bubble bath in the USA in 2140.

Sarah came to her senses in a house she did not recognise, in front of a mirror. "This wasn't planned," she protested and added, "Oh, my God," as she saw Zak's nose and at the same time felt the pain. She had no idea where she was until Carmen came hurrying in asking if she were all right and fiddling with her mobile. She was turning the recording app on, but Sarah did not notice this.

"*I'm* all right. What have you done with Zak?" She pointed at his face in the mirror.

"What have *I* done? It was your stunt yesterday with the syringe that got Zak injured! Sean Miller has given him three days to find the antidote. I've had to move him in here with me for his own safety."

"That must have been soooo difficult for you."

"Actually, it was. There's Karl to consider."

"Karl?"

"It's complicated. What were you thinking yesterday? Don't you know if Zak gets killed, it might be fatal for you too?"

"I wasn't thinking. An opportunity came, and I took it. I don't understand; there's no way Sean should be up to attacking Zak after the amphycetylene I gave him yesterday. It's not physically possible."

"He sent Skunk to do his dirty work."

"Shit. Skunk is a problem. I should have drugged him too."

"No, I don't think so! Try, 'I should have stayed away from both of them!'"

"You wouldn't be saying that if Zak had told you what Sean did to me, to him, to both of us, while his friends watched."

Carmen was about to speak but stopped because Sarah was right; Zak had not told her yet what had happened that time, just that Sarah had had a bad experience.

"Don't worry," said Sarah. "From what I've seen, Skunk will do what Sean wants, and I can guarantee you that before three days are up, what Sean wants will change."

"How do you know that?"

"Because I sometimes work with sex offenders. I know what amphycetylene does to them. It's worth years of therapy, believe me. Sean Miller's priorities and values are about to change. He won't be interested in harming anyone anymore – except, possibly, himself. The guilt people feel with amphycetylene can be excessive; the manufacturers need to work on that. Only problem is it takes 48 hours for all the effects to be felt. I should have thought of that."

Carmen was suddenly fascinated. As a research scientist, she had loads of questions. How could a drug affect emotions like guilt? Were there side effects? Would the effects wear off? Had the drugs company had difficulty in getting it licensed? She could not imagine such a drug being cleared in her own time. All she could say was:

"Don't you think this is going a little too far? I mean, it seems a little manipulative."

Sarah did not need to think about her answer.

"Manipulative? Do you want Sean Miller to keep shoving his smelly dick into women's mouths at knife point? That's what I call manipulative."

Carmen's jaw dropped open. Then she took Zak's familiar arm and led Sarah to a chair. "I'm sorry, Sarah, I didn't know." Coffee was produced and for the next half hour Sarah told Carmen what had happened to her in Zak's body in Campsfield a few weeks earlier.

Birmingham, England, Late September 2026

Carmen and Sarah were now getting on so well that Sarah showed no signs of swapping back with Zak. They wondered what she should do. Should she transfer back with Zak, or should they just stay in each other's bodies for a few days? It was Carmen who decided it when she pointed out that it might be safer for Zak to be in Sarah's body in 2140 in three days' time if Sean or Skunk came looking for him. It might also be a chance for her to interview Sarah, as a reincarnater, for her research.

Sarah did not need to think about this for long. She felt she owed Carmen for looking after Zak after she had put him in danger. Plus, she had known this was coming and had even committed some impressive facts from the future to memory – Zak had already asked her if she'd be prepared to help Carmen's research. She agreed, on condition that Carmen did not go public yet. She did not want to make Zak's life any more difficult than she'd already made it.

For his part, Zak decided to stay in Sarah's body as he felt safer there. He was also annoyed that she had got his nose broken and thought it was only fair that she should suffer the pain. Carmen led Sarah into her laboratory for the first time the next morning, past a sullen-looking Karl, who brightened up when he found out that it was Sarah, not Zak, in Zak's body and that she planned to stay for a whole week.

Carmen soon saw that Sarah was surprisingly comfortable doing pieces to camera. She found out that in her own lab work, Sarah often did reports, and even interviews, to camera. After four hours, including one long coffee break when Karl joined them, Carmen had pretty much all she needed. At one point, she described Sarah as a 'conjoined time twin' which she was particularly pleased with as it was off-the-cuff. It was a phrase that would return to haunt her in the coming days.

The interview covered, matter-of-factly, Sarah's early life; when she had first swapped bodies with Zak; what life was like in the 2130s; how she found being in the early twenty-first century; and crucially, how she could prove that she was

Sarah Templeman from New Palm Springs, USA in the twenty-second century and not some hoaxer from Birmingham, England in 2026, hoping to get rich. Sarah gave no details here, just saying that she would predict events which would come true later in 2026.

After a brief introduction, Carmen recorded the 'proof' promise first to grab people's attention, although personally, she was more fascinated by the details of everyday life which emerged when Sarah was describing her childhood experiences of swapping bodies with Zak: the fact that everyone was afraid of the ground and saw it as dangerous, while buzzing about between tower blocks in small personal drones was considered safe; the advertising holograms everywhere; the family trips to space satellites to gaze into the outer reaches of the Cosmos; and the giant red daffodils, visible from the air.

For the proof part of her thesis, Carmen persuaded Sarah to do a second interview to divulge facts about events just a few weeks into the future. This was a time she did not remember, long before her own, and Zak had needed to explain why they wanted it before Sarah had agreed to do the necessary memorising. This interview would be circulated to a select few academics who Carmen had met at conferences or collaborated with on research projects. It would have a far greater impact than, say, twenty-second-century inventions, because it could be proven so quickly. Universities would take Carmen's research seriously and she would get guaranteed funding. She could then dedicate her life's research to the science underpinning reincarnating behaviour and help people like Sarah and Zak to live a more normal life. All very good on paper, but not the way things turned out.

Carmen was in her kitchen the next morning making coffee when a face appeared outside. He looked pleased with himself as he took a picture of her in her PJs and slippers through the window. Other photographers bobbed up like meerkats to do the same. In shock, Carmen let down the blind to cover the kitchen window. She was just breathing a sigh of relief when the phone rang, there was banging at the door and her mobile went off, all at the same time. What was happening? She ran to Sarah's room to see if she was OK and met Sarah in the lounge coming the other way to check on her.

"What's going on?" asked Sarah, also in PJs, Carmen's baggiest pair which were still a bit tight on Zak's body. "Is it to do with the interview we did yesterday?"

"Can't be," Carmen replied. "Only the project staff have access to that part of the cloud."

"And you trust them?"

"Absolutely." Carmen looked thoughtful. "We do update our blog from that cloud, but I'm sure the link was disabled yesterday." She found her mobile, which was still ringing, and called Karl's number. The ringing stopped. Karl picked up.

"Carmen, why aren't you answering your phone? I've been trying to contact you. There's a problem."

Carmen pulled aside part of the blind, provoking renewed frenzy among the meerkat photographers and more banging on the window.

"Could it be a media-related problem, Karl?"

"'Fraid so. How do you know?"

"They're camped outside my house now. What did you do?"

"Oh, shit. Sorry, Carmen. Believe me, it was a mistake. I meant to update the Project blog with just my bit, but somehow, I uploaded the whole cloud."

"Karl, you klutz! Thanks to you, Sarah and I are now stuck in my flat!"

"I'll come and get you."

"Damn right, you will! Call this number when you get here; don't knock on the door. And come around the back, by the bins."

After she put the phone down, Carmen kicked the waste bin across the room. Owen Farrell would have been proud of it. It smashed a glass ornament she had cherished for years.

"Bloody Karl. So stupid. He's never made that mistake before, and he chooses now to do it?"

"Yeah, it's a bummer. What can we do? Should I speak to them?" Sarah pointed to the window.

Carmen sat down at the old oak table which dominated her kitchen and cradled her chin in both hands for some time before replying.

"Let's think this through. It's way too early to go public with my research. I've only got one proper case study, you. On the other hand, we do seem to have their attention, so perhaps we should try and make the most of it. We were going to do the predictions later, I know, but how much can you remember of the facts from late 2026, which Zak asked you to memorise?"

"All of them, I think."

"Good. Let's hit them with that. It will buy us some time. But not like this." It was Carmen's turn to gesture to the window. "I'll call a press conference in two hours' time at the University. We'll put a sign up at the window and let them read it."

"Great idea, have you got marker pens?" said Sarah, and started working on the sign straight away. Carmen was still thinking.

"We'll also need to know what angle TV and the papers are using. I'll call Karl and get him to bring some of today's newspapers."

As Carmen was doing this, Sarah finished the sign, which read: "Press Conference at Carmen Fry's Laboratory in two hours' time. No Comment until then." She stuck it in the window, provoking angry shouts from the press men and women outside. Then she switched on the TV and clicked on the News channel. The main story was about the Pope resigning but the red banner underneath had:

BREAKING NEWS: – Midlands academic interviews 'time traveller' – Dr Carmen Fry blogged last night that she had brought someone back from the future into a friend's body.

"At least three mistakes there then," said Carmen, looking over Zak's shoulder. "Not bad for one sentence."

They had to wait ten minutes for the story to come up. TV clearly did not have access yet to this morning's kitchen window photos, for which Carmen was grateful. Instead, they had a standard talking head webcam shot of yesterday's interview, quite poor quality, backed up with some better moving images of Carmen delivering papers at conferences. The tone was worrying. 'Dr' Fry's claims were described by fellow academics from rival universities as 'rash', 'unsubstantiated' and even 'scurrilous'. She was in deep shit.

Carmen's mobile rang. The ring tone was one Zak had found for her, the march to the scaffold from Berlioz's *Symphonie Fantastique*, he had told her, which she thought appropriate at that moment. It was Karl. She let him in the back door, and he plopped a pile of papers down on the table. Without exchanging pleasantries with Karl, who was responsible for their current dilemma, Sarah and Carmen dived straight in.

They were the headline story in nearly every paper. *The Mirror* had, 'Back from the Future', as its headline and a photo of Zak and Carmen in close conference from the webcam. *The Times* had, 'Conjoined Time Twins'. In the absence of a photo of the real Sarah, they had creatively used a female silhouette head-and-shoulder shot next to a head-and-shoulder shot of Zak from his Facebook page. *The Mail* had, 'Why Fry Lies', over an article claiming Carmen's funding had been withdrawn so she had set up an elaborate hoax to get money from the tabloids. This would not go down well with the Dean of the Faculty, nor with the Vice-Chancellor for that matter. Only one paper, Carmen noticed, had even featured the reincarnation angle. *The Observer* headline was 'Soul Survivors. One Soul, Two Bodies'.

"It gets worse, Carmen, I'm afraid," said Karl. "Professor Williamson wants to see you in his office first thing Monday morning."

Carmen was expecting this reaction from the head of her department, her employer. "Did you at least tell him that it was your fault?" she asked.

"I guess I must have left that bit out," said Karl, looking uncomfortable.

Her job was on the line now. What could Carmen do? She texted Professor Williamson with an apology and urged him to watch the press conference. "I will explain everything on Monday," she promised.

****

Carmen and Sarah were standing outside the Great Hall, about to go into the hastily arranged press conference. They had asked Karl to join them for moral support, but he had refused point blank, saying the media wouldn't know who he was. This had annoyed Carmen as it had been Karl's mistake which had dropped them in this shit in the first place. They rehearsed their answers one last time. They had agreed that they should not admit that the leak was a mistake, as no one would believe them anyway. They would pretend that they had planned it like this. Carmen turned to a technician and asked if the projector was switched on. He nodded and put his thumb up. Zak's face was wearing a nervous expression Carmen had never seen on it before, when Sarah's voice asked:

"Have you got the envelopes I prepared?"

Carmen held up her hand with the envelopes in. Each was addressed to a different newspaper editor or TV News Desk. They looked at each other and went in.

It was not an academic audience, so Carmen decided to get straight to the point (where normally she would have held back her most impressive research finding until the end of a paper).

"I am Ms Carmen Fry," she stated simply, as cameras flashed. "Thank you all for promoting me, but I am not a doctor."

There were a few laughs. *Very clever,* thought Sarah, *she is using humour to break the tension and get them on our side.*

After a pause, Carmen continued, "At least, not yet. My doctoral research is what has caused all this fuss." She smiled and there were more laughs.

"The more thorough researchers among you may have recognised the person standing next to me as Zak Emblin, with whom I started going out earlier this year—"

That caused a ripple of texting and tweeting.

"And you'd be right. But you would also be wrong. I am going to play you now a recording of Zak's voice. Please ignore what is being said. That shouldn't be too difficult for some of you." She fixed her gaze on the tabloid editors and there were some forced smiles and nervous laughs. "Instead focus on the voice itself." Puzzled frowns greeted this.

A video recording shot on Carmen's mobile appeared on the screen behind her. Zak's voice rang around the hall. He could be heard saying: "Is that my coffee?" and adding playfully, "You didn't put sugar in it, did you, like last time?" The clip ended.

"I will now hand you over to my friend, Sarah Templeman, from New Palm Springs, USA, in the year 2140."

She pointed to Zak's face. She and Sarah had decided that for maximum impact Sarah should introduce herself immediately after the press had heard a different voice coming from that same mouth. Sarah started speaking. There were gasps from some journalists. Although not especially high, her voice was a lot higher than Zak's rich baritone and had some sort of American accent which no one could quite place.

"I am Sarah Templeman. This is what I look like most of the time." A photograph of the brown-haired, brown-eyed, short and ever-so-slightly-squat figure of Sarah flashed up on the screen. It had been taken from her work ID lanyard, which she had had in her hand during a previous transfer and left behind. Carmen had kept it in case it came in useful. What a good decision that had been. She was wearing what looked like a Tudor England flat cap with a feather in it.

"The voice you have just heard, Zak's voice, which belongs to this body" – Sarah pointed at herself – "is now coming out of this body" – she pointed to the screen – "in the year 2140. In other words, we have swapped bodies." She paused for effect. "Don't ask me how this has happened. I'll hand you back to Carmen for the science bit."

They did not want to be handed back to Carmen for the science bit. A volley of questions shot out at Sarah. Among them, she heard:

"How do we know you're not Zak putting on a funny voice?"

"What happened to your nose?"

"Prove you are Sarah Templeman!"

"How do we know you are from the future?"

She homed in on that one.

"I can prove I am from the future. In fact, this is easier for me to do than to prove I am not Zak Emblin doing a funny voice. For that, I would need to produce Zak. I can't do that. I've never seen him face to face because I share his body. As I said, Zak Emblin is in my body right now in 2140, but I can't prove that."

"How convenient!" shouted someone.

Sarah ignored it and carried on speaking.

"Carmen, the envelopes, please."

Carmen distributed the envelopes to the newspaper editors and TV news desks they were addressed to. She spoke as she did this:

"Each one of these sealed envelopes contains three predictions. Some are football results. Some are celebrity news items. Divorces, marriages, maybe names of new-born celebrity children. What they all have in common is that they occur later this year. Check that they are sealed, then lock them away in a safe somewhere."

"How will we know when to open them?" asked the BBC *Midlands Today* reporter.

"On the back of each envelope is a single date, different for each of you. On this date, you should open the envelope. You will find that the predictions Sarah has made will come true on that day."

"And if they don't?"

"They will."

Barrymore Pegg stood up and introduced himself. He had a reputation for establishing the truth in a series of hard-hitting TV documentaries. Politicians and business moguls alike feared him. He spoke confidently, even arrogantly:

"I'll tell you what will happen if they don't come true. This man here" – he emphasised the word 'man'– "will be exposed for the charlatan that he is. In fact, he'll be exposed as a charlatan *in any event* because there is nothing new to this magic trick. Stephen Frayne, better known as Dynamo, did the exact same thing more than ten years ago. He may never have divulged how he did it, but he did admit that it was a magic trick and not clairvoyance!"

He looked at Sarah, expecting her to protest but she seemed distracted. Since he had introduced himself, she had been staring at Barrymore Pegg with what appeared to be an expression of pity on Zak's face. Nobody expected what she said next.

"You like Caribbean food, don't you, Barrymore?"

There was a stunned hush.

"Yes, why?"

"Just stay away from El Nino's."

"That's my favourite restaurant! How did you know that? I've never allowed myself to be photographed there, not even on fans' mobiles."

"Just stay away. It's dangerous for you there."

"Is that a threat?" asked Barrymore, outraged.

"Not at all. I just don't want anything to happen to you."

Clearly not mollified in any way by this reply, Pegg was about to speak again but Carmen stood in front of Sarah and announced loudly to the gathered press that that was it for today, that they would take no more questions until after the first date on the back of someone's envelope arrived.

"What was all that about, with Barrymore Pegg?" asked Carmen as soon as they were alone in the office room behind the Great Hall. Sarah decided to tell Carmen the truth.

"He's going to die."

"What? Zak didn't ask you to predict deaths, Sarah, it's too macabre! It won't help us."

"It's not one of the official predictions. I just noticed it online when I was learning all the other stuff. And by the way, I have included deaths. You need to grab people's attention to keep your funding."

"We'll just have to agree to disagree on that one as the envelopes are already sealed and distributed. But you say Barrymore's death is not one of them?"

"No, it just grabbed my attention as it was such big news. He died, I mean will die, of food poisoning. The restaurant, El Nino's, gets closed. It's a celebrity restaurant, two Michelin stars. Loads of famous people go there. They have no need to cut corners in the kitchen but do anyway. Result – salmonella. Not usually a killer but Barrymore's not in the best of health; you saw how overweight he is. He just isn't strong enough to fight it off."

"Christ, this is bad."

"What do you mean? I might have just saved his life!"

"Believe me, the tabloids won't play it that way. If he dies, they're going to say you killed him. You will be portrayed as some sort of demonic force who killed him because he questioned your integrity just now."

"Are you sure?"

"100%. I've had to deal with these media clowns before."

They were silent for a few seconds.

"You guys really have some issues with press responsibility in the twenty-first century."

"Tell me about it."

"OK," said Sarah and started to explain that press and media risked being put out of business in her world if they published unsubstantiated stories.

Carmen stopped her, smiling. "No, I didn't mean *literally* tell me about it. It's just an expression. It means 'you're right'."

Sarah smiled back. "We don't have that expression anymore," she said. "I guess the language changes quite a bit between your time and mine."

"Anyway, back to matters in hand. How long have we got before Barrymore *pegs* out?" asked Carmen and then started laughing. It was a release of the tension which had been building inside her ever since she had seen the first reporter outside her kitchen window that morning. She expected to have to explain the joke to Sarah, but she was also laughing.

"Now that expression, we do still use."

"Odd that you do, it's a much older expression than 'tell me about it'. It dates from the seventeenth century when cribbage was invented. Pegs are used to keep the score. When you reach the finish, you 'peg out'."

"Yeah, language is funny. But don't you think it's a little disrespectful talking of the soon-to-be-dead in that way?"

"Nothing about Barrymore Pegg earns my respect while he's alive. Why should that change when he dies? Anyway, assuming he doesn't heed your advice, which I'm sure he won't, arrogant so-and-so that he is, how long has he got?"

"One month exactly. And I don't think he's arrogant, just Pegg-headed."

They both laughed again.

"That's really terrible," said Carmen. "Why didn't Zak warn me about your awful puns?"

Sarah didn't take this criticism to heart as Carmen was smiling as she said it.

"You started it," she said.

Birmingham, England, Late September 2026

Sean Miller was drinking alone in the Cross Keys, feeling down. Some feminist cunt from the next century had taken away his libido, and there was nothing he could do about it except threaten Zak, her body in the present. Then he saw her on the news – rather he heard her voice coming from Zak's mouth. She was here now. They even told him where she was: Dr Carmen Fry's laboratory at the University of Birmingham. He could go there and deal with her directly; yes, that would be much better. Renewed hope surged in Sean's chest as he called Skunk and told him they were going to the University right away. Skunk was not happy – he hated intelligent people – but agreed anyway.

Great Hall, University of Birmingham, England, Late September 2026

Sarah asked Carmen if it would be safe to leave yet. Neither of them wanted to run a gauntlet of photographers or get followed by reporters.

"The best thing about this Hall is it's old. It has been changed many times. As a result, it has lots of exits. There is even a surviving underground passageway which comes out in the Students' Union building. I think that's our best bet."

"Is it safe?"

"Completely. I've done loads of visitor tours down there."

"OK, then lead the way!"

****

The grandeur of the Edwardian dome of the Great Hall, an iconic building of the University of Birmingham, was lost on Sean Miller. To him, it was just a place where rich kids went to do a bit of reading and get laid. He surveyed the bunch of photographers crammed in around the main entrance to the Great Hall. No way in there. He sent Skunk to check out the First Floor and Lower Ground exits. There was only a slightly smaller crowd at each of those.

"How am I going to get to her through this lot?" Sean asked Skunk, not expecting an answer, just thinking aloud.

Luckily for Sean, Skunk had been playing Cluedo on his smartphone the night before with his ten-year-old niece in Australia. The Great Hall looked a lot like the building in the game to him. He had only lost because his niece had used a secret passageway to get from the Library to the Hall, something he didn't even know you could do.

"What you need is a secret passageway," said Skunk and laughed.

"You're a moron, do you know that?" Sean was not in the mood for jokes and found Skunk's good humour very irritating at a time like this when his manhood was on the line. Then he remembered the last time he had come to this University.

"Correction," he said, "you're a genius. Skunk, follow me."

Sean turned and headed back in the opposite direction towards the Students' Union building. Skunk followed, struggling to keep up.

"Where are we going?" he asked.

"You know that rich student with the cocaine habit who's one of our clients?"

"You mean Timothy Allsop?"

"That's the one. I met him last month in that building" – Sean pointed to the Students' Union – "where we are going now."

"But surely Zak, I mean Sarah is in the Great Hall not the Students' Union?"

"There's an underground passageway between them! A real one. That's why you're a genius."

"How do you know?"

"Allsop insisted we meet down there to do business. Didn't want to be seen handing over a bundle and receiving a package. Wanted privacy to test the merchandise. Can't think why. I asked where it led. He said the Great Hall. Dates back to World War Two, apparently. They used it to hide artworks in case the Germans invaded, some shit like that. Hardly anyone uses it now or even knows about it."

"That's good, isn't it?"

"It is, Skunk. It means we can surprise them. They won't know how we got in. I'll threaten to expose her as a fraud to the newspaper guys if she doesn't get me the antidote."

They were descending the stairs to the Students' Union basement now.

"Sounds a good plan." And Skunk really was impressed until they came up against an old oak door which Sean kicked, swearing.

"What's the matter?"

"Can't you see, moron? It's f***ing locked. It had been open last time. Allsop must have had a key."

They were standing there, staring at each other, not knowing what to do when they heard a sound coming from the other side of the door. Someone was fiddling with the lock. Suddenly the door opened. And out walked Zak Emblin and that Dr Fry from the television. Sean Miller smiled. *Talk about luck.*

"Going somewhere, ladies?" he asked.

Skunk stepped in front of them. Skunk smiled when he saw the state of Zak's nose and admired his own handiwork.

"I hate to point this out, Sarah – yeah, I know it's you in there – but shouldn't you be working on an antidote for that drug you tricked me into taking, rather than developing a television career? You've only got until tomorrow before that body you're in gets destroyed forever. That's the ultimatum I gave Zak."

Carmen pulled Zak's arm and tried to make a run for it, confident that she could outrun Skunk at least, and that she and Sarah together might be able to take care of Sean Miller (for she had guessed that that was who he was). But Sarah just stood there, icy calm, forcing Carmen into a decision – stay with her new friend or run for safety; after all, it wasn't her they wanted. No contest. She went back to Sarah, who was arguing with Sean – *something of a risky strategy*, thought Carmen, particularly as he was almost certainly armed.

"Go on then, kill me," said Sarah. "You can do it tomorrow or you can do it now, makes no difference. Either way, you will be destroying my only connection with this world and, with it, the only chance you have of ever getting the antidote."

Carmen was incredulous that Sarah would put Zak's body at risk like this so soon after what had happened to him the last time that he had met Sean Miller and Skunk. She prayed that Sarah did not get so worked up that she forced a transfer and left Zak facing Sean again. But there seemed little danger of that happening. Sarah was ridiculously calm and in control of the situation.

Sean clenched his fists. Sarah was not sure whether this was aggression or frustration.

"OK!" he said. "I admit you've got me there. I can't kill you, but I *can* cause you a lot of pain."

"Yeah." Skunk interrupted. "How's your nose?"

"Leave this to me, Skunk."

Sean turned back to face Sarah and passed a hand across Zak's face as you do to check if someone is daydreaming. "Can't you go back now? Just swap back with Zak, get another syringe from your lab and come back! It should only take a few minutes. Then everyone walks away happy. Can't you see? I really need women. I love women."

"You hate women. That's why you rape them. What you love is sex. And power. Anyway, the transfers don't work like that. I need to get angry to transfer, and believe me, you are nowhere near annoying enough. I see you more as pathetic."

"Are you angry now?" Sean screamed in Zak's face. "I want that drug! If you don't get it, I'll expose you to all of those journalists as a fraud!"

"Oh, yeah? And how are you gonna do that?"

Carmen could not believe her eyes. Sarah poked Sean in the chest as she said this. *Talk about provocation!* And she could have sworn she had seen a smile on Zak's face when Sean screamed at her. What was she playing at? Sarah continued calmly spelling out the situation to Sean.

"Are you going to produce a photo of me with you in this time and not my own? Don't think so, this is Zak's body, remember? You have no proof of my existence here and you know it."

"I've got the syringe."

For a moment, Sarah looked troubled, but the moment quickly passed.

"Produce it then. It proves me right. It's an entirely new narcotic which can only have been developed in the future."

"They'll say you and Dr Fry here have been developing it in the here and now, in her lab." Sean pointed at Carmen.

"It's not that kind of lab. It's full of computers not test tubes. And you are forgetting that you are the narcotics dealer here. The police will assume you have been experimenting and got lucky. Besides, they don't know what it does."

"I'll tell them."

"You don't know what it does yourself."

"I do. You told me."

"I didn't give you all the details. I didn't tell you, for instance, that exactly 48 hours after you'd taken it, you would experience a last surge of aggression; that it feels good to get this out of your system; that you might scream at someone, for instance, like you just did, at me. Sometimes it helps then if someone you know provokes you a bit, as I just did by poking you in the chest. This gets every last drop of aggression out and maximises the feeling of well-being which floods over you as the amphycetylene takes full effect. How are you feeling now, Sean?"

Sean Miller was looking around as if unsure where he was.

"I feel fine," he said, smiling now. "Never felt better."

"Of course, you haven't." Sarah smiled back at him.

"What were we talking about?"

"Let me remind you. You were just saying that if I don't get you the antidote to amphycetylene by tomorrow, you will kill both me and Zak. And in the meantime, you promised to cause me a lot of pain. That's right, isn't it, Carmen? Did I miss anything out?"

"No, I don't think so." Carmen was smiling now, along with Sarah and Sean, as she understood what was happening. Only Skunk looked confused.

"How could I say such a thing to someone as nice as you?" said Sean.

"I don't know. Why would you threaten me, Sean?"

"I think you did something bad to me. I remember now, you gave me this drug from the future and—"

"And why did I do that, Sean? Why? Think hard! The transition has confused you."

Pain registered on Sean's face as he recalled what he and his cronies had done to Sarah behind the Cross Keys in Campsfield. "Oh, my God." He put his hands over his face in shame. "Oh, my God," he repeated. "How could I do that? *That's* why—"

"That's why, Sean." Sarah put Zak's hand on Sean's shoulder. He was crying now.

Skunk stared, open-mouthed. He had never seen his 'boss' cry before.

"That's why, Sean Miller. But you don't have to worry about it anymore. It will never happen again. All the badness has gone now, forever."

This didn't seem to reassure Sean, who was now crouching on the floor, hugging himself, as he recalled all the violence, criminal and immoral activity he had been involved in since…since as far back as he could remember.

Carmen watched, fascinated and concerned. "Is he going to stay like that?" she asked Sarah.

"No. The guilt rush is strong with amphycetylene. Plus, he's got a lot to feel remorseful for. This mood will come over him often to start with. It will alternate with euphoria, as you saw just now. Over time, things will settle down and he'll experience fewer extreme emotions."

Sarah turned to Skunk. "As his friend, I think you'd better take him home now; he's not well."

"I can see that." Skunk was in awe of this lady from the future who could occupy Zak's body and reduce his boss to a quivering wreck. Everyone he knew was afraid of Sean Miller. Not Sarah.

"What now?" Carmen asked Sarah.

"We could go back to yours, I suppose, maybe get a takeaway?"

"No. I mean what do we do about Sean Miller?"

"Do? Nothing. That's it. 'Sorted' as I think you say in this time."

"We can't leave it like that, Sarah!"

"Why not?"

"Is there no aftercare in your social welfare system in the twenty-second century?"

"What's 'aftercare'?"

"You know, when you follow up on someone you've treated to make sure the treatment was successful and to see if they're OK."

"I can see the treatment was successful. And I don't care if he's OK or not."

"But you were so gentle with him just now; you even put a hand on his shoulder! If you don't care, what was that?"

Sarah hesitated for just a moment before replying. "I suppose that was 'aftercare'. But that's as far as we take it."

Carmen noticed that Sean had not left yet but was still sitting on the floor with Skunk trying to comfort him.

"Can I speak to him?" she pointed to Sean.

"Sure, if you really want to. I may have changed him a bit but the man's still a scumbag."

Carmen ignored this. "Is he suggestible, in his current state?"

"Very."

Carmen marched over to where Skunk was comforting Sean who looked confused.

"Sean, you might want to think about a career change."

"I might?"

"You're a drugs dealer. It's dangerous for you and your clients."

"I know. All this bad stuff keeps coming back to me from way back. What can I do?"

Carmen looked at Skunk. "What is he good at?" she asked.

"He's not bad at computer games. And phones," Skunk offered after a few seconds.

Carmen thought.

"I suppose you could try buying and selling online. You're good at buying and selling. You know about profit margins. In fact, you know how to run a business. It's just been the wrong one."

Skunk and Sean looked at each other. Each saw that the other was willing to give it a try. The difficult bit would be convincing existing customers and suppliers that they were out of the business forever without getting dead. They would have to start afresh somewhere completely new.

Carmen left them discussing it and went back to join Sarah. As a scientist, she was very curious about what she had just witnessed. She had a few questions. Did amphycetylene permanently change a lifetime of bad habits, a career of crime? Were these things really rooted in chemical imbalances in the brain rather than in environmental influences? In other words, was it really all nature rather than nurture?

Or was the stunt Sarah had just pulled only a veneer, a papering over of the cracks from Sean Miller's inadequate and unhappy childhood? Were those beginnings bound to push him in the criminal direction again at some point in the future? Were there side effects? After all, this type of treatment had been tried before and abandoned. About a decade ago they had used anti-androgens to prevent erections and remove the capacity to ejaculate from repeat sex offenders. But there had been too many problems with osteoporosis and coronary side effects. And some men had become 'menopausal women', exhibiting hot flushes and mood changes and growing breasts. She remembered reading about it.

On a more mundane level, she was also dying to know how Sarah had managed to stay so cool with two violent men facing her. Had she been 100% sure the drug would take effect exactly when she needed it to?

Above all, Carmen needed a drink. Fortunately, Sarah did too. They went off arm-in-arm to the Gun Barrels.

"That took some balls!" said Carmen two drinks later as they both sat on high stools propping up the bar.

"To face a guy with no balls, you mean?" replied Sarah and laughed.

"At least, not anymore, he doesn't!" added Carmen and they laughed again.

Sarah had the feeling that she had just missed the chance to say something funny, then it came back to her through an alcoholic haze. *What did they put in these cocktails in the twenty-first century?*

"Anyway, if it took balls, I got balls, don't I, big, hairy ones?" she pointed at Zak's crotch and nearly fell off the bar stool, laughing.

"They're not hairy; they're shaved," said Carmen, smiling a wicked smile.

"Oh, I forgot, you've seen 'em, haven't you? Do you want another look?" She gave the giggling Carmen a quick flash, and this time did fall to the floor, laughing.

Birmingham, England, October 2026

Zak and Sarah were in each other's bodies. It was not time yet for the first of the envelopes to be opened but Sarah had pointed out to Carmen and Zak that Barrymore Pegg was about to die. This meant that she should be in Zak's body to face the music. It had proved impossible for Sarah to get leave from work again so soon after her last transfer with Zak, so she had called in sick, running the risk that friends might call around to see how she was, friends who didn't yet know of Zak's frequent occupations of her body.

Sarah was watching television at Carmen's when the shit hit the fan. It was the main news item. Renowned journalist and TV personality Barrymore Pegg had lost his fight with salmonella in a Birmingham hospital, where he had been admitted two days earlier following a bad reaction to his green fig with salt fish menu choice at his favourite restaurant, El Nino's. He was only 65.

"The sense of shock we all feel," intoned the newsreader, "is compounded by the fact that this death, exactly this death – by food poisoning from this very restaurant, El Nino's – was predicted last month, live on TV, by someone who claims to come from the future. Mr Pegg's immediate family declined to comment last night but we did speak to his nephew, Calvin Holmes."

The report cut to an angry young man with the build of an English Defence League hooligan and a posh voice who shouted at the camera.

"She did this! That Sarah who is Dr Fry's girlfriend (or boyfriend, or whatever), she did this. She told him she would kill him…on TV, in front of millions. You all saw it. And now she has done! Where is she? I want her brought to justice!"

Until this outburst, Sarah was hoping it might somehow all blow over. Now she knew this was just wishful thinking on her part. OK, she had warned Barrymore Pegg not to eat there, but he was never going to heed advice from her, was he? Like most people's, his mind was closed to the possibility of a reincarnated soul connecting across time with a former self. Now she was going to have to do another press conference, this time for damage limitation.

****

At this hastily arranged press conference, Sarah began by running footage of the previous one, a month earlier. This was supposed to prove to her tormentors from the press that she had *not* threatened Barrymore Pegg in any way, merely warned him. It backfired. Sarah clearly remembered telling Pegg that she was not threatening him, but as the video played, that part was barely audible because the crowd were still responding angrily to Barrymore's, "Is that a threat?" comment.

Things went downhill from there. In the back row, recording on his mobile, sat Inspector Nigel Sandford from the local CID, who was most definitely not a believer in future echoes or reincarnation, subjects he would lump together under the general heading of 'New Age mumbo jumbo'.

He was particularly interested when Sarah was asked, "Why did you tell Barrymore to stay away from El Nino's if you weren't threatening him?" These guys were doing his job for him!

"Because I knew what would happen to him," replied Sarah.

Yeah, she knew all right, thought Sandford, *because she was planning to contaminate the food herself.* And now he had her on tape saying confidently that she knew what would happen before it did. OK, it wasn't a confession, but it was the next best thing; it did hint at pre-meditation. It was time to bring her in.

Birmingham, England, October 2026

They were in a small grey room sitting either side of a cheap grey table. Sarah was on one side. Detective Inspector Nigel Sandford was on the other. His female colleague was observing, but Sandford alone was asking the questions. There was a camera above filming the whole interview.

"Do you have any forensic evidence that puts me at El Nino's on that day?" Sarah yelled at Inspector Sandford, her impatience growing, two hours into the interview.

"No, but you knew that, of course. We *can* put a friend of yours there, though, on the night Pegg died. Did you two plan it together?" Sandford deliberately left out the name, hoping 'Sarah' would fill it in and incriminate herself. She didn't. She spoke calmly now.

"What do you mean? I am pretty sure I don't know anyone who was there that night. The point you haven't grasped, Johnny English, is that I live in the future. My friends are all in 2140 in New Palm Springs, California Peninsula, USA. I know hardly anyone here."

Sandford moved his face uncomfortably close to hers across the table.

"What about Dr Karl Frideriks? Do you know him? He's American, like you say you are. We have his prints at the table next to where Barrymore Pegg was sitting. Did you know that?"

Sarah did not know it. It was a bolt from the blue. It hadn't been her, so it must have been Zak, had been her first thought. But no, it had been that stupid Karl. What was he doing at the only restaurant in Birmingham she had wanted them all to avoid?

****

"Having a meal," explained Karl later to Carmen. "The food's really quite good there, you know, except they obviously have some hygiene issues. She made it sound intriguing in the first press conference. I didn't know we had an upmarket Caribbean restaurant in Birmingham. I went to try it."

"Karl, you idiot. Your being there makes you a suspect. And Sarah. The police think she killed him, for Christ's sake! It will land both of you in prison. Why did you have to go there on the day Barrymore Pegg died?"

"How was I supposed to know he would choose that particular day to die?"

New Palm Springs, California Peninsular, USA, October 2026

Zak was in Sarah's totally transparent bath again, this time by choice. It was more of a jacuzzi really, a step up for him, although Sarah told him that all her friends had one. He was doing her a favour, bathing her body, but if he was honest, he was also curious to see how the jets of warm water would feel around his – well, Sarah's – clitoris. Answer? Amazing. They were so lucky, women. How could you get so many nerve endings into such a small organ? OK, so he wouldn't swap genders by choice. There were too many negatives – breasts flopping everywhere and PMT to name just two – but as he was forced to rent out this body from time to time, he might as well enjoy it. He closed his eyes, lay back and massaged himself to increase the pleasure. And then he heard someone open the front door. Shit.

"It's only me; I've let myself in. Are you there, Sarah? It's Kate. I heard you were ill, so I brought pizza."

"I'm in the bath, be out in a minute," said Zak, turning the tap on to hide his voice and at the same time trying to make it sound higher, yet still natural.

"OK. You sound different. Are you all right?"

"Yeah, it's just a covid. Throat's a bit sore."

"Then what are you doing in the bath? You'll make it worse."

Zak was no longer in the bath. He was rapidly putting Sarah's clothes back on and trying to plan an escape. Why hadn't Sarah warned him about Kate coming around? And that she had a key!

"I thought the steam might help."

"Yes, you do sound bad. I might have some Lemon Parafen sachets in the gyro – had a covid myself last week – do you want me to fetch them in?"

"Oh, could you Kate? That would be great."

"OK, back in five," said Kate, and Zak heard the door slam.

He jumped to his feet and ran to the door, dripping water everywhere from Sarah's hair, opened it as quietly as he could and set off in the opposite direction from Kate, hoping she would not turn around. It was lucky Sarah's gyro was parked in the opposite direction from Kate's. He unplugged the charger, jumped in, set the SatNav to 'Malin's', and the machine slowly took off. He would never get bored with this! *Mental note, I must ask Sarah if I can use her gyro, since I do anyway.* (What else was he supposed to do in a city where most people had stopped walking anywhere decades ago?)

Once in Sarah's favourite café, he ordered an Americano Deluxe and stared at it. He bathed in its warmth as Sarah's wet hair was making him feel cold. He took in the rich promise of its cinnamon aroma, wondering what Kate would do when she came back in and found him gone.

****

Meanwhile, back at the police station, Sarah was beginning to appreciate just how deep the shit was which she was in. The police did not believe her and an alibi from her own time would be no good. That was why she had turned down the offer to have a lawyer present. It would be just one more person to convince that she was not Zak. Maybe Zak could provide an alibi. Sarah had no idea what he had been doing on the night Barrymore Pegg died. He was so hopeless, he never left her the information she really needed in his notes for her.

Sarah was just thinking that maybe this was a little harsh on Zak, when she found herself back in her own time, at Malin's café, two blocks away from where she lived, a large Americano Deluxe in front of her. *Malin's, good choice, Zak,* she thought, although she would have preferred Latte. Something cold and wet dripped down her neck, and she realised that she had wet hair – very wet hair. This was weird. Why would Zak shower, then leave the apartment so soon before drying her hair? He must have had to leave suddenly. Clutching the Americano Deluxe, Sarah followed the trail of drips back to the gyro bay and recognised her own dear vehicle. She fought off rising indignation, not wanting to end up back in that police station. It was better for Zak to sort that business out. She told herself that Zak must have had no choice but to take her gyro. Anyway, how else was he supposed to get about? She didn't want him paying for taxis with her money or walking the dangerous streets at ground level.

As soon as she was indoors, she started a note to Zak. "What happened, Zak? Why was I sitting at Malin's with my hair soaking wet?"

"Who's Zak?"

Kate's voice made her jump. Sarah had not seen her come up behind her and look over her shoulder at what she was writing.

"Sorry, Kate, didn't know you were here."

"Yes, you did! You spoke to me from the bathroom. I went back to my gyro to get you Parafen for your sore throat, and when I got back here you were gone…for a coffee by the looks of it! And I have been waiting 15 minutes. I told you I'd be back right away. What's going on, Sarah? You're acting kinda weird. And your voice is back to normal again."

Sarah sat back on the kitchen chair, which was connected to the table but not to the ground. She put her arms behind her head. Should she tell Kate? If anyone deserved the truth, Kate did. But would she be able to handle it? Sarah went for it.

"OK, Kate, you're a good friend, so I'll tell you, but it's weird shit, believe me. That's why I haven't told you before; I knew you wouldn't believe me. Now you've seen it happen, you just might. What you witnessed today was someone from the past swapping places with my body. While he was here, I was in his body in Birmingham, England, in the year 2026." Sarah paused as she wondered how Zak was doing in the police interview.

"His name's Zak. He doesn't know about you. That's why he was outta here so fast."

"No, shit!"

"Yes, shit. It was Zak, not me, who bought this coffee. We swapped back before he could drink it. It was still sealed so it seemed a shame to waste it."

"So how…why are you guys connected, you and this dude? He is a dude, right?"

Sarah nodded agreement.

"In your body?"

Sarah nodded again.

"You're right, that's really weird."

Not once you got used to it, thought Sarah. Anyway, it was all she had ever known. It was a relief being able to tell Kate everything. She was a loyal friend who had been let down on many occasions because Zak and she had changed places when she was about to call her or go somewhere to meet her. Now she would understand.

She certainly asked enough questions over the next two hours to understand, although Sarah felt she was a little bit too preoccupied with the physical aspects

("What's it like having dangly bits between your legs – did they get in the way? Is it easy to pee standing up?") She liked to think that, in Kate's shoes, she would have been more interested in the fact that she could watch past events unfolding as they happened. Maybe not.

****

He looked around and took in the police cell walls. This was clearly not a good situation Sarah had put him in, but he was not annoyed. It happened. It was difficult explaining yourself when you were in someone else's body. He knew. He sympathised. A mutual respect had grown between him and Sarah since they had been communicating by notes and pre-arranging body swaps. It had never been stated openly, but they both got a buzz from not knowing where they were going to end up next. They quite welcomed these little adventures, secure in the knowledge that whatever happened, whatever scrapes they got into, they would be temporary ones, provided they didn't get killed, of course. An out-of-shape policeman in his forties, sporting facial hair to hide his double chin, barked a question at him, Zak sensed not for the first time.

"Do you know Karl Frideriks?"

Sure, I know him, thought Zak. *He's the annoying American who keeps moving in on my girlfriend.*

He said, "I know *of* him. He's my girlfriend's, er, work colleague."

Sandford spun around, astonished at the deep voice he had just heard and the sudden cooperativeness of his suspect.

Zak spoke again, "Now can you please tell me why I'm being held because I'm very tired and would like to go home. Constantly switching centuries, gender and body can be quite exhausting, you know."

Sandford folded his arms and stared at Zak in disbelief. Diversionary tactics. Going into his 'other personality'. It had to be deliberate. He was obviously uncomfortable talking about Frideriks.

"You're not going home until you've answered some more questions."

"Can I have some coffee then? I had this beautiful Deluxe Americano right in front of me, untouched, cinnamony, smelled delicious, and then she…disappeared me."

Not understanding a word, Sandford motioned to his colleague to get coffee.

"Do I need a lawyer as well?"

"You have already turned down the offer of legal representation. But you won't need it anyway if you can prove you were nowhere near El Nino's the night Barrymore Pegg was killed. But I've already asked—"

"Oh, that's easy," cut in Zak.

"Easy? You've just spent the past two hours telling me you can't provide an alibi and now you say it's easy?"

"Sorry about that. It wasn't me who said that about the alibi; it was Sarah. She didn't know where my body was that night. She's safely back in 2140 now and should give you no more trouble as long as you don't annoy me too much."

Sandford looked irritated by this but said nothing.

"Now, about that alibi, I usually play tennis on Friday evenings—"

"We know, we contacted your regular playing partners. They all said you didn't show up, without any explanation, leaving them short by one player. And they haven't heard from you since."

"I know. It's sometimes difficult being me. I can't contact friends in this time if I myself am in 2140. Just doesn't work – I've tried it. Anyway, I was at the vet. 'Paws Plus' they're called. My dog, Psycho, had diarrhoea. I had to get her some emergency tablets. They're the only vets around for miles and they're very good. The queues were enormous. I was there from seven till nearly ten. I couldn't contact my tennis pals that night because my phone wasn't charged. You should check it out."

"Don't worry, I will," said Inspector Sandford through gritted teeth.

He called his colleague back in and whispered to her for a while. There followed an awkward few minutes during which Sandford shifted about awkwardly in his chair but said nothing, and the other officer, whose name Zak didn't know as she'd been introduced to Sarah, plonked a coffee down in front of him. He sipped it, although it was nothing like as good as the one Sarah was enjoying at Malin's (which was fair enough when he thought about it, as she had paid for it). The female officer did her own share of whispering before leaving.

Sandford looked Zak in the eye and said, "Your story checks out." He sounded disappointed. "You are free to leave, but before you go, let me tell you this." He glowered at Zak, who smiled back at him. "I don't like you. I don't like games players. I am watching you. You could have given me that alibi two hours ago. Pull a stunt like that again and I'll have you for wasting police time."

Zak picked up his jacket and left the room. He breathed a sigh of relief, glad to be leaving that claustrophobic square room with no windows. In the doorway, he turned to Sandford and said:

"Why would I need to waste police time, Inspector, when you are already doing such a good job of it?"

****

London, UK, Late November 2026

Kyle Flanagan arrived at work early so he could smoke in the office before anyone else arrived and chucked him out. He switched on his PC a little nervously. As usual, the ten-year-old virus-ridden piece of junk took ages to log on. Today was the day Sarah Templeman, or rather, Zak Emblin, would be made a fool of in his paper when the predictions he had made two months previously failed to come true. Kyle's paper, *The Sun*, would be the first to open their envelope, and there was a keen sense of anticipation across the whole media – rather like in 2012 when the Mayans had predicted the end of the world would come. And of course, the world had not ended.

Kyle had not waited to open the envelope. He had needed the information to write the articles in advance, and this he had done the very next day after Carmen Fry's press conference. Colleagues at one or two other papers, who had also opened their envelopes early, had prepared two lots of articles: one set for if the predictions came true and one set letting Dr Carmen Fry and Zak Emblin have it with both barrels for wasting everyone's time, if the predictions proved inaccurate.

Kyle had not bothered with the 'true' set. He was so confident these predictions were not going to happen. I mean, really, Robbie Kent? The cleanest living, most sanctimonious sports presenter on TV (who, everyone knew, had a gorgeous, trophy wife) caught snorting cocaine with high-class prostitutes? Wasn't going to happen. Why would he? He had too much to lose. And as for an unknown 16-year-old Welsh pole vaulter becoming the first woman in history to clear six metres, he hadn't been able to find *any* 16-year-old female pole vaulters in Wales, let alone world class ones (and he'd put the word out at all the biggest athletics clubs).

He did admit the third one might happen. Some young violinist was supposed to die in a plane crash. He had never heard of her but had to admit she was quite fit. It would be a shame to lose her. That was straightforward obit stuff; he had that one ready.

****

Montreal, Canada, October 2026

Clint Morgan called his sister over and showed her an email from his former coach in Cardiff saying some geezer had been looking for a 16-year-old Welsh, female pole vaulter – something to do with breaking records. The coach wanted to know how high Cerys could jump these days.

"Maybe it's one of those Guinness World Records events they want you for. You should go, Cerys. It's about time we let you loose on to the world of athletics. You're already better than me and I've been jumping for years."

"I'm fine here, Bruv, with you, but I'd love them to know how high I can jump. Could we film it and upload it?"

Clint knew his sister well enough to know there was no point in pushing it over getting her to appear in public at a big event. Maybe she would in time, but she was acutely shy and just not ready for it yet. The local meets were all she could handle. "Great idea. Let's get an independent witness too; the internet's full of bogus claims."

They arranged for Canada's international athletics coach, who was also based at Montreal's Olympic Stadium, to attend the filming. He was, coincidentally, a paid representative of the Guinness World Records franchise, which Clint Morgan did not know. The bar was set at exactly six metres, and Cerys Morgan cleared it at her third attempt, as she had done many times before in training. The low-key footage, shot at a local indoor meet in a nearly empty arena, was uploaded later the same day. By this time, it was about 7 pm in the UK.

At 7:40 pm the same day, Kyle Flanagan got a call. His friend and sometime rival at *The Mail*, Sandy Rice, had found it on YouTube simply by googling 'Pole Vault record attempt'.

"Fuck me!" was Kyle's reaction. Several colleagues in the crowded news office stopped what they were doing to glare at him. Kyle didn't care; he had the front page now.

"Kind offer, Kyle," said Sandy, "maybe some other time. Is that the full set?"

It was. Kyle had opened a file sent to his mailbox anonymously that morning to find indisputable video evidence of a naked Robbie Kent scoring a line from an equally naked blonde girl's navel. Kent looked completely wasted. The girl had since materialised, claiming to have been paid £800 by Kent and demanding another £10,000 for her story.

And Miranda Harper, one time a child prodigy, apparently, had perished late last night in a light aircraft crash, "on her way to appear as soloist in the Sibelius *Violin Concerto* at The Concertgebouw in Amsterdam." Tributes were pouring in and the web was awash with images of her and her 'best friend', her Stradivarius violin.

Suddenly, Kyle had a story, a big one. He didn't care that the material he'd already prepared was now useless. She had got it right. That bitch from the future had got all three predictions right! He checked the internet, nothing yet. Kyle got to work immediately, one eye on the TV news, which hadn't picked up on the pole vault video yet, so 'Fry's predictions' was still only third item on. Curious that they had become known as 'Fry's predictions' when it was supposed to be Sarah Templeman who had made them…or Zak Emblin, pretending to be Sarah Templeman. He thought it was probably because the great British *Sun*-reading public couldn't handle all that shit and just focussed on the mad scientist. Mad scientists sold papers – the madder the better. You couldn't get much madder than claiming people had swapped bodies across two centuries! Best of all, in the paper selling stakes, was a truly mad scientist *who turned out to be right*, especially if she was young and hot like Carmen Fry. Kyle had a sudden fantasy about putting the lithe red-haired Carmen in his paper wearing matching glasses and bikini bottoms and nothing else. He decided that would probably never happen outside his own brain.

****

London, UK, Two Weeks Earlier.
Editor of The Sun Newspaper's Office.

"Marcus, I've called you in here to do some undercover work for me, the type that pays well. Do you understand me?"

Marcus, who looked and sounded like a walrus, nodded.

The editor, Piers Henry, continued, "Sometimes in this business, we need to oil the wheels, you know, to make things happen that are supposed to happen."

Marcus nodded agreement.

"That's where you come in. Two weeks ago, a Dr Carmen Fry predicted that certain events would take place. This was supposed to prove that she'd got some woman from the future to swap bodies with her boyfriend."

"I saw that press conference," said Marcus drily.

"Then you know about the envelopes. Kyle opened ours straight away, of course. That God botherer Robbie Kent, of all people, is supposed to be caught doing a line of cocaine with naked call girls. 'That'll never happen', says Kyle straight away, 'but it would be huge for us if it did'."

"Yes, it would, I thought. It gave me an idea, Marcus; let's *make* it happen. No offence to the Fry woman but I don't trust her to come through for us on this one. She's off her trolley. Kyle doesn't need to know; I don't want to cause trouble for him. He's a good reporter but a bit by the book. You'll be working for me directly. You can't discuss this with anyone else, you know the drill. My contact number is the same as before. Can you do it?"

Marcus said nothing and sat motionless in his chair with his huge arms folded beneath his drooping moustache. For a minute, Piers Henry looked confused, not understanding why he was getting no response from his faithful bloodhound. Suddenly he understood – 'give the dog a bone' – reached into his briefcase and handed over three sealed, bulging packs of pink notes which looked like they had come straight from the studio of the *£100K Drop*.

"That 75 grand?"

The editor nodded.

"Then I can do it," growled Marcus, and slowly ambled off, stuffing the notes inside his jacket.

****

London UK, Channel Four News Studio, December 2026

After Carmen and Sarah got all three of the Sun's predictions right, there was even more attention and speculation surrounding the second set of predictions. Channel Four News had these. The nation was on tenterhooks, waiting to see if Sarah Templeman, the woman from the future, who many more believed in now, could do it again.

As with *The Sun*, Sarah had not specified when exactly during the day each prediction would come true. This brought Channel Four News, normally a cure for insomnia, their best viewing figures, as curious people tuned in at all hours of the day. Channel Four's envelope also contained three predictions. The producers had decided to make an event out of opening the envelope on live TV. This added to the suspense, the thinking went, and proved they had not opened it in advance, as some suspected had happened at *The Sun*.

They had even invited in a famous actor to do it, which had provoked criticism from some serious commentators that they were pandering to the masses. The actress chosen was Emma Watson. The producers were delighted and not a little surprised, when she accepted. She was a Hollywood A-Lister, after all, and could have been forgiven for saying she was too busy, whether this were true or not.

As live television, it could not have gone better. Emma Watson made a great show of opening the envelope, as was expected of her. And then she completely lost it, standing there motionless for way too long, ignoring the autocue, her mouth wide open with a sequin-covered gloved hand over it.

"I don't believe it," she eventually managed when the host prompted her, "the first one's about *me*. Apparently, I am to be offered the part of James Bond, only it will be 'Jamie' Bond, obviously, and I'm going to accept it. I'll be the first woman to play the role in the character's 64-year history on film." Emma looked up, smiled and accepted the applause as if she'd already accepted the part. The other predictions she was supposed to read out seemed forgotten in the moment.

Carmen was watching at home with Sarah. She swore at the TV. When Sarah asked why, she explained that this had not been a good choice for a prediction. It was flawed; it left them open to the accusation that they were manipulating events to fit the predictions. When Sarah still looked confused, she added:

"Seeing this, the producers of the James Bond films will now want her on their project even if they hadn't thought of it before. They know she's got great pressure on her to accept now. And she's a big draw."

"I disagree. No need to be a Fry-Baby yet, over this, Darling. Wait for the reaction."

"What do you mean?"

"I think most people watching will have been more impressed by the fact that the very actress who is in the prediction *was invited to open the envelope* – it's like part of the plan, our plan, when in fact it was sheer luck!"

They were both proved right by events. Channel Four tweets expressing delight at the extra, unexpected twist to the prediction regarding Emma Watson far outnumbered the more cynical ones implying it was all a fix. The *Today* programme on Radio Four and *The Guardian* newspaper on the other hand, both made Carmen's point at length and with much research evidence to back it up.

Sarah was happy with the way things were going. She sensed that the popular mood was one of wanting to believe. In her view, they had turned things around since the bad publicity surrounding Barrymore Pegg's death.

Carmen saw things differently. She felt she needed the big guns, the broadsheet newspapers and the respected highbrow TV and radio programmes, on her side, to convince her professor and Vice Chancellor of the viability of her research. That was three lots of bad publicity now: first, the insinuation that her research colleague was somehow responsible for Barrymore Pegg's death; then suggestions that she might have colluded with the Sun to stitch up a famous and respected sports presenter; and now the Emma Watson, James Bond thing – all of them bringing the University of Birmingham into disrepute.

She need not have worried. The days of 'bad' publicity were long gone. Nowadays nearly all publicity was good publicity. At the very moment she was having these worrying thoughts, her Vice Chancellor was in his office calculating what effect the Emma Watson publicity might have on applications next year – how many more could he expect? He rubbed his hands and poured himself a celebratory malt. This was only the second set of envelopes to be opened! He was one very lucky man, and in his view, Carmen Fry was a shoe-in for the Member of Staff of the Year award, although traditionalists on the panel might need some convincing.

****

Birmingham, England, December 2026

Carmen and Sarah agreed that they had to fill Zak in immediately with what had been happening, but Sarah was so into it all that she found it difficult to get annoyed enough to re-join her own body. She finally managed it by focussing on the infuriating Inspector Sandford, at the same time wondering what was happening now in the murder investigation in which they were all suspects. Suddenly she was holding open the door to her own refrigerator, which looked remarkably empty. *Zak! I left you money; can't you shop occasionally?*

Zak found himself in Carmen's kitchen. Carmenstood opposite him, arms folded. Policemen and cameramen were outside, but he was only mildly curious. He just kept seeing that dishevelled bed from the day his nose got broken. There was so much to talk about yet neither of them could say anything. Carmen knew instantly that Sarah and he had switched because of the sudden increase in tension in the room. That and the fact that Psycho came bounding into the kitchen, tail wagging, and licked Zak's hand, something she would never do while Sarah was occupying his body, as if she somehow sensed that Sarah was a cat person.

"We need to talk," said Zak.

"You're right there. So much has happened since you were last here. You won't believe what—"

"I mean about Karl," Zak interrupted her.

"No, not that again, Zak. I've been over that with you! It's not the right time. You don't want to swap—"

"I *know* about you two."

"Exactly what do you know?"

"I know you sleep with him. I saw the bed that day I came here with a broken nose. He said he was here to help you move in some big plant, so where is it? Plus, he stopped me coming in when I first arrived, then drove slowly enough for you to pass him on the dual carriageway, so you could both pretend you had come to the hospital from another direction. And you gave him a shirt at the hospital."

"Ah," said Carmen, all the tension gone from her voice.

Zak knew then that he was right. Until that moment he had hoped she could provide an alternative explanation.

"Zak, it's not you, please believe me. What we have, you and I, is wonderful. I really care about you."

Carmen's soothing tones brought tears to Zak's eyes. He turned away so that she couldn't see them.

"So why did you lie to me when I came out to your parents' house? You had a chance then to tell me you and Karl were…together!"

"I didn't lie to you, Zak. That time, Karl and I…we…hadn't done anything yet."

"What? You mean you've started sleeping with him since we've been going out? That's worse."

"Believe me, Zak, Dearest, it's nothing. With Karl, it was purely physical. I don't even like him anymore! He was always borrowing money from me and never paying it back. And he's really dropped me in it by uploading my research to the public space on the cloud and he's done nothing to try and help sort it out. You and me, we are different. We have something really special."

She tried to hug him, but he pulled away and made for the door. Outside bulbs flashed and microphones were shoved in his face. He just strode through them all, barely noticing the questions and drove. Just drove. First, it was houses and traffic lights that flashed past, then fields and villages. He had no idea where he was and didn't care. He was losing Carmen. That was all that mattered. He tried to tell himself that this was a good thing but got nowhere. "All for the best," as his mum would say. It just didn't work. He knew they were supposed to be together, why else would she have been able to help him with his schizophrenia, no, his reincarnating behaviour, from the very first day they had met? That was fate, surely?

A dark thought entered Zak's brain which he tried to resist but there was no fighting it. Maybe Carmen had known all along who he was, had even been searching for him. That was why she had signed up to the same chat service; it wasn't coincidence at all. She had done it so that she could get to know him and use him in her research. He was her Lab Rat and nothing more. They used to call him 'Lab Rat' at school because of his schizophrenic episodes and because of the hospital tests he had to go through. He had made a promise to himself back then that he would never again let anyone use that term about him, Zak reminded himself. Carmen had used it the first time they had chatted. He should have heeded the warning and got out. She had denied seeking him out, of course, but could he trust her word anymore after the Karl thing?

Maybe even the sex was a sham. She seemed to be enjoying it, but hadn't she just admitted she was physically attracted to Karl? They'd started sleeping together after he and Carmen had first ended up in bed, so that experience must have been lacking something for Carmen, or wouldn't it have been enough?

OK, maybe he was overreacting. What she had said was that what she had with Karl was 'purely physical'. Zak tried to imagine 'purely physical'. He failed. There had been plenty of girls he had found sexually attractive in the past, but he had never tried to get any of them into bed unless he had come to know and like them first. During lovemaking, all their little quirks, the habits he liked in them, formed part of the pleasure. After sleeping with a girl, he had always thought about her differently, more affectionately. Surely Carmen thought about Karl differently too. He simply could not imagine shagging someone because they looked great and then moving on. He knew that Carmen was trying to make him feel better with the 'purely physical' remark, but it only made him feel more jealous.

****

Birmingham, England, December 2026

Unable to placate Zak, Carmen decided to tell him the truth when he came back (if he ever came back), to reveal her big secret, that she was a sex addict. By revealing this personal secret, which she was receiving treatment for, she would admit Zak to a special club which contained only two other people who knew this about her, apart from her counsellor – Sarah and her father. She hoped this would take some of the edge off the jealousy he clearly felt and allow him to see how privileged this made him – see it as proof of how much she cared for him.

With that decided, Carmen realised how tense she had been feeling and slumped into the purple Isadore sofa. She needed a drink but could not summon the energy to go into the kitchen and pour one. She tried to focus on the original paintings she had purchased at galleries in St Ives. The one with the bottles and the one with the ship which was a house if you rotated it through 90 degrees. Why was it that so many talented artists lived in Cornwall? She could not concentrate. For a few minutes, she wondered what to do and how to cope if Zak never returned. Then she realised that he had no choice. Sarah would want to see her again, and she knew she could persuade Sarah to swap bodies with Zak.

Zak came back about three hours later. Carmen did not ask where he had been. He would not have been able to tell her anyway. Instead, she put her plan into action straight away and told him her secret. Zak still misunderstood. He was too busy fretting about whether she was attracted to Karl because his own sexual performance was lacking.

"It's not about you!" she found herself shouting. "Why do men always think everything is about them? I just need…variety." She admitted to Zak that Karl was physically attractive, and because Zak had just irritated her, added unhelpfully, "and he has so much energy."

"I can be more energetic," said Zak, immediately, before she could correct herself.

This time she thought before speaking. "Not necessary," she replied, "you don't need to compensate."

In his current vulnerable mood, even this was not enough for Zak.

Carmen had to spell it out for him that his penis was bigger than Karl's. "Why do you think he needs to do all that working out? It's compensation!"

"So, why then?"

Carmen sighed. "I'm a scientist," she said. "I think like a scientist in everything I do. Think of it as experimenting. Have you never wondered what sex would be like with someone who is really into you but you don't find attractive at first?"

Zak thought of all the times women had responded to his natural beauty with offers, some of which he had accepted only to be disappointed when he had found out that they were only interested in his body. If anything, he had been the experiment for them.

Seeing she was getting nowhere, Carmen opted for analogy. She asked Zak if he could stay faithful to just one composer.

"Suppose you heard the *Rose Adagio* from *Sleeping Beauty*, which you introduced me to, as your first piece of Tchaikovsky, wouldn't you want to hear some more Tchaikovsky? I bet you could not resist. You wouldn't stay faithful to your beloved Brahms and Beethoven then."

Zak protested that music was different, but even as he said it, he was beginning to understand Carmen better.

"Is it different, though? Think of the times you've tried to get me into classical music. You talk about moments, climaxes that affect your whole body, make the hairs on the back of your neck stand up – I've even heard you describe them as 'orgasms'!"

Zak got it now. Carmen would have accepted nearly all the offers he had had, not just a few, for the sake of those physical sensations alone. Even as he was thinking this, she asked:

"Can you honestly say you've never thought about experimenting sexually, when in Sarah's body?"

Zak coloured up, thinking of his behaviour the other day in Sarah's bath, and protested too much.

"No! Of course not! She's a woman. I have no desire to shag futuristic men, no matter how 'luminous' they are!"

"Luminous?" Carmen was smiling now.

"It means 'hot', attractive. I keep seeing it on twenty-second-century hologram adverts when I'm in Sarah's body."

"Find a woman, then. I'm sure they still have homosexuality in the twenty-second century!"

This comment was a real eye-opener for Zak. He found the idea intriguing, but also guessed that Carmen had probably slept with his body while Sarah was in it. He put this to Carmen who, in their new-found spirit of honesty, admitted it.

"What was it like? Was it better?" he asked her, more out of curiosity than jealousy this time, which Carmen misunderstood at first and started berating him about being ultra-sensitive.

"No, no. It's OK. I'm not jealous – you were doing it with my body, after all – just curious. What was it like?"

Carmen considered for a moment and decided to be honest.

"Only in one way was it better. Sarah is a woman. When she is in her own body, she has the same anatomy as me. She knows exactly where to touch me, lick me, suck me, how much pressure to use…"

"OK, OK, TMI, I get the picture," said Zak, annoyed with himself now for getting jealous again when he thought he had got that under control.

"No, don't get upset, you haven't got the full picture! It's not the same with Sarah, somehow. It's less erotic, maybe because I know she's really a woman."

Sarah blurted this out because Psycho was barking the signal, but it was too late for Zak to hear it. He was gone. Sarah heard it instead.

"I see. Well, I'm glad you got that off your chest, Honey. I'll try and be more manly next time. Let's see, would fake pecs and chest hair work for you? Zak sure as hell doesn't have any." She pulled open Zak's shirt to prove the point.

"That's not fair, Sarah, and you know it. You can't tease me for things I thought I was saying to Zak!"

"Fair comment. At least, he knows about us now, I suppose. I hate secrecy."

****

"In Everett's approach, everything that is possible, quantum-mechanically speaking (that is, all those outcomes to which quantum mechanics assigns a non-zero probability) is realised in its own separate world. These are the 'many worlds' of the Many Worlds approach to quantum mechanics."

Brian Greene, *The Hidden Reality,* p211

Birmingham, England, December 2026

Over the coming weeks things only got better for Sarah and Carmen. All their predictions came true. Why wouldn't they? For them not to have done would have meant a mistake or memory lapse by Sarah, and Sarah had an excellent memory. Still Carmen was not happy. She was a scientist, a good one. She wanted recognition in her own field, and she did not have that yet. It was probably true to say that the British public were now convinced that Sarah was from the future, and that she was somehow occupying Zak Emblin's body. But academics required more rigorous proof. Academics were a lot more suspicious, and one particular one, Dave Adams, got to her.

Carmen had socialised with Dave Adams at various conferences – they had even ended up in bed together at the Belfast one – and while she didn't count him as a friend, he would have been on her Christmas card list, if she'd had one (she didn't because she preferred to donate to Greenpeace instead). She respected his opinion and felt uncomfortable having him in the opposite camp. And that is very definitely where he had put himself by writing an article for *The Guardian* which rubbished her research and showed 'beyond reasonable doubt' that each recent prediction was a trick. It must have got to her because she could remember it, almost word for word. It had read:

I won't go into Pegg's alleged murder. That one is still with the police, but I would say that it seems a bit too much of a coincidence that Carmen Fry's close research associate Karl Friderikѕ was there the same night and that he's never been there before or since. No, others have gone into that case in far more detail than I have space for here, so I will concentrate on the more recent predictions. Number One, the devout Anglican, and TV sports presenter, Robbie Kent. The police have decided not to press charges. Why not? I hear you ask. Wasn't he caught naked on camera snorting cocaine with call girls? Proof enough, surely?

Well, is it? Let us take another look at that now infamous, 'incriminating' photo. When the police examined it, they found several interesting things. First, he has no erection. If this were a sex game as the tabloids implied, shouldn't he be enjoying it? Secondly, look at the cocaine and the tube – look closely and you'll see a small gap between the white powder and the bottom of the tube. Kent is not snorting it up, he's just hovering over it with a tube in his hand, a hand which is being held tightly closed around the tube by one of the girls. Now look at the other girl's left arm. She is holding him up! That arm is bearing far more weight than it should be if he were an active participant. And that is my point, he is not active. Look at his face; his eyes are closed. In my view, he is unconscious. This would explain why he remembers nothing, as he has always maintained when interviewed about this event. I do not doubt that the prostitute was paid the money she admits to receiving, but it did not come from Kent. He was clearly set up. Kent is innocent. He should be reinstated in his job as a sports presenter.

Now I don't know who did that, or why they would do it, but I do know who has a motive: Carmen Fry and Zak Emblin. Could they be trying to legitimise her bogus research by predicting events that they know they can make happen? All it required to set up Robbie Kent was a journalist unscrupulous enough to open the envelope in advance. And if this did happen, which does not seem that unlikely at The Sun, that same journalist would also have seen the other predictions.

Let us assume he got lucky with Miranda Harper's death on the way to a concert performance (because the alternative is frankly too horrible to contemplate). That leaves Morgan's pole vault world record. I see two possibilities here. Either Fry and Emblin knew of her and her achievements in training and used the Sun reporter to coax her out (knowing he would open the envelope ahead of time). Or the vault itself was a sham. There weren't that many witnesses, after all. Not that many people to collude with.

And as for the most recent so-called successful prediction, Emma Watson getting the part of 'Jamie' Bond, well, sorry Emma, but you had to be in on that one. Or if not you, then the producers of the franchise were.

What hurt Carmen most was the accusation that she was dishonest. It had never occurred to her that she might be able to exploit her access to someone from the twenty-second century for personal gain. Yet that is what everyone, including her former lover, was assuming she had done! Worse than that, they wanted her to become even more self-centred to prove that she was right, that Sarah *really was* from the future. Dave Adams' article had concluded:

It is no secret what nearly everyone on the planet would do if they could travel back in time – they would take the winning lottery numbers back with them and get stinking rich. Come on, you know you would. Anybody who says they would not is either a liar or a saint and there aren't too many of those around (saints, I mean!).

So I, Dave Adams, challenge you, Sarah Templeman, to win the jackpot in the official national lottery, two weeks in a row, both here and in the United States, then I will believe you. Any other predictions, frankly, aren't worth the paper they're written on.

This annoyed Carmen but also gave her the chance to prove herself right. She decided to accept Dave Adams' challenge. Within minutes of reading his article, she was looking forward to seeing the expression on his face when she succeeded. She would enjoy making him eat his words.

The trouble was Sarah took some persuading to do it.

"Don't you think that would be grandstanding? (Do you have that expression in your time?)?" was her first reaction.

Carmen agreed. She was not comfortable with it from that point of view. However, once they had provided conclusive proof that the predictions her research on quantum entanglement naturally led to – that multiple personalities from the same soul really can communicate with each other across generations – were true, then the tabloids might leave her alone.

She had not even had a chance to voice this thought, before Sarah revealed it to be a delusion by saying, "And if we did win the lottery twice, we'd be inundated with requests to do the same thing for others. We would never escape. We'd become hounded celebrities overnight. I don't want to put you and Zak through that."

They were in Carmen's kitchen. Both loved spending time there. Carmen had bought a huge oak table, for a bargain price of £199, at an auction when she had first moved in. It looked ancient and was probably originally a small banqueting table from a Tudor manor. She had had enormous difficulty getting it in. She and her friends had had to remove the front door from its frame. Still, it was worth it. Everyone loved it and people were drawn to it. The kitchen had become the place for coffee and conversation.

She and Sarah were sitting there now as Carmen thought about Sarah's celebrity status point. There was no denying it was true, but the alternative, their current situation, seemed far worse to her.

"Believe me, Zak and I are willing to take that risk."

"And there's another problem I've only just thought of," Sarah continued.

"What is that?"

"The truth gets in the way. We can't do it because we didn't do it. We didn't win the lottery or I would know about it – my ancestors would have been rich, and so would I be, probably."

"But how do you know for certain that we don't win it? Have you looked it up? Maybe we gave all the money to charity?"

"If we'd done that, it would surely have been front page news. I don't recall seeing it."

"It was before your time, Sarah. Why don't you check when you get back to your own time? We will put off our decision until then. I don't think we should accept the challenge, if we didn't win it."

"I see what you mean. Wouldn't we be opening up an alternative universe if we accepted the challenge, knowing that we didn't win the lottery in the future?" asked Sarah.

"Ah, the good old multiple worlds theory. We have Schrödinger and Everett to thank for that one. It's such a beautiful idea, I'd love it to be right, but unfortunately, there's no evidence for it."

"So why don't we test it now? I'll check, and if we didn't win the lottery, we'll win it this time around and we'll see if we end up in a parallel universe."

"It can't be done, Sarah. Believe me, I've been over this thousands of times with students. Proof is the problem. If we do end up in a parallel universe, we won't know it. It will be a different you and a different me from the ones who are talking to each other now, but they won't know that. To them, they will be the same as they have always been and in the same universe which they've always been in. Each decision you make takes you in a different direction. But in Everett's theory, *every decision you could have made, but didn't* is also played out in its own parallel universe."

Sarah had put a smirk on Zak's face. Zak used this expression when he thought of something funny. Carmen knew that when Sarah did it, she was planning something mischievous.

"If I understand you right, Carmy darling, you are saying that proof is the *only* problem. You're not saying that we *wouldn't* end up in an alternative universe?"

Carmen looked worried but said, "Yes, that's right. Why?"

Sarah jumped up and down like a child who has just been promised ice cream. "Then let's do it! Sod the proof. I just want to know that I'm in a different universe and there's another me out there in the old one. How cool would that be? Just think how cool it would be!"

"You wouldn't know," said Carmen, and shook her head, resignedly.

****

New Palm Springs, California Peninsular, 2140

That shake of the head irritated Sarah so much that she found herself back in 2140, crossing the airways in her gyro and had to manoeuvre quickly to avoid a collision. A drunken Kate was alongside her. Sarah quizzed Kate about what she had been doing with Zak, but before long Kate fell asleep, so Sarah took her home.

This was frustrating. She had just been persuaded by Carmen to win the lottery (just think – to knowingly go into a parallel universe!) when Carmen seemed to be having second thoughts. Her tummy was rumbling. *That Zak, you could never trust him to look after your body for you – for instance, by putting food into it at regular intervals! OK, lunchtime.* She glanced at her watch. The Public Library building was still open. She could grab a bite to eat there (but no drink, her woozy brain was telling her that Zak had already taken care of that!) and make use of her unexpected time back in the present to memorise the next two lottery results after the date Carmen was living in now.

Ensconced between the stacks, out of sight of all other library users, Sarah also looked up who had won them. This proved annoyingly difficult, both for the US and UK results. There was just no information for those weeks. There were loads of pictures of smiling or bewildered faces, champagne corks popping all around them, for the weeks just before and just after the ones which she was interested in. Perhaps she and Carmen had ticked the 'no publicity' box? Unlikely, they wanted publicity, that was the whole point.

After nearly an hour, Sarah got lucky. She abandoned all lottery-related searches and searched on people instead, Carmen, Zak, and herself, to see if there was anything about what they were up to at that time. The headline she found was: "Zak Emblin Fraud Case." She read on:

US officials request extradition of Zak Emblin and Carmen Fry, who both face charges of fraud over their recent claims to be able to predict the future which culminated in the suspension of National Lottery draws for two weeks in both countries. Inside reports suggest that Fry and Emblin 'won' jackpots in four successive draws, two in each country, prompting a Federal investigation.

They had won. Why the secrecy? She was curious now and eager for Carmen to respond to that Dave Adams guy. Nice day though it was with the sun setting behind the Microsoft building, showing off its five black turrets, she hoped that Carmen was at this minute trying to annoy Zak, so that she could get back and tell her the news.

Earlier That Day

Zak was eating pizza which he had found in the huge black 1950s' style fridge with those lovely, rounded corners. He was bugged by Boudicca, who felt so entitled to some he wondered whether Sarah sometimes shared it with her. The taste was disappointing, given the Americans' reputation for delicious pizzas back in his own time. The beer, on the other hand, was a revelation. They were probably world leaders now in this market. The lager he was enjoying was smooth, with the tiniest of bubbles which caressed your tongue, so he was already feeling drunk and it was only 11 am.

His reflections were interrupted by the sound of the front door opening. *Oh, no, Kate again.* There was no time to hide, he just put a weak smile on Sarah's face, said, "Hi," and waited to see how Kate would respond.

"Hi," said Kate. "Still got that sore throat then? How many weeks is it now?"

Zak blurted out something about chronic symptoms which even he had trouble believing, but it didn't matter because Kate interrupted him with the surprising words, "Hello, Zak! Pleased to meet you again. Sarah has finally told me all about you, so there is no need to run away this time."

She sat down at the table opposite Zak on one of those chairs which seemed to be suspended in mid-air. It was, of course, connected to the table, but the connection was designed to pick up the colours in the room so that it was camouflaged. It was almost invisible unless you were looking for it. Nearly everyone had one, apparently. Kate asked if there were any more beer in the fridge. He handed her a bottle, noticing as he did so that she was dressed in men's clothing. She looked like Diane Keaton in *Annie Hall*, only older, say mid-30s, with shorter, glossier hair which was swept back from her face. The total picture was not unattractive. Kate saw him looking at her and smiled mischievously. Zak thought of Carmen's advice – almost an order, really! – to 'shag a woman', if he did not feel like experimenting with a man while in Sarah's body.

"Sorry you missed Sarah."

"I'm not. I was hoping to bump into you, Zak." She fixed him with her light brown eyes and caressed Sarah's foot under the table, making him start and sending Boudicca scurrying from his lap. Sarah's face blushed.

"Now I'm 100% sure you're not Sarah. Nothing embarrasses her."

"Do you play footsie under the table with her as well?"

"I try. Sarah would have moved her foot away at the slightest contact. But I can tell you're interested."

Zak said nothing.

Kate smiled. "Let me fess up. I've fancied Sarah for years. She has just the sort of short, plump body which drives me wild. But she won't share it with me. She's not here, though, is she?"

Zak had to think what to say.

"This is a bit fast for me, Kate. Shouldn't we get to know each other first?"

"I already know loads about you. But I can give you a brief autobiography if it would make you feel better."

"Thanks, it would. It's not just that, though. It's…I've never used this body before for…you know. It would be kind of like a first time for me. I still don't know Sarah's body that well."

"I can help you with that. I've got one that's nearly the same. You just relax and let me drive."

With that, Kate leaned over the table and kissed Zak full on Sarah's mouth. It was not that many seconds before tongues were involved. When Zak pulled away suddenly, he saw such a sad expression on Kate's face that it tugged at his heart. It was an expression which said, "I've been here before, and just when I had my hopes up, you, Sarah's body, are going to disappoint me again."

Zak smiled and spoke gently to Kate. "It's OK, I do want you…but life story first, please. OK, I'll settle for just some of it," he added when he saw mock disappointment on her face.

Kate stood up quickly, a bright smile on her face.

"Sorry for being so pushy, Zak, that was wrong of me. We can do this later if you are still, you know, curious. But now," she said, "I'm gonna take you to the Swamp! They have live music there all day. And you can learn all about luminosity." She reached into her handbag. "First, we have to take these."

Zak looked unsure about the pills.

"It's OK, they're harmless; no side effects. Take one or you won't glow in the dark. The Swamp is perfect. The music is loud, so no one will notice you're not Sarah. All you need do is smile at everyone and dance. We'll take Sarah's gyro; mine needs to charge. You can drive if you like. Now, come on." Kate grabbed Sarah's hand and off they went.

Zak had no idea what to expect but was looking forward to it. Sarah could not show him the sights of twenty-second-century New Palm Springs as she was always in his body back in England whenever he was here. Kate's invitation was just what he needed.

The Swamp turned out to be a night club, a 24-hour one. The first thing he noticed was the music. If he were asked to describe it to someone from his own time, he would have said a Cajun and reggae fusion, but it was really a lot more original than that, at least to his ears. Above all, it was danceable, and boy, were people dancing. They appeared to be dancing around giant luminous cacti. When he looked closer, he realised they were also dancing through them – the cacti were holograms which changed colour and location. Kate bought him a cocktail, which was blue but tasted like Sangria. They danced. It was so dark in the Swamp that when they were sitting down, Zak could only see the luminous people. Once they were on the dance floor, he realised that a lot of the people he thought were dancing alone, were really dancing opposite someone, or even in a group, but the others were not glowing…or not yet glowing, for he noticed that two girls dancing near him suddenly started to glow, one yellow, one pink. You could see their body shapes through their clothes.

"You, too," said Kate, noticing him looking at the girls, and pointing at Sarah's body.

Zak looked down and saw his, Sarah's, whole body glowing green.

"That's what the pill does," Kate added, indicating her own body starting to light up, also green.

Zak felt strangely self-conscious, at first, feeling more exposed than ever before in his life. After two hours, all inhibitions were gone, and he was having a great time. He found he could really lose himself in the music and not worry about injuring other people with his long limbs, as usually happened in night clubs.

He was a little disappointed when Kate leaned into him to be heard over the music and said, "Time to go, Honey. I don't want you using up all Sarah's energy on the dance floor. For a doctor, she's not that fit, you know."

On the way back in Sarah's gyro, Zak could not help glancing at Kate's body because you just couldn't tell, in daylight, that she'd taken a luminosity pill at all. Another gyro had to swerve to avoid them and beeped loudly.

"Maybe I should drive," said Kate, and then recalled how drunk she was herself, as she had been drinking at twice the rate Zak had. "I wish Sarah would get this bloody SatNav fixed," she mumbled to herself, drifting in and out of sleep.

"I've booked it in for next week," said Sarah, grabbing the throttle.

Kate sat bolt upright in her seat. "You're back, Sarah!"

"Don't sound so pleased. Where have you been with Zak?"

"I took him to the Swamp."

"Now let me see, you take him to the only place where it's dark in the middle of the day, where lots of writhing, apparently naked people get luminous and drunk – yes, I feel drunk – you weren't trying to seduce me, were you? Kate, I know you."

"Of course not, how could you think that of me? I was trying to seduce *Zak*, but you had to come back early like some spoilsport parent."

They both laughed before Kate fell asleep.

****

London, UK, December 2026

Dave Adams was doing something he had never done before, watching nervously as the National Lottery numbers were drawn. As a renowned scientist and academic, he would have set himself up for ridicule had he played the lottery. The chances of winning a significant sum of money were so small that no scientist worthy of the name would ever enter, but he had to admit he was enjoying the suspense. He clutched two pieces of paper in his large, hairy, hand, both with predictions of the winning numbers from Zak Emblin (well, supposedly from Sarah Templeman), one for the US lottery due later in the week, and one for the UK one which was on TV now.

The very first number drawn was wrong.

"Hah, I knew it, chicanery, all of it!" When the second number drawn was also wrong, he added, "No wonder they haven't turned up, it's all a bloody trick!"

A production assistant on The National Lottery Live leaned in at this point and took the paper from his hand. She swapped it around with the other piece of paper. On this sheet, the first two numbers drawn were clearly visible. Adams looked again at the back of the scrap of paper. It said, "UK Draw 1." He had mixed them up.

Carmen Fry and Zak Emblin were led in, to cheers, complaining of traffic hold-ups, and he managed to force a smile. They did not seem at all nervous. "How we doin'?" asked Emblin in an unexpectedly high voice.

"Er, OK, so far," said Adams. This was an understatement. While Fry and Emblin were coming in, two more correct numbers had been drawn.

When the sixth correct number was drawn, the audience erupted into applause which almost drowned out the bonus ball draw. Carmen and Sarah also got this right. Dave Adams regretted accepting the invitation to the live studio draw. What should have been a moment of triumph was now one of embarrassment in front of a TV audience of millions. How could Fry and Emblin be that lucky? No, it was a trick; he just hadn't rumbled them yet. When put on the spot by the host for his immediate reaction, the experience he had gained from all the conferences he had been to where he'd had to respond immediately to unanticipated, difficult questions got him through. He said:

"I chose four consecutive lottery wins as my challenge for a reason. There was always a chance, admittedly a small one, that Carmen Fry here might really win one (or even two) draws. It is also possible that a trick has been played on all of us which we have yet to work out. If this is true, again, having four draws so close to one another, in different countries and time zones, will make it highly unlikely that these con men, if they do prove to be con men, can reproduce the feat on all four occasions."

"You're saying you won't believe them until they've got all four lottery draws right?" asked the host.

"That's exactly what I'm saying. But if they can get all four draws right, they will have met my challenge. I'd even start supporting them then."

****

New York, USA, December 2026

Wayne Ferrer checked his manicure and practised his smile. He was a little nervous but happy. Today was the big day the world was waiting for when Carmen Fry and Zak Emblin (or was it Sarah Templeman? He still wasn't sure) would probably win the jackpot in the fourth successive National Lottery draw in the UK and the USA. The show had been promoted on billboards for weeks and a global audience topping 100 million was predicted. It was going to be massive. *He* was going to be massive. He let his mind wander to the deliciously curvy and tanned body of Nadia, one of the assistant producers who had been flirting with him a bit more recently. If that didn't happen, he could always select someone from the enormous amount of fan mail he was bound to get after this show. Life was good.

They were just rehearsing their lines for the last time before the show went live. And that is when his world collapsed. Five uniformed and armed soldiers marched in unannounced. Behind them were four other men built like bouncers and wearing shades. They were followed by three suits, the one in the centre belonging to a middle-aged woman of medium height with dyed auburn hair who quickly let it be known that she was in charge.

"We are from the Defence Department," she said, in a rich, deep voice, holding up a badge. "We are here to prevent this live broadcast in the interests of National Security."

"National Security? On what grounds?" demanded an indignant Wayne Ferrer.

The woman from the Defence Department smiled at the presenter. "We don't need grounds," she stated simply. "However, you do deserve an explanation. The draw will go ahead – we are not authorised to stop that happening – only it will go ahead behind closed doors. Please proceed. We'll explain afterwards."

The producer was furious. "But what about the Live show? What about our ratings? Our advertising clients? We'll lose millions over this!"

"We all have to make sacrifices from time to time in the national interest. Pretend it's a technical fault, for now. If you need compensation, I suggest you talk to these two guys – they've come into quite a bit of money recently." She barely lifted her forefinger in Carmen's direction.

No one knew what to do. The draw just did not work without an audience. Wayne Ferrer started off announcing the numbers as usual but soon just looked at them as they rolled out of the machine. They were, of course, the ones Carmen and Sarah had said they would be, but no one outside the studio knew that. There was a sense of anti-climax after the bonus ball was drawn and an awkward silence, broken eventually by Sarah, who asked:

"Is this where you arrest us for fraud?"

The lady in charge wore the smile of someone accustomed to power as she answered, "Not why we're here, but it sounds like a good cover story. Make a note of it, Corporal Matthews."

"Yes, ma'am," said one of the soldiers and tapped something into an iPad.

"I want this studio cleared of everyone except these two, or should I say 'three'," the woman ordered.

Immediately, the soldiers did her bidding while the 'bouncers' formed a ring around them, facing outwards.

Carmen was over her initial shock now and getting angry. "Who are you exactly?" she demanded.

"Sorry, didn't I introduce myself? I am Commander Eleanor Levy, Defence Department, Special Ops." She turned to look directly at Zak's tall figure.

"Now let me guess, you got the 'arrested for fraud' idea from tomorrow's papers?"

Sarah nodded, surprised.

"You see, we at Special Ops don't think that all this is fraud." She turned to face Carmen again.

"We believe in your research, Dr Fry—"

"I'm not a doctor."

"You will be, if I have to see to it myself. You're not under arrest. You're not in trouble, but we can't allow your research to continue as before; it's too dangerous."

"I think Professor Williamson might have something to say about that," said Carmen, still angry. "His department funds the project."

"Not any more it doesn't." Commander Levy had their attention now and paused before she continued.

"You are right, of course. Professor Williamson did have something to say, but his objections disappeared very quickly once we offered him $5 million for other research programmes run by his department. We also informed him that your own research funding would be doubled, subject to rigorous scrutiny of your evidence so far. I'm sure you have questions."

Carmen had so many questions she did not know which to ask first.

"Am I to understand that you are offering me a US Government Defence Department research contract?"

"Yes, for five years initially. You can operate out of the UK if you prefer, provided you file regular reports and attend meetings when asked to. Oh, and your salary will be tripled."

"Will I get any of this in writing?"

"No. We need to keep this programme secret, so no paper trails. You can trust me. Here is my card and contact number. Memorise it and destroy it. Officially, I will be your supervisor, but in practice you will run your own research, as I believe you have been doing anyway. Professor Williamson complained of your unwillingness to consult regularly."

Carmen smiled at this.

"What happens to my friends, Zak and Sarah?"

"They, you" – Commander Levy corrected herself and looked straight into Zak's eyes – "will receive generous expenses allowances, but we cannot recruit you directly to the programme nor do we have any desire to. Our interest is better served with you continuing your normal lives as far as possible. And that brings me to the delicate part."

"As I have said, this is a secret programme. The implications are huge. If Dr Fry really has discovered a mechanism for seeing future events, perhaps even for communicating with people from the future, any country or Alliance which has this capability will have an enormous advantage, both economically and militarily. Everyone will want it."

"Militarily? I don't want this research used for military purposes! I won't agree to that."

Commander Levy calmly put up her hand in Carmen's direction.

"As I was saying, everyone will want it. At whatever cost. And believe me, Dr Fry, they will come after you to get it. Your wishes in this matter are of little consequence at the end of the day, whether you like it or not. That's why we're taking you in, for your own protection and to give you the freedom to work, unmolested. You will be relieved to hear we have no military ambitions for this research at present; we just want to keep it under wraps so other, shall we say, 'less reasonable' parties can't get hold of it."

Sarah asked, "What does 'taking you in' mean exactly?"

"That's the bit none of you will like. We need you to participate in a cover story, maybe a pretend trial for fraud following your earlier suggestion, Sarah. We need to get the public's attention away from your discovery, Dr Fry, by giving them an alternative explanation for the lottery wins. Too many people are starting to believe you. That's dangerous – for you, mainly."

"My problem there, Commander, is that I only have your word for that," cut in Carmen. "None of us have experienced any danger, have we?" she looked to Sarah for confirmation.

"Absolutely not. Can't see what the fuss is, myself. I'm enjoying all the attention," her new friend agreed.

Commander Levy thought for a minute then sent one of the soldiers to fetch something and called one of the studio staff back in to set her up with a PC. The corporal returned with a memory stick and connected it to the PC.

"Watch this," instructed Commander Levy.

She showed them four different clips, each containing a death threat to either Carmen or Sarah. One was from a group calling themselves Vigilantes Against Greed. Another was from an extremist Fundamentalist Christian Sect which claimed that Sarah returning from the future and predicting events was interfering with God's will. They promised to 'break the circle' by executing Sarah and, with this act, proving her wrong, even about her own future. There was one from a fan who wanted to be with Zak and promised to kill first, Sarah, to reunite Zak permanently with his own body, and then Carmen, presumably because she was his girlfriend. Finally, there was one from Muslim extremists, saying pretty much the same as the Christian Sect, that Sarah had no right to predict the future as this was God's will, and then anticipating that same God's will by saying that Sarah must die.

"Shit and double shit. How come we didn't know about any of these?" asked Sarah.

"We intercepted them. We've been…monitoring you, and we didn't want you to know the danger you were in."

"Why not?" Carmen was angry again now.

"That's simple." Commander Levy spread her arms to indicate the studio, in an isn't-it-obvious gesture. "We couldn't risk you pulling out of the lottery draws. We wanted to see if you could do it."

"We could have been killed!"

"Yes, but you weren't. We've arrested Zak's lovesick fan, who had bought weapons recently. The rest are still out there somewhere. That's why we couldn't take the risk with the fourth live draw."

Everyone was silent for a moment. It was Sarah who spoke next:

"Suppose Carmen agreed to a pretend trial (and by the way, I didn't suggest it, I just saw when I was back home in 2140 that that's what had happened) would she have to go to prison?"

"No. The cover story will be that she has gone to prison, but she won't really go. We will produce some footage of her in prison uniform. We will also pay some real inmates to say they shared a cell with her. For the duration of the supposed sentence, she will have to stay out of sight, of course. We will help with this."

"And Zak?"

"Must also be seen to do a prison sentence. The public will expect it. They have seen him alongside Carmen at all four – sorry, at three live lottery draws. They will not accept that he's not part of any conspiracy we 'discover'. The shortest sentence for fraud is two years. We should be able to 'get both of you out' after 15 months. For that time, you will have to lie low. We can provide safe houses for each of you. Or if you prefer, you can be in the same one."

"What about our jobs?" asked Carmen. "Imprisonment for fraud would lose anyone their job. It just won't look right if I suddenly turn up at my desk again 15 months later."

Commander Levy stroked her chin as she thought about this.

"You're right. This fraud idea has only come up this afternoon, and it needs some details ironing out, but I am sure it will work. We should go away now and think about the employment angle and a few other things. But have I got your agreement in principle, Dr Fry?"

Carmen asked if she could sleep on it. This was agreed. She regretted it almost immediately as she had to run the gauntlet of paparazzi outside the TV Studio and again, to get into her own house, holding Zak's hand all the while to stop Sarah being separated from her. The 'no comment' Commander Levy had insisted was all they could say only incensed the media crews. These crews need not have worried. Commander Levy was already preparing a very newsworthy press statement detailing the elaborate hoax inflicted on the public in both the UK and the USA by these 'skilled crooks' who were 'motivated by greed and a desire to lead a celebrity lifestyle'.

****

London, UK, Late December 2026

Dave Adams read this statement in *The Guardian* the next day over his coffee in his study at home, surrounded by bookshelves and leather furniture. He immediately found it suspicious. He should have been pleased that they had been caught (and the statement he had already given to the press had said exactly that), but something felt wrong. After the third successful draw, Dave Adams had spent most of the next three days researching magic tricks of this type. He had found out how Stephen Frayne, better known as Dynamo, had done something similar back in 2012. And there was no way Frayne's method could have been used in two different countries and time zones, with so little time between them. He had found himself wondering about some of the other predictions and had had to look himself in the eye and admit that he was persuaded. Carmen and Sarah were right. Sarah *was* from the future.

When he thought about it, this was the only thing that could explain their sudden disappearance. The press statement, supposedly from the police, was short on detail, although it did say that Carmen had got the numbers right again. There was no explanation of how they had committed the 'fraud'. And why were they not in custody? Their assets had not been frozen. There was no mention of bail, so presumably they could skip the country whenever they wanted to with their ill-gotten gains. No, it did not add up. They must have reached some sort of agreement with the authorities to keep the truth quiet.

I haven't, though, he thought and immediately set about writing an article for *The Guardian* declaring them to be victims of a government conspiracy. The article stated that he had set them a challenge to prove the veracity of their claims and that they had successfully met that challenge. He now felt duty bound to protect them from Government censure. He headlined it, 'Where Is the Fraud?'

Dave Adams was a regular columnist for *The Guardian* and had built a reputation which had earned him the right almost to publish at will. He could not remember the last time an editor had rejected a piece from him, although he did occasionally have to shorten them. So he was completely unprepared for the rejection which came by text and email the same day he submitted the article. There it was, sandwiched between a request to launder $250,000 from somewhere in Nigeria and an invitation to part with all his personal details for a forthcoming copy of Global Who's Who, which he would, of course, be appearing in. This scam did not even carry a signature, purporting only to come from the 'Editor in Chief'.

The reason given for the rejection was lack of evidence. He was informed that although *The Guardian* regularly criticised the Government, it never did so without evidence of wrongdoing, preferably from several reliable sources. Reluctantly, he admitted to himself that the News Editor was right. All he had was a hunch. But he had given them loads of articles before with just as little evidence to back them up! That was why they used him. He was not an investigative journalist. He was a columnist. He made it clear in every article that he was voicing an opinion not presenting facts. Usually, the paper loved it. Under the cloak of free speech, they could print things they wanted to say but had too little evidence to prove. What was different this time? He could just imagine a phone call to the Editor from some faceless security official instructing the paper not to print any more about Carmen Fry and her research. The Government clearly wanted to kill the story. Why?

Dave Adams was at a loss as to what to do next until he remembered the police investigation into Barrymore Pegg's death. The officers involved with that might know what had happened to Zak and Carmen. Immediately, he phoned to make an appointment. Eventually he was put through to Detective Inspector Nigel Sandford. When they met in a cafe three days later, the police officer spent five minutes evading all questions. Adams was used to this. It was normal when the police were speaking to someone who worked for the papers, in whatever capacity. It did not matter that he was a respected columnist, working for a broadsheet and not some hack from a tabloid. He persevered because he sensed Sandford was just following protocol and was really dying to tell him something. Why else would he have agreed to meet?

His hunch proved correct. Suddenly Sandford blurted out:

"They've dropped the case. I can't believe it. Gave me some crap about targeting more winnable, less high-profile cases to improve statistics. Bollocks. I think they were leaned on by someone high up. Fry and Emblin are as guilty as sin, but don't quote me on that. Haven't they just been done for massive lottery fraud? Couple of crooks if ever I saw any. Of course, they murdered Pegg."

"Did you have any proof?"

"Just circumstantial stuff. But I am sure one of them would have confessed before long – it didn't take 'em long to own up to that Lottery scam, did it?"

"But why would your bosses want them to go free, if they're guilty?"

"Search me. Nobody liked Pegg. He made life difficult for all coppers with that undercover documentary series a few years back, 'proving' we beat up prisoners. Maybe that's why. Fry and Emblin have done us a favour, and now we're returning it."

****

“A less than widely appreciated implication of Einstein’s work is that special relativistic reality treats all time equally. Although the notion of ‘now’ plays a central role in our world view, relativity subverts our intuition…and declares ours an egalitarian universe in which every moment is as real as any other.”

Brian Greene, *Fabric of the Cosmos,* p131–2.

Birmingham, England, Late December 2028, Carmen's House

Without much enthusiasm, Carmen switched the Dictaphone she had given to Abigail Moran to Playback. She had taken to giving subjects who claimed to have lived past lives (and it was always past lives, never future ones) a Dictaphone or mobile to record what they could recall of their past life. It did not take long, usually, to rule out these subjects. She suspected that they knew they were lying and were motivated by the money or, more likely, by an acute need for attention. But she was not their therapist. She lied when rejecting them for the research programme, usually saying that she already had enough participants and asking them if they would like to be 'reserves', to let them down gently.

Carmen sat up quickly and replayed the introduction. This one was different. Abigail Moran said:

"The following is what I recorded when I became Private Harry Roberts last night. Sorry I didn't tell you when we met that I become Harry. I thought you might think I was just saying it to copy Zak and Sarah…"

A click, then, in a sing-songy but unmistakably tenor male voice, what sounded like fresh memories followed:

"Whilst asleep during the night, we were frequently awakened by rats running over us. When this happened too often for my liking, I would lie on my back and wait for a rat to linger on my legs, then violently heave my legs upwards, throwing the rat into the air. Occasionally, I would hear a grunt when the rat landed on a fellow victim."

"Then there was the trench foot. If you have never had trench foot described to you, I will explain. Your feet swell to two or three times their normal size and then go completely dead. You can stick a bayonet into them and not feel a thing. If you are lucky enough not to lose your feet and the swelling goes down, it is then that the most indescribable agony begins. I have heard men cry and scream with pain and many have had to have their feet and hands amputated. I was one of the lucky ones, but one more day in that trench and it may have been too late."

"The water in the trenches through which we waded was alive with a multitude of swimming frogs. Red slugs crawled up the side of the trenches and strange beetles with dangerous-looking horns wriggled along dry ledges and invaded the dugouts in search of the lice that infested them. There were times when we had to scrape the lice off our faces with the blunt edge of a penknife."

"Unsurprisingly, to get a 'cushy' one is all the old hands think about. A bloke in the Camerons wanted a cushy bad! Fed up and far from home he was. He puts his finger over the top and gets his trigger finger taken off and two more besides. 'I'm off to bonny Scotland!' he says laughing. But on the way down to the dressing station, he forgets to stoop low where an old sniper is working. He gets it through the head."

Carmen leapt from the chair, rejuvenated. Her many abortive attempts to find other reincarnaters seemed over. The interview with Abigail Moran had been promising, and the recording was an unqualified success. Such detail! How could anyone who hadn't been there, in the trenches, know about the rats stopping you sleeping? What it was like to have trench foot? The red slugs and the horned beetles that fed on the lice infesting the soldiers? And that poor guy deliberately getting his fingers blown off, only to get shot in the head on the way to the dressing station – that had the ring of truth about it.

She was already looking forward to her second interview with Abigail Moran. Even the timing seemed right. Sarah was going to be born about a hundred years after Zak. Abigail's former life as a soldier in World War One had begun just over a hundred years ago. Perhaps this was the natural period over which entanglement between lives occurred.

Excited and dying to tell Sarah and Zak about her success, she made herself a raspberry infusion (she did not need caffeine; she was already hyper) and brought up the internet on her PC. Light from the PC lit up Carmen's face. She was working late and had not got around to turning the light on. Experience had taught Carmen Fry that no matter how plausible a subject seemed, they had to be checked out. This part of her research was like journalism. (Quality journalism at any rate, not the stitch-up job the tabloids had done on her and Sarah when they had first found out that Sarah was from the future). Like conscientious reporters, Carmen had to be 100% sure of her sources. She googled 'memoirs from the trenches' and scanned the results. It wasn't a pleasant thing to be doing this behind Abigail's back, when Carmen already believed her; it was just one of those things that had to be done.

The first two hits revealed nothing surprising or interesting. Carmen mechanically clicked on *Memoirs from the Trenches – History Learning Site* expecting the same outcome. Almost immediately her heart sank. The first page was divided into boxes with different coloured backgrounds. The first box gave soldier R.L. Venables' account of rats waking him at night. The second box described Harry Roberts' relief that he personally had never experienced the agony of trench foot. By now, Carmen knew what would be in the third box – sure enough – red slugs and horned beetles feeding on lice from the soldiers in the dugouts. Of course, the fourth box had the story of the soldier from the Camerons' Regiment who had got himself killed on his way to get treated for getting his fingers blown off.

Carmen let out a deep sigh. It was insulting. The recording had copied word for word what was on the web site. How stupid did they think she was? They had not even bothered to change the regiment's or the soldiers' names! She made a mental note to reduce the amount of money she offered research subjects in her adverts. Better still, she would not offer any money at all, just expenses. That should keep out all the wackos.

There was a knock at the door. (Carmen despised doorbells.) Feeling discouraged, Carmen answered it and nearly shut it again immediately when she saw who it was. Karl Frideriks was standing there. For a moment, they just stared at each other in silence.

"I thought you were in jail for fraud. I tried to find you in jail."

"They let me out after two years, on parole."

With this, Carmen stood back from the door and allowed Karl in.

"It's late, Karl. How did you find me? I am supposed to be off the map. They couldn't re-employ me officially."

"I persuaded Professor Williamson to give me your address. I had to tell him I wanted to make it up to you for dropping you in it two years ago."

"And is that why you're here?"

"Yes, absolutely, Carmen, I – hey, can I have some coffee?"

"No. I'm fresh out of coffee."

"What's that you're drinking?"

"Coffee. Now just say what you have to say and leave."

"OK, but it's not easy for me, I—"

"Just spit it out."

"All right. I set you up, Carmen. I contacted the press deliberately. There were cuts. There was too much competition. I wanted you removed from the picture before the next funding round. You were an easy target because your research was so way out. Everyone thought so. But it got out of hand. I never meant for you to get into trouble over it, not beyond the confines of the university, anyway. I never meant for you to go to prison and lose your career over it, at least, as far as the public is concerned."

Carmen said nothing and just stared at Karl. It was what she had always suspected.

Karl continued, "I suppose you could say you have me to thank for the Department coming into all that money. None of us have to worry about funding for a few years."

"Karl, you jerk, you must know I didn't get any of that money."

"I'm not stupid, Carmen. I know the Department would not have come into £5 million overnight if there hadn't been some sort of deal. I know you have funding from somewhere."

"Too right, I do. My salary is £100K a year plus expenses. I have automatic tenure. And I never have to deliver a single paper nor take on a single student, for life. You could have had some of that, Karl, if you had worked *with* me, instead of against me, but you blew it. As you knew about Zak and Sarah, I would have invited you on to the team. But no, you had to do your own thing."

"You're right, though, I was there at the beginning. If it wasn't for me, you'd never have won all that lottery money." Karl tried to sound casual as he added, "What happened to that by the way?"

"Now I know why you're here. What happened to the money? Let's just say accommodation is never a problem for me as I travel the world looking for reincarnaters. I always have a place of my own to stay in. It's all tied up in property, and you'll never see a cent of it. Now get out."

She pushed him towards the door.

Once Karl had left, disappointed and still protesting, Carmen felt particularly pleased with herself for not letting on that she, Zak and Sarah had not been allowed to keep a single penny of the lottery money.

Birmingham, England, January 2027

It was cold and snowing outside, so Carmen and Zak were watching a romantic comedy together at Carmen's flat, while sharing a Hawaiian pizza. The film was not very good. Their minds kept wandering, and there was a weight of something unsaid between them. They each felt hurt by something the other one might have done, but because they only *might* have done it, each was reluctant to bring it up, in case they had got it wrong.

Zak was worried that Carmen might have only been interested in him because of his reincarnating behaviour, that she might have tracked him down on purpose and was only still with him because he was useful to her research.

Carmen had found a note from Sarah to Zak in his jeans pocket. It read: "Zak and Kate, sitting in a tree, K-I-S-S-I-N-G! 'I didn't know you had it in yer, boy', as your mom might say."

Carmen was surprised by her own reaction – she was jealous. This was out of step with previous similar situations. Twice before, Carmen had confided in a partner, once out of necessity, once by design, that she had other lovers. Both times it had caused her partner pain, but she had been able to alleviate this by encouraging them to do the same as she did and sleep with other people. A more open relationship had developed in both cases which Carmen had convinced herself was an improvement. Now she was not so sure. She wondered for the first time if the change she had brought about in both relationships might have contributed to their early ends.

On neither previous occasion had she felt jealous when her lover had heeded her advice and found an additional partner. So why now? Was she in love with Zak? It was important to know the answer to that because she might have put her relationship with him in jeopardy – if it were true that making those other lovers accept an open relationship had been the beginning of the end for them.

Neither Carmen nor Zak wanted to embarrass themselves nor start a fight. As the more troubled of the two, Zak found the courage to speak first.

"Carmen, I have to ask you something."

The tone of Zak's voice told Carmen it couldn't be good.

"What is it?" she asked.

"I need to know where I stand. Would we be in a relationship at all, if I weren't a reincarnater? I need to know if you knew about my medical history before we chatted online the night we met."

Carmen jumped up from the Isadore sofa and started pacing about.

"It's not important, Zak. The only thing that matters is that we are together now and that I love you now." It was a complete surprise to Carmen that she had said that last part. Now that she had said it, for the first time, she knew it was true. Zak appeared not to have noticed it.

"It is important to me. I need to know why we started going out in the first place. I—"

"That doesn't matter. All that matters, is how we feel now. I love you."

"So, you did know about me before, then?"

"Yes, yes, all right I did. I wasn't entirely honest with you to begin with because I needed to gain your trust. I couldn't just invite you to help with laboratory tests in our very first conversation; you would have said no."

"Why not? At least it would have been honest. You sound a bit like Commander Levy, you know."

"Now, that's not fair! I've just told you I love you. Twice. Does she do that?"

"I'm sorry, Carmen, I'm just feeling very insecure. First, I find out that you've had a thing behind my back with Karl, then there's the whole sex addiction thing, and now I find out you weren't physically attracted to me; it was my reincarnating behaviour which you were interested in from day one."

"You silly boy, I was, *am* physically attracted to you! And I'm not just saying it. I really do love you! OK, I knew about you as a potential subject for my research before I met you, but when I first saw you, you very quickly became a real man, a hot one, who I wanted to be with. And I can prove to you that I love you. Ask me how."

"How?"

"You've made me jealous, insanely jealous. That's never happened to me before. Now I need to know something."

"What?"

"Did you sleep with Sarah's friend, Kate, while in Sarah's body? I saw one of the notes Sarah left for you."

"No, I didn't. I was going to, but Sarah swapped me back before we got the chance. Anyway, it was you who told me to do that!"

"I know, I know. I think that was a mistake now. I take it back. I don't want you to sleep with other people—"

"But what about you? Am I supposed to turn a blind eye while you—"

"I was coming to that. No. You are *the* one. I know it now. I am prepared to give up relationships with others. I have a real incentive to do this now because I know that if you find other lovers, it makes me jealous, so that must be how you felt when I was with Karl. I'm sorry, Zak."

Carmen waited for Zak to say something, but he didn't.

"What do you say, Zak? Are you prepared to forgive me for not telling you at the beginning that I was looking for you to help with my research? If you do, I will forgive you for whatever you have done or are about to do with Kate from the future, so long as you don't tell me about it. Is that a deal?"

Zak looked reluctant and still concerned, but he said, "Yes."

"So, what do we do now?" asked Carmen.

Zak smiled at last. "I suppose we should rush out and get married or stay in and go to bed."

"I'll let you choose."

"Stay in and go to bed," said Zak, and suddenly all conversation was over as their mouths found other occupation.

Or rather, it was postponed because, feeling more committed to each other, Zak and Carmen stayed in bed all evening, mostly talking and getting to know each other, while sipping merlot.

Zak described the isolation he had felt throughout his life. No one had known how to deal with a schizophrenic – fear of the unknown had led to discrimination at every turn, he told Carmen. He'd had to fall back on his own resources and inner strength on more occasions than he would like to remember. Unfortunately, he could remember them all. He'd had no parental support and no sibling support to help him deal with his condition. In fact, his mum, brother and sister had all been very unsupportive.

Carmen contrasted her excellent parental support but still partly blamed her mum and dad for her sex addiction. "It's the name. What were they thinking of?" OK, so at primary school it was quite cool to be named after a famous operatic character, but kids grow up. In her late teens, it had been decidedly uncool. Guys had expected her to be more of a slut with them because of her name. Ironically, some other guys expected her to be frigid or prudish because of her high intelligence. She had decided to live up to her name to prove one set right and the other set wrong and had started sleeping with more guys. To her surprise, she had found that she enjoyed it a lot. But then she found that, once in a committed, stable relationship, she could not give up sex with other people. She had become deceitful, which she had found demeaning and which had led to isolation.

Zak said he had had to hide his condition from new friends. Carmen said she had hidden her addiction from everyone except her closest friends (which included her father). Each felt sorry for the other and recognised a kindred spirit. They felt that in choosing each other, they had made the right choice.

Zak opened up to Carmen about his insecurities. One was over his level of intelligence. "I've never had the opportunity to prove my intelligence," he explained. And without a complete education he felt stupid.

"Normal academic schools wouldn't have me. I had to start work at 16 when I couldn't find an FE Institution to take me. A full education gives you confidence. Social inclusion gives you confidence. I had neither of these."

Carmen reassured Zak about his intelligence. "Just look at the stand-up comedy you do," she said. "That requires intelligence and wit."

She repaid his frankness by telling him how she now realised she might have destroyed two previous relationships by insisting on them becoming open relationships.

They fell asleep in each other's arms at two in the morning.

After this glorious evening of passion and soul-searching, Carmen was inspired, against her nature, to commit to monogamy. And because she really did love Zak, she succeeded, with only very occasional lapses.

For Zak, almost once was enough, as far as playing away was concerned. He felt he had ticked that box. His feelings for Carmen ran so deep that he experienced no desire to sleep with other women, either as himself or when in Sarah's body. This was despite plenty of opportunity, especially in Sarah's world, and despite the twin twenty-second-century attractions of luminosity and hair which could be any colour of the rainbow or even all of them at once. Most of the time, his own hair when he was in Sarah's body was the colour of rape flowers in April, her favourite colour.

****

Snowdonia, Wales, UK, May 2036

Carmen was half-sitting, half-lying on the couch. Zak was in a similar position, opposite her on the surprisingly comfortable sofa bed. It was a beautiful day outside, with tulips and fuchsias resplendent in the garden and the equally resplendent snow-capped Cader Idris in the background. They hardly noticed any of it. The babies were both asleep. It was a rare thing for the boys to sleep at the same time, so it was a welcome, peaceful moment for both parents, but they were too exhausted to do anything with it, having been up half the night on feeding and nappy-changing duties. There was no conversation between them; they just stared blankly into space.

Carmen noticed that Zak had started crying, and her first thought was, *Don't wake the twins,* especially as he had set Psycho off. She could hear the dog barking in the next room. Then she realised that it was Sarah who was upset and not Zak.

"What's the matter Sarah? What has upset you?"

It was not the first time Carmen had seen Sarah upset, but she had never seen her *this* upset before. Sarah had not even noticed the sleeping baby boys, Stephen and James.

"I shouldn't have done it," sobbed Sarah. "I should never have looked it up. I was curious, that's all. I am so annoyed with myself, that's why we transferred."

Sarah looked even more concerned as she thought of Zak, back in her apartment.

"It's OK, he won't see it," she said suddenly to herself, relaxing a little. "I switched off the light pen just as I was transferring."

"Won't see what?" Now there was real concern in Carmen's voice.

"I can't tell you, Carmen. It's too upsetting. I've already said too much."

Carmen's mind was racing. Something 'too upsetting' about Zak, which Zak must not see, and which Sarah should not have looked up. Her eyes found Zak's dear eyes and she saw the answer there.

"He's going to die, isn't he?"

Sarah said nothing. She got up and walked to the window to hide Zak's face from Carmen. This was too difficult. She wanted to swap back now, even tried to, but her mind was a mess, and she could not do it. Carmen broke the silence.

"Sarah, tell me you haven't looked up when Zak dies. Please. You promised me you would never do that. You promised!"

Sarah turned slowly. Tears were streaming down Zak's face as she said very quietly, "I'm sorry," and tried to hug Carmen, but Carmen pushed her away.

Sarah pleaded. "Nothing's changed. I don't have to tell you when. I—"

"Everything has changed! Of course, you have to tell me."

Stephen woke briefly, then fell asleep again. Carmen realised she had been raising her voice and made a conscious effort to speak more softly.

"Can't you see? It's bloody obvious he's not going to make old bones or you wouldn't be so upset. I need to know how long he's got."

"Why do you need to know? Surely it will be easier if you don't know exactly when—"

"Sarah, if Zak is going to die young, I need to know how long I have with him. I need to make sure the boys spend as much time with him as they can. Please tell me."

At first, Sarah resisted, but it was a persuasive argument, especially after Carmen had repeated it a few times. Sarah succumbed, needing to share the pain with someone, and told Carmen. Carmen had a figure in her head for the number of years she had left with Zak, but the truth was even less – a lot less. It hit her hard and she cried out involuntarily, waking the babies:

"To lose both of you so young, it's too cruel!"

As soon as she had said it, she knew it had been a mistake. She looked up quickly and registered the new expression of shock on Zak's face.

"Oh, my God, you don't know, do you?"

Sarah sat down gingerly and put Zak's face in his hands before speaking.

"What do you mean, 'lose both of us so young'?"

Carmen tried to cover her tracks. "It's nothing, Sarah, really. I'm just upset by the news about Zak. I mean, once he's gone, I won't be able to see you anymore, will I? So you'll be 'lost' to me too."

"Oh, no, no, no, that's not what you meant. You knew you had said something you shouldn't have. You knew right away! You have to be honest with me now, Carmen, especially after I've just done the same for you!"

Carmen did not know what to do. She picked up the crying Stephen and fed him. James was also crying. It was hard to think. She felt less annoyed with Sarah, now that she had made the same mistake herself. Didn't the same logic apply? Didn't Sarah also have a right to know how long she had left? She was still deciding what to do when Sarah said:

"It's my 29th birthday, isn't it?"

Carmen did not get the 'how the hell did you know that?' expression off her face fast enough.

"I have nightmares about that day," Sarah continued, "and hallucinations. But how do you know? It's way into the future for you. It doesn't make any sense."

Carmen put the pacified Stephen down and picked up James, who stopped crying immediately. She put him down again, unfed for now, so she could take both Zak's hands in hers.

"It does make sense, Sarah, Darling. How old are you now?"

"Twenty-five."

"Zak has had some unplanned swaps with an older version of you. He's seen it happen."

"Seen what happen?"

"I'm not going to tell you that. And I don't want to know what happens to Zak. We know how long you each have now. That's enough."

They hugged for a long time. Carmen looked up and said, really trying to reassure herself more than Sarah:

"We have done the right thing, telling each other, haven't we? It is better to know, isn't it?"

"Oh, yes, of course it's better to know," replied Sarah. "We can plan now."

There was a pause as they looked into each other's eyes. They both said at the same time, "Don't tell Zak!"

As she said this, Sarah got annoyed with herself again for telling Carmen about Zak and so finding out about her own early death. Zak arrived back in his own body to find Carmen inconsolably sad.

"Don't tell me what?" he said, finding himself back on the sofa bed.

"That I miss you so much every time you're away from me because I never know when, or even if, you'll be coming back. I love you, Zak Emblin. I love you."

"Where did that come from?" said Zak, smiling and hugging Carmen. "I love you too."

This time there was enough truth and emotion in what she had said for Carmen to cover her tracks successfully.

****

“Coleman and De Lucia found that, much as is the case for a single particle, a universe can do what classical physics forbids: it can jitter its way – it can quantum tunnel – through the barrier.”

Brian Greene, *The Hidden Reality,* p158.

****

Gwynedd, Wales, May 2039

Carmen brought up her emails and got a shock. Her 'boss' Commander Levy wanted a meeting.

This could only be bad news. Carmen had spoken with Levy just three times in the 13 years since the US Government had started funding her research. At the last two meetings, she had been able to sound optimistic because the sample of subjects interviewed had still been quite small, so it was not that surprising that no more 'reincarnaters' had come to light. This time she was in deep trouble. Thirteen years, over 1,800 candidates interviewed and researched, and nothing to show for it.

Except a PhD which she did not deserve as it was based on a single case study. Carmen knew that her PhD would never have been granted but for American Government money oiling the wheels of other research programmes in return for it. She particularly remembered the look on Professor Cummings's face at the viva as they were congratulating her. When no one else could hear, he had almost whispered to her:

"I'm giving you this doctoral thesis but you and I both know that you don't deserve it. Who are you? How did a young, skinny girl like you get so powerful that a government minister visits me at Oxford and calls in a favour?"

It was a bad time for Carmen to be flying to Washington. Zak had just lost his mother. The twins were only three years old, and Rachel had recently returned to Nottingham. She hated leaving them. Needs must. As she packed for her interview with Levy in Washington, she felt resentful for being dragged away from her family, but also guilty because she had not found any more reincarnaters yet. Almost as an afterthought, she packed the light pen.

****

The Pentagon, Washington, USA, May 2039

When you see it for the first time, The Pentagon is a very imposing building. She knew about the iconic shape, of course, but Carmen was unprepared for the scale of it. It was a lot bigger than she had imagined. The entrance lobby alone was the size of a railway station concourse. The entire floor was polished marble. How expensive must that have been?

On the flight over, Carmen had worried about not being in uniform and if this would make her stand out. It did. She felt naked among all the uniformed personnel hurrying this way and that. At home in Wales, she could put to the back of her mind that her research had military backing, something she had never been comfortable with. Standing here in this lobby, wondering which way to go, she could not escape it. This was going to be a tough interview.

Commander Levy showed Carmen into her office very warmly, offered coffee and asked about her family. For some reason, Carmen did not find this reassuring. She looked around Levy's desk and office and saw no framed family photos, nothing personal at all, only portraits of famous generals. The request seemed perfunctory to Carmen. A moment later she was proved right in this assumption as Eleanor Levy got straight to the point.

"Thirteen years, Doctor Fry, and only one 'proven' case of reincarnation. This puts us in a difficult position. We had hoped for more, much more."

It dawned on Carmen that Levy might be about to pull the plug on the whole project. She had expected a new, tighter deadline but not unemployment. It was time to plead her case.

"We have tried, Commander. Over 1,800 candidates have been interviewed. At first, we only considered 'reincarnaters', but they all turned out to be bogus or delusional. We widened the net and included schizophrenics from all over the globe, who exhibited similar symptoms to Zak Emblin. So far, we have drawn a blank. But we press on. I mean the Zak and Sarah case – that tells us that what we are looking for is out there somewhere. I—"

"I disagree."

"What?"

"The situation is worse than you know, Doctor Fry. To begin with, the real total of candidates interviewed is nearer 15,000. We took a lead from your programme and did some of our own field work – also including schizophrenics. We drew a blank too."

"But that won't work. I can't include your case studies. The questions must be the same or the results are skewed. It's—"

"They were the same. We used your questionnaire." Commander Levy smiled as she said this.

"How did you get—"

"Remember your annual electrical equipment safety checks?"

"Yes. What about them?"

"Bugs and cameras being installed, replaced."

Carmen was shocked but not surprised.

"Why the subterfuge? Why didn't you just ask me?"

Sitting on the edge of her desk now, Levy opened her arms in a placatory gesture. "I'm not the unreasonable woman you take me for, Doctor Fry. We wanted you to feel in control of your own project. If I had asked you, you might have said no. It was easier for everyone this way."

Carmen was speechless. She felt angry and violated but she needed this woman's funding to continue her research.

"So, what do we do now?" asked Levy, after Carmen had been silent for a while. "17,000 interviews, no hits. This cannot go on. We now doubt the veracity of the Sarah Templeman case. We have brought you here to tell you that we are going to pull in Zak Emblin – for tests. To find out once and for all how he has fooled everyone. Even that information might have some military benefits which will mean we have not been completely wasting our time. Then we will terminate the project. You should start informing your staff now—"

"Wait! Don't do this. I can prove Sarah is real." In desperation, Carmen pulled out the light pen.

"Zak brought this light pen back from the future." She handed it to Commander Levy, who immediately looked fascinated, turning it in her hand.

"Before I show you what it can do, I need an assurance from you that this interview is not being recorded."

Eleanor Levy looked offended.

"Of course not. This is an informal chat between just you and me, a chance for me to forewarn you the project is closing before you get the official letter. Why would I record it?"

"OK, in that case, you will find on here hologram footage of—" Carmen hesitated. "You know what? Just watch this."

She flipped open the Smart Slimline, and a hologram bubbled out of herself, looking about 60, talking to Zelda and a young Sarah, about five. The voice coming from Sarah's mouth was a boy's of about the same age. It had an English accent. Towards the end, Dr Fry talked about a light pen and the boy's voice got upset, but there was no visual image for this part.

They both sat back in their leather chairs, thinking. It was Carmen who broke the silence.

"Put it under a microscope. You'll find some micro buttons to press, clearly labelled. This will reveal my DNA, that of Sarah Templeman, and that of her mother, Zelda Templeman, all from the year 2121."

Carmen could see that Levy was fascinated and itching to get a closer look at the light pen with the help of her team of experts, but she was trying to hide this.

"Why haven't you shown us this before?" she asked, sounding annoyed.

Now there was a good question. Carmen herself did not know the answer. It had just seemed the right thing to do, to sit on it until she absolutely needed it, as a sort of insurance.

"You haven't questioned the integrity of my research before," is what she said.

"Surely you realised the implications this item has?" snapped Commander Levy. "If what you say about it is true, we're looking at an object which has been transported backwards through time. Not to mention the advanced technology of the 'light pen' itself. Didn't it occur to you that we might have an interest in this? It has clear military potential."

"That's what worried me. In any event, we made an agreement to try and find you another reincarnater, nothing more. That is all we are contracted to do. I had no obligation to show you this light pen."

If Levy's anger moments before had been feigned, now it was totally genuine. She thumped the table and made Carmen jump.

"May I remind you, 'Doctor' Fry, that the US Government is funding your project. You have an interest in US security. How *dare* you criticise our leaders' motives! Who do you think pays for all those trips around the world you go on – yes, I know – trips to interview the odd one or two reincarnaters who always turn out to be frauds or deluded?"

Carmen held up her hands in apology. "You're saying don't bite the hand that feeds me. I get that."

"Damn right, I am. And I resent your sarcasm. Show some respect, woman! If it were up to me, you would be singing *The Star-Spangled Banner* and saluting the US national flag every morning. You academics always think you're so superior. Don't you realise the special treatment you're getting, the compromises we've made?"

"What do you mean?"

"I mean that we could have demanded more militarily sensitive information from the future from your lover, Sarah – yes, we know. We haven't done that because we respected your desire to keep her out of danger, so we concentrated on the search for new reincarnaters."

"I didn't realise."

"Well, now you do. Remember, Doctor Fry, respect is a two-way street. Right now, I feel a need to contact Sarah directly and give her new instructions."

It was Carmen's turn to get angry.

"She won't help you. She's more anti-military than I am, more left wing."

"Oh, you think so?"

"I know so. What about her attack on the tabloid newspapers when they stitched us up back in 2026?"

"What about the direct action she took against Sean Miller in the same year? Any marine would have been proud of it."

Carmen realised that Commander Levy had a point.

"Just leave her out of it, OK. Except for what you get through me and Zak."

There was an awkward silence.

"I will agree to that, Doctor Fry, for now. So long as this" – she held up the light pen – "is as good as you say it is. If not, Sarah's going to have to get a lot more active."

With this, Commander Levy stormed out of the room, taking the light pen with her. She did not say goodbye or even look back. Carmen was not sure if she was free to leave until a corporal came in and announced coldly that the interview was over.

Carmen had mixed feelings. On the plus side, she had saved the project and, more importantly, prevented Zak from being brought over for 'tests' whatever that meant, she dreaded to think. On the minus side, she no longer had the light pen. Still, it had served its purpose. And she had had the foresight to make a copy of the recordings from it, which was safe back in her lab. It would be a much more relaxed flight back to England than it was coming.

****

The Pentagon, Washington, USA, June 2039

To Carmen's surprise, Zak was summoned to Washington anyway. She was outraged.

"Levy promised me they wouldn't call you for tests," she told Zak, and immediately called Commander Levy for an explanation.

"Calm down, Doctor Fry; I was expecting you to call."

Levy explained that it was really Sarah she wanted to interview.

"What about your promise to me to leave Sarah out of the project, except for what you get through me?"

"I'm afraid I'm going to have to revisit that promise. Don't worry, I just didn't want to distract you from the search for more reincarnaters. It's just nickel-and-dime stuff we want from Sarah – you know, major rival economies' Gross Domestic Product, investment tips, stuff like that. I could have emailed the request to you, but I thought that Sarah might enjoy the trip."

Carmen was not happy about it, but Zak and Sarah were keen to go. There was nothing she could do. Two days later, Sarah was on the plane, feeling insecure about trusting her life to such an antiquated flying machine as a 747. *It should be in a museum.*

Carmen had been right to be worried. After greeting Sarah obsequiously and following closely her instructions for making a twenty-second-century style latte, Levy hit Sarah with a question:

"How would you like to be responsible for Carmen losing her entire funding? That's the way things are heading. Carmen has shown me conclusive proof that you do have access to the future. So why have we had so little useful information from you for the past 13 years? We need more from you, Sarah."

"What do you mean, conclusive proof?"

"A light pen."

"Ah, I see. So, you don't want these?" interrupted Sarah, holding up the list of mainly economic forecasts and investment tips for the next 15 years which she had been asked to provide by Levy's secretary, just a few days' earlier.

"Yes, I, I mean we, do," replied Levy, looking embarrassed. "But what I really want you to concentrate on is names of future leaders, their political affiliations, and weapons development technology in nations which are a threat to us. We need to know what the Chinese, Russians, Arabs and North Koreans are working on."

"What? How am I supposed to get access to that? It's all classified! And what makes you think I'd agree to provide you with militarily sensitive information anyway?"

"Why wouldn't you, to help your own country's defence interests? It's every American's God-given duty."

"And if I refuse?"

"If you refuse, the plug gets pulled on your dear 'Carmy's' project. I've already warned her." Commander Levy pressed a button and Sarah was treated to selected parts of her recent interview with Carmen, the one she had promised Carmen she was not recording.

"You have until next week to think about it. I am depending on you to come through for us, Sarah. Carmen is convinced you won't help me. As you have just heard, she thinks you're 'anti-military'. I've seen the marine in you, and I know better. I also know how much she means to you and that without the Reincarnation Project, her life means nothing. Now do the right thing, Sarah."

****

On the plane on the way back to the UK, Sarah did not know what to do. What Levy was asking of her seemed impossible. Experienced international spies would struggle. Jason fucking Bourne would struggle. Yet she did not want Carmen to lose the project. Levy was right; it did mean everything to Carmen. It was her life's work. God, what an infuriating woman that Commander Levy was!

Zak suddenly found himself on a 747 flying across the Atlantic. He checked the date and time and the direction the plane was headed and realised what must have happened.

"It didn't go so well with Commander Levy, then?" he wrote on the notepad he always carried with him and left it half-sticking out of his jeans pocket. Then he took a swig of Sarah's wine and thought about how she had been the lucky one who had got the expenses-paid, First Class flight across the Atlantic. Thinking about losing that coin toss, supervised by Carmen, was just annoying enough to get Sarah back to read his question and send him back to toddler bathing.

Sarah wrote a reply:

"Gross, Zak! Stephen just splashed soapy water all over me, I mean us. What am I gonna do? About Levy, I mean, not the water. She wants me to do all this dangerous espionage stuff. If I don't, the plug gets pulled on Carmen's research. Help me think of a way out, Zak, please, and don't tell Carmen."

She went on to describe the interview with Levy in some detail, on the pad Zak had left for her. He was always so much better prepared for swaps than she was. How annoying!

Finding himself back on the plane, Zak read Sarah's note and worried about how Carmen would cope if she lost her job. She wouldn't. But then it was not exactly ideal working for a bully like Levy either. "That's it!" said Zak out loud, getting some surprised looks from fellow passengers.

Levy was a classic bully, and Zak realised that he knew how to deal with bullies. His childhood had prepared him for it. He recalled how he had gained revenge on the much older Owen Flynn when only eight himself. You had to outsmart bullies, stay one step ahead. A plan started to form in his mind, which he outlined in a note to Sarah. When he had finished writing, he reached for Sarah's rather tasty wine, a Rioja, he suspected, only to find that she had drunk it all. This annoyed him sufficiently to put him back on toddler duty.

Sarah was happy to be relieved of childcare responsibilities and even happier when she read Zak's note. Straight away she knew it would work. It would take a lot of time and dedication, but it was doable. And it was a plan which would keep Levy off her back for years to come and allow Zak and Carmen to sleep easily at night. "Be one step ahead," Zak had written, "that is how you outsmart bullies." Looking out of the window at the clouds, she pondered this. With Zak's help, she realised that coming from the future, she was, by definition, one step ahead. Levy would have no way of knowing if the information she would be provided with were true or not. The Commander would get the information she craved. And just enough of it would be accurate to avoid arousing suspicion. But in every significant regard, in all the details about rival major economies' weapons research programmes for decades into the future, not a single byte of data would be true. It would take a lot of research and attention to detail to work, but she knew that she could do it. The flight back to the UK suddenly felt a lot more comfortable. She asked the steward for some more of that delightful red wine.

Zak watched his beautiful wife bathing his beautiful twin boys. Losing someone made you appreciate the close ones around you. Psycho forced herself into the already crowded blue bathroom and barked six times. And six times more.

"How did it go with Commander Levy?" Carmen asked Sarah. "I know it's you in there because the dog just barked the signal."

Sarah looked down at the happy, splashy boys in the bath and said:

"Not good. I'd like to discuss it on the plane now, with Zak."

"You'll be in and out then, for a while, so I won't ask you to entertain James while I wash Stephen's hair."

"No problem, I can still do it," said Sarah and bent down to show James his little toy boat floating past. James chose this moment to raise both his hands high and bring them down hard on the surface of the water, thoroughly drenching Sarah, who started spluttering, her eyes closed. Everyone else was laughing so Sarah felt obliged to join in, but what she said was:

"I don't know how you cope, Carmen. I couldn't do it. Give me cats, any time."

"Oh, come off it, Sarah, I've seen you with the boys a few times now. You love children. I think the cats you've owned are just baby substitutes."

"Yes," agreed Sarah, to Carmen's surprise, "excellent baby substitutes," and found herself back on the 747, crossing the Atlantic.

****

"Immortality like this is about as useful as sunscreen on a submarine."

– Elisabeth Marx, *All's Fair in Vanity's War.*

The Pentagon, Washington, USA, June 2039

Commander Levy was sitting in her intimidating office watching the holograms from Carmen's light pen, over and over. With her were a team of three hand-picked advisors, all smartly dressed and nervous, people she could trust to keep the discussion secret. One was in military uniform. They heard:

"Tell him he can't go home. Ever. Quickly, tell him now!"

"Zak, you must stay in this new world now. Forever. You can't go home. You can never go home." Zelda's last words were drowned in her own sobs. The recording ended.

Commander Levy leaned back and looked around the table, waiting for comments. Getting none, she added:

"I can tell you that we've had the voice analysed. It's Zak Emblin's. We've also had the hair samples analysed. They do not match Emblin. In fact, they don't match anyone living. The air quality they have been exposed to is considerably worse than ours. It is consistent with what ours might be if pollution continues at the current rate for the next hundred years. Fry says the air quality is poor in Sarah's city in the twenty-second century. Could these be a match for Sarah Templeman and her mother? Yes, they could. We certainly can't rule it out. What do you think, gentlemen?" Levy asked the room.

One of the yes-men enthused about the light pen and its possible future uses and another one joined in, making the same points and wishing he had spoken first. His boss interrupted him.

"Yes, yes, of course," said Eleanor Levy, irritated. "Of course, that's true. But you're not seeing the bigger picture, Sergeant Howard, gentlemen. This part is much more significant. Listen again, carefully."

She played again the part of the recording where Carmen told Zelda about the Eternity and Mortality Programmes. When her subordinates were still looking confused, she explained:

"Don't you see? Now we know which direction to go in. We can get Sarah Templeman to fill in details, but the detail is not that important. We already know enough. We can start planning now. First, we prioritise funding on research into isolating the ageing gene. Then we take charge of the first human trials. Later, it will be someone's responsibility to decide, *really decide*, who gets access to the treatment, who lives, who dies. Think of it. That's where I—" Commander Levy quickly corrected herself, "That's where we come in, gentlemen."

"Shouldn't we get Presidential approval first?" asked Sergeant Howard, bravely.

"Where's your vision, Tom? You're a good committee man, but I've always said you lack vision."

Stern generals looking down from portraits all around the room seemed to share Commander Levy's disapproval and added to Sergeant Tom Howard's humiliation. H looked down at his papers.

"Of course, we'll have Presidential approval," said Commander Levy, "from whoever's in the White House. Presidents come and go. The longest they are ever in office is eight years, and they spend the first four trying to get re-elected! No, this is a long-term project which requires continuity of funding and management. It cannot be left to politicians. The Defence Department must take it on. *We* must take it on. As far as Washington is concerned, we just need to emphasise how beneficial for everyone a cure for ageing will be. They'll buy it, it's a natural vote winner. 'Vote for me and you'll live forever', who couldn't resist that?"

"What about the Mortality Programme?" asked the only man who had not yet spoken. Levy's reaction made him pleased that he had found the courage to speak.

"Good question, Richard, and I thought you were asleep. We play it down, at least to begin with. Pretend ignorance, maybe. Yes, that should do it. We will volunteer to head up a Working Party looking into the implications for the future of the Eternity Programme. Of course, everyone around this table knows where it inevitably leads – to the Mortality Programme; we have seen the light pen recording. Let's make sure it stays that way, stays in this room, just us four, at least until the Eternity Programme is well-established. Give me six months to get it set up."

The yes-men all nodded, as yes-men do. Commander Levy stood and offered handshakes all around.

"One last thing, gentlemen. If any of this discussion ever gets out, it will have the most severe consequences for whoever leaks it. In the interests of national security, it will mean retirement, and I do not mean the kind that comes with a pension. Is that understood?"

"Yes," said the yes-men.

****

Wales, UK, April 2040

Carmen was online, sitting in the kitchen. She liked to sit there because she could see the tits and finches, and occasional yellowhammers, on the bird feeders just outside the back door. Zak was outside chatting with the architects about the plans he wanted drawn up for the double garage. He, Carmen and Rachel had decided to turn it into a small self-contained bungalow for Rachel to move into. Rachel herself was with Stephen and James in the lounge, showing them pictures of Sugar, the horse she had ridden that morning at the pony-trekking centre at Coed y Brenin, ten miles away, and promising to take them next time.

Carmen had a little time to herself and used it to catch up on the news. She had set up a feed to notify her of any developments in research into ageing. She had decided to do this after watching all the recordings from the light pen again once she had come back from Washington the previous year. She had been a little concerned about what exactly she might have handed over to the dangerous and unscrupulous woman who funded her research. For the first time in six months, an article popped up on the left-hand side of her screen. She clicked on it. It was from yesterday's *Washington Post*. Carmen read:

In addition to her other roles, Commander Eleanor Levy of the Defence Department has been given the responsibility, by the Senate, of leading a United Nations and US Government funded research programme into ageing and population control. Its brief is to work with other similar bodies from UN Security Council countries to identify the genetic process behind ageing, with a view to developing a cure for this 'disease'. The remit also includes a requirement to investigate the implications developing such a cure might have on population growth, to recommend solutions and to develop an Action Plan. Commander Levy is to have overall control over finances and staff recruitment to the programme which, according to our source, will have national security status.

It begins, thought Carmen.

Wales, UK, August 2047

Zak was talking to Rachel in the kitchen, sharing tea over the same old oak table Carmen had bought at an auction all those years ago in Birmingham. Carmen herself was away at a conference in Prague, where she had been invited to speak. Zak and Rachel had had to put a lot of pressure on her to go. Ever since New Year, she had been unusually clingy, not wanting to let Zak and the boys out of her sight. She had not agreed to go at all until Zak had promised to stay at home, on the hill, and not go down into Barmouth for anything, for the whole weekend. She had been phoning every three hours.

The boys were outside, shooting water at each other from colourful, plastic water pistols shaped like machine guns. They had already got him twice and Rachel once, but the adults were now wise to their tactic of ringing the doorbell and popping up to shoot them when they answered it. They had a plan.

Rachel and Zak were busy thanking each other while they dunked home-made cookies in tea. *The cookies were surprisingly good*, thought Zak, considering Stephen and James had made them under Rachel's and his supervision. He just wished they could have made them all the same shape, but they didn't have a template. Rachel was thanking Zak for introducing her to this lovely part of the country. How could she not have fallen in love with it and wanted to spend more time here?

Zak was thanking Rachel for taking on the role of 'nanny' and moving into the self-contained bungalow they had converted from the old double garage.

"It's been a godsend to us, particularly since Martin became too ill to look after them whenever I swapped with Sarah. And when Martin died this year, we were in no fit state to—"

"I know, I know. It's OK, Zak. I love it here. It took me a while to find my own pony and stables not too far from here, but I love it now. And don't forget, you are paying me, you know."

"Are we, really?" asked Zak in mock surprise. "I'll have to have words with Carmen about that."

They both smiled. The doorbell sounded. Rachel and Zak nodded conspiratorially to each other, and Zak picked up a newly loaded water pistol as he ran to the door. He swung open the door with his left hand, while firing with his right, shouting, "Gotcha!"

"No, I got you!" replied Skunk, as he looked down momentarily at his wet chest before unleashing seven bullets into Zak's head and body.

"That's for the past 20 years," he said.

He walked calmly to the bottom of the field below the house, where he turned the gun on himself.

Hearing the gunshots, the boys came running to find Rachel cradling Daddy's head and getting covered in his blood, her face contorted in a silent scream. So much blood. James fainted. Stephen calmly asked Rachel:

"If we could get all this blood back into Daddy, would he be all right again?" It was the last thing he said for months.

****

Birmingham, England, 2047, One Day Earlier

Skunk Phillips was sitting in his caravan, trying desperately to stop his old TV buffering during the Blues' game. Life was shit and he'd had enough. Nothing had been right since he'd lost Sean – since Sean had dumped him. Yes, dumped him, after all his loyal service! Said he kept reminding him of all the terrible things they had done together. Said they had to separate so they couldn't accidentally lead their old employers to each other; that way they would only end up dead, Sean had said. But it wasn't the real Sean who had said those things. Sean had never been the same since that future-bitch had taken his balls away.

Skunk didn't know what to do after that. Gangs was all he had ever known. Sean's gang was *his* gang. You couldn't change that, no more than you could change your football team. He, Skunk, was a Blues supporter and would be till the day he died. How could he ever become a Villan, an Aston Villa fan? So although he'd tried over the years, he just didn't fit in to any other gang.

They would always give him the shit jobs, like beating up young, trafficked women who didn't want to become prostitutes. They were all whores, he'd been told, but some of them had just been kids. No, he preferred drugs. You beat up a client if he didn't pay. That was fair. Even most of the clients thought it was fair. The slave trade just made him feel bad. And he didn't want to feel bad anymore.

He stood up quickly, picked up his bags and walked to the local station. He took a local train to New St Station in the City Centre and slept overnight on the platform before taking the early train to Barmouth. Something had to be done.

****

The Pentagon, Washington, USA, September 2047

Dr Carmen Fry had been summoned to the Pentagon for the first time in eight years, and she had a good idea why. She had been useful to Commander Levy in two ways: as the possible route to other reincarnaters (although she had searched in vain so far), and as the friend of Zak Emblin and Sarah Templeman, who possessed the world's only known shared soul. With Zak gone, there was no longer any access to Sarah and the information she could provide from the future. The Reincarnation Project was dead, unless she could find alternative funding.

To be honest, she did not really care. She was hurting too much and kept going only for the sake of her two 12-year-olds who had taken the loss of their father very badly, particularly Stephen. He said nothing and stared at the wall all the time. They were both receiving counselling, of course, as their father's death had been a violent one.

She nearly had not come at all, but Rachel had persuaded her. "It will give you time to yourself, to grieve. You've been putting on a brave face for Stephen and James. You need a break from that," she had said.

Carmen's thought process was interrupted by a secretary's voice inviting her into Commander Levy's Office.

"I am sorry for your loss," said Commander Levy, shaking her hand and gesturing for Carmen to sit down. "Why didn't you warn us about Skunk Phillips? We could have watched him."

"I know. I will never forgive myself. I underestimated him, just did not see him as a threat. To be honest, I'd completely forgotten about him."

Commander Levy shook her head in sympathy.

"Let me tell you why we've asked you here."

"It's OK, there's no need to explain. I can see the project has to stop, now that Zak is gone."

"No, no, that's not it, Doctor Fry. Your work trying to find new reincarnaters is even more important to us now that we have lost contact with the only ones we knew about, Sarah Templeman and your late husband. No, I want to talk to you about the Eternity Programme. I want you to join the team."

"The Eternity Programme? Wait, how do you know about that name?"

"You gave me the light pen, remember? It has been very, very, useful to us. And we have you to thank for that. Co-opting you on to the Management Team of the Eternity Programme is our way of rewarding you for that help."

"Sorry, my brain is a bit slow. I can't stop thinking about Zak and Sarah; I miss them so much. Exactly how does joining the Eternity Programme Management Team reward me?"

"Everyone involved in running the project is guaranteed treatment once it has been successfully trialled on humans. You won't die, Doctor Fry."

"But surely, you won't reach that point for decades?"

Eleanor Levy could not resist smiling. "You need to meet Methuselah."

She turned and produced a rodent cage from a cardboard box. She put her hand in and picked out a black and white rat.

"As you know, rats normally live for two years. He's very lively. Feel how lively he is."

Carmen took the rat from her.

"He is six. It has worked on pigs, too. Needs a daily tablet, but it works."

"How did you get this far so quickly?" asked Carmen, handing back the rat.

"Once your light pen showed us it was possible, we threw money at the research. Closed a few other programmes to make it work. Simple as that. What do you say, are you in?"

Carmen's conscience was troubling her. At a gut level, she felt she should say no. And immortality was the last thing she wanted, missing Sarah and Zak as she did. But her maternal instinct was pushing her in a different direction. From the recordings on the light pen, she knew that not everyone would get access to treatment under the Eternity Programme. If she wanted to make sure that her boys were included, then surely it would be better to be on the inside. Who knows, she might even be able to exert some influence when it came to decisions about which people lived on. Left up to Eleanor Levy, the chosen ones would probably all be soldiers. She said yes.

****

Washington DC, USA, August 2077

Carmen was in Washington doing something she had been putting off doing for the past two years. Stephen and his girlfriend, Lauren, who he had met years ago at medical school and recently re-discovered on Facetime, had travelled with her. So it was part family holiday, to see New York, and part business trip.

She arrived on foot at the FEMA offices, having walked the last ten minutes from L'Enfant Plaza Metro station, for an appointment with Fernando Salgado, Head of the Disaster Prevention Unit. Since Eleanor Levy's death, Carmen had come to realise that, tyrant though she had been, she had also been a useful contact to have. She was not expecting the coming interview to go as smoothly as it would have done had Levy set it up.

She was right. Salgado just did not believe her when she tried to warn him of the impending disaster facing Louisiana, Alabama and Mississippi in about seven years' time.

"Why should I take your word for it, that the water levels will rise that much, when I have my own team of experts saying they won't."

"Because I have had access to data from the future, as you will know if you've read the files on the Reincarnation Project which I sent you."

Fernando Salgado stretched his long legs out in front of him and leant back in his chair, clutching a mug with hot coffee in it. Carmen noted that she had not been offered any.

"Yes, the Reincarnation Project, I did read that. Headed up by the late Commander Levy, wasn't it, the woman who, craving immortality, treated herself first in the human trials of the Eternity Programme and ended up dying anyway of a stroke?"

"That's right, although it was I who managed the project from day to day."

Salgado leaned forwards. "I'm not supposed to tell you this, but I don't want you to embarrass yourself in front of any other Government officials. I have it on authority from a long-standing friend in the Defence Department that Eleanor Levy was under internal surveillance for the last few years of her life. Since her death, she has been discredited as both corrupt and power-hungry. Everyone who worked with her will come under scrutiny, including you. You might be safe because of your involvement in the Eternity Programme which has produced real and startling results in its first few decades. But the Reincarnation Project looks less good for you. It has been running for decades with nothing to show for it except one, rather dubious, case. There is suspicion now that it was essentially a money-making scam, set up by Levy to line her own pockets."

"I can't speak for Commander Levy's personal morality, Mr Salgado. I avoided her company as much as possible because I did not like the woman, but I can tell you that it was I, and not Eleanor Levy, who set up the Reincarnation Project. And I can vouch for Sarah Templeman. She really exists – I mean will exist. I have met her and spoken with her on many occasions. That is why we need to take seriously what she said about the 2084 natural disaster, which for her had already happened."

"Why should I believe you?"

"There are many reasons why you should believe me, Mr Salgado. Do something you obviously haven't done yet – read the whole file on both the Reincarnation Project and the Eternity Programme, in its early years, and you will find much documented evidence of our contact with Sarah Templeman from the twenty-second century. I was married for 20 years to the person she shared a soul with. Above all, you should believe me because you are not talking to a wrinkled and white-haired 72-year-old but to someone who looks and feels about 60."

"What does that prove? Everyone knows about the Eternity Programme. It has been so successful. It only shows the wisdom of Government research funding decisions in the '40s, which has nothing to do with Sarah Templeman or the Reincarnation Project."

"On the contrary, it has everything to do with both. Your ignorance is staggering. You should ask your friend in the Defence Department to get access to Top Secret files from the '40s. These will show that the Eternity Programme was set up specifically because of information provided from the future by Sarah Templeman who was discovered by the Reincarnation Project. You need to ask about the light pen she brought back from the future and the recording Levy made from it. The Defence Department still has that light pen somewhere. Levy confiscated it from me."

Salgado was honest enough to admit that he had been found out not preparing the interview thoroughly. Maybe he had been too caught up in the scandal surrounding Levy's alleged misuse of Government funds and written off too hastily everyone she had been involved with.

"OK," he said, "supposing that what you say is true and a quarter of a million people really are going to die in 2084, what can we do about it? I've seen enough time travel movies to know you can't alter events retrospectively. For Sarah Templeman, these events had already occurred, and if I understand you correctly, they exist independently as 'now' moments etched into the fabric of spacetime waiting to happen. There's nothing we can do, anyway."

"So you did read that part of the files and you were paying attention. But you are wrong; we *can* change things, a little. What I have come to realise is that when massive tragedies are reported, the news always gives the numbers of the dead in round figures. When the young Sarah studied climate change at school, she learned that 'a quarter of a million people' had died, but how many is that *exactly*? It could be 262,000, but if it were 238,000, it might still get rounded up by the news media to a quarter of a million. And that's a potential difference of 24,000 which is a lot of lives you could save."

"And just how would we do that?"

"I don't know. I'm not here to teach you guys your own job. How about by evacuating vulnerable areas as early as possible. Just promise me you'll look into it."

Salgado spun around in his chair. "You know what?" he said. "You didn't have to come all the way out here. That counts for something. I will look properly at the files you mention, and if everything you say is true, I will make sure we save as many people as possible."

"Thank you, that's all I ask."

Carmen returned home to look for more lost souls.

Two weeks later she received a package by FedEx. Not guessing what was in it, she opened it with some trepidation. A light pen fell out, looking a bit the worse for wear. There was a handwritten note with it:

I believe this is yours. Fascinating. Thanks for the insight, and sorry for not believing you. About the floods, we'll save as many as we can.

Regards, Fernando.

Birmingham, England, April 2026

Zak Emblin was doing a stand-up comedy routine on Open Mike Night at Birmingham's Glee Club. If he got through, it would be an extra source of income, one night a week. If not, well, at least he would have given it a shot. Zak had always been able to make friends and family laugh. He believed this was because his reincarnating behaviour gave him a different perspective on life. When you don't know when you wake up if you're going to stay in your own body for the whole day, that tends to put the rest of your problems into perspective and allows you to see the funny side of things. Now it was time to see if he could make a bigger audience laugh…

"Found myself watching daytime TV yesterday," he told the audience, most of whom he could not see in the dark upstairs venue. "Yes, I know, always a mistake. There was this black and white film on about the Second World War. God, it must have been hard for those guys. In the days before colour, everything looked the same. 'What are we bombing, Sarge?' 'That grey building over there'. 'Do you mean that grey building or that grey building?' Very difficult."

Zak got a laugh, and his nerves settled a bit. He continued:

"We're all too young to remember, of course, but I think colour came in, in about 1970. I think it was a Tuesday. The Hippies and the Glam Rockers demanded it. Since then, the world's been in colour. So, what I want to know is, if the world is all in colour now, why are the cows still black and white?"

This got an even bigger laugh, and Zak started to enjoy himself, sometimes departing from his prepared material.

"Colour can be a tricky concept, know what I mean? Blokes wearing orange, just doesn't work, does it? Why is that? Women can do it, not guys. There are only two situations where a guy looks right in orange: US State Penitentiary or Buddhist monk."

The audience laughed again.

"I saw some monks recently on Caldey Island, near Tenby. They make their own chocolate and perfume which they sell on the mainland. They can mix with the tourists visiting the island, although it is a silent order at night times. Some even work in the kitchen of the main tourist cafe. We were introduced to the monk doing All Day Breakfasts. He was the friar, obviously, and helping him was the guy in charge of French fries – the Chip Monk."

Getting more groans than laughs for this, Zak moved swiftly on.

"That was a great holiday we had in Pembrokeshire, South Wales. As well as visiting the monks on Caldey Island, we went to see the new lions they have at Folly Farm and Zoo. The big male had a magnificent mane, rich golden brown it was, biggest I have ever seen. And he knew it. Boy, did he know it. The female and the four cubs were all huddled together against the unseasonal cold wind, but not him. Oh, no. He positioned himself apart from the others in just the right place for the wind to ruffle his mane. It was a real look-at-me moment. It was like he was under a hair dryer, all that was missing was the back combing."

"But the zebras were my favourite. Why? I hear you ask. Because I was able to realise an ambition I've had since childhood. I've often wondered, 'Can you scan a Zebra with a barcode reader? And if you can, what price are they?' So I borrowed a barcode reader from a friend who works in a shop. Answer: most were £4.99, and the little one was on special offer at £2.50 with 50 bonus Nectar points."

This went down well, and Zak's confidence grew.

"No, it's true, honestly. 'Many a true word spoken in jest'. Have you heard that? Well, I swap bodies with an American woman from the future." Zak just got blank looks from the few people in the audience he could see. "Yeah, right, none of you are buying that."

He finished with a visual gag about how to distinguish Scottish country dancing from Irish dancing using what he called the 'good deodorant/bad deodorant' technique. First, he donned a tartan skirt (too small to be a kilt) and sash and did a few steps of highland dancing to imaginary music, with his arms confidently raised aloft above his head, the hands curling slightly inwards. "Good deodorant!" he declared and stopped dancing. Then he did a few *Riverdance* type steps, his arms down firmly by his sides and declared, "Bad deodorant!"

This got the biggest laugh, and applause followed. The managers offered him a warm-up slot on Friday evenings, and Zak returned home wired and feeling pleased with himself.

****

Wales, UK, 5 July 2121

Carmen took a walk out to her favourite spot, from where she could see almost the entire Mawddach Valley to the East, stretching to Dolgellau. To the West was Cardigan Bay; to the South, the foothills of Snowdonia, with mountains rising behind; to the North West she could see her own farmhouse, perched alongside the 'Slabs', a local name for the pair of near vertical rock faces frequented by climbers and abseilers. She loved seeing the cloud patterns develop along the valley; it was like watching a film on fast forward. It was a panoramic view which had been voted many times into the top ten views in the UK, and a sight which had given the walk its name, Panorama Walk.

The view was so wonderful that Carmen wondered why she did not come up here more often. Ah, of course, because of the visit, she remembered. She had had to be in this year for Zak's visit. Well, that was done now.

She looked back on her life. She tried to focus on happy thoughts about Zak and Sarah and, with a smile, recalled laughing at Zak's stand-up routine at the Glee Club. Mostly, she considered how Zak and Sarah, her two Best-Friends-in-One-Body, had ended up destroying each other by intervening in each other's worlds. She thought about the pain and the exciting times, in equal measures, which they had given her. She missed them a lot. That time, most of which was over 70 years ago now, seemed so recent, almost like it had been happening last week. She considered the fact that Zak and Sarah were almost unique, that there were so few others out there like them that she had not been able to find any, and that this was probably a good thing.

She thought about her dear, sweet father, Martin, and how he had set her on the path of learning, not with any particular end in view, just learning for the sheer joy of learning. Tears came into her eyes as she recalled his brave seven-year fight against cancer – a battle he had almost won. Just when his body had been declared free of any cancers, weakened by chemotherapy, it had succumbed instead to pneumonia in 2046.

Way too soon after that, it had been Zak's turn to go. Commander Levy had been as good as her word and had provided protection for Sarah, Zak and Carmen from the forces that had issued threats to kill them. All except one, that is, and his threat had only ever been issued verbally, in Zak's hearing alone, although Zak had told her about it later. Once Sean had disappeared to start a new life somewhere else, she, Zak and Sarah had simply forgotten about him. If anything, Skunk had been even more forgotten. A mistake, obviously. She knew that now, but for all the privileges in relation to time fate had given the three of them, even they could not turn it backwards. They should have remembered that Skunk had broken Zak's nose once and therefore remained dangerous. They should have shared information about him with Commander Levy's security team, but they had not done that.

Carmen realised tears were streaming down her face. She tried to re-focus on happier aspects of her life. She had two lovely lads, Stephen and James, who would have been in their 80s by now, had they been allowed to age naturally. They both still looked about 35. She was proud of the fact that her influence had kept them alive when the Eternity Programme had first come in and when they had been considered just too old to qualify. It was just a pity that both had put career before family, meaning that she had no grandchildren. That would have been a little complicated anyway, although not impossible, in James's case as he was gay. James was the only dental surgeon on the General Medical Council, a body he often said would be 'toothless' without him. Stephen was a much published and well-regarded surgeon, gunshot wounds being his speciality. "I wish I could have saved Dad that day." She had heard him say that so many times.

And she had proved the existence of reincarnation, albeit for only an infinitesimally small number of people, maybe only one in half a million. Still, with the strong implication that even those who don't reincarnate did have a soul, and at a time when death was being assigned to people as easily as the writing of a prescription, this must have provided some comfort to many. It did for her. She took out a pill bottle and examined its contents. They were daily tablets, affectionately known by almost everyone as Peter Pans. Well, no more for her. She opened the bottle and scattered the contents to the wind. It was time to go.

Shen Yang Province, North East China, August 2232

The young woman glanced behind her on the bike to see if her child had his face covered. The dust storms blowing in from Mongolia at this time of the year were so strong that you had to protect your eyes and skin with a sheer scarf which you could breathe through. The local population had been doing this for centuries. The boy was saying something, but she could not make out what it was. "蓋住你的臉" she shouted, "蓋住你的臉" ("Cover your face, cover your face.")

The boy did not hear. He was chanting something she could not understand. It sounded like a European language, maybe English. How could her four-year-old who had never had a day's schooling in his young life know English? Jūn Yì took out her mobile and pressed record, making her bicycle wobble and narrowly missing the pile of watermelons beside the road. She would play the recording later to her husband, and he would take it to his friend, who taught English at the local college. The friend would translate it into Mandarin and the astonished parents would hear:

"莎拉，扎克，我與你我聽到你，莎拉。我聽說你扎克我聽到你，拉狄克. 你出來玩嗎？我希望有人一起玩你在那裡，莎拉？你在那裡，扎克? (Sarah, Zak, I am with you. I hear you, Sarah. I hear you Zak. I hear you, Radek. Are you coming out to play? I want someone to play with. Are you there, Sarah? Are you there, Zak?")

They would hear it, but they would not make head or tail of it. Not for a few years, anyway. Not until little Bao-Zhi revealed the detailed memories he had of both Sarah's and Zak's lives and of the connection between them. Not until, at the age of seven, he started swapping places with Radek Forss, who was also seven and lived in Prague, in the year 2365.

****